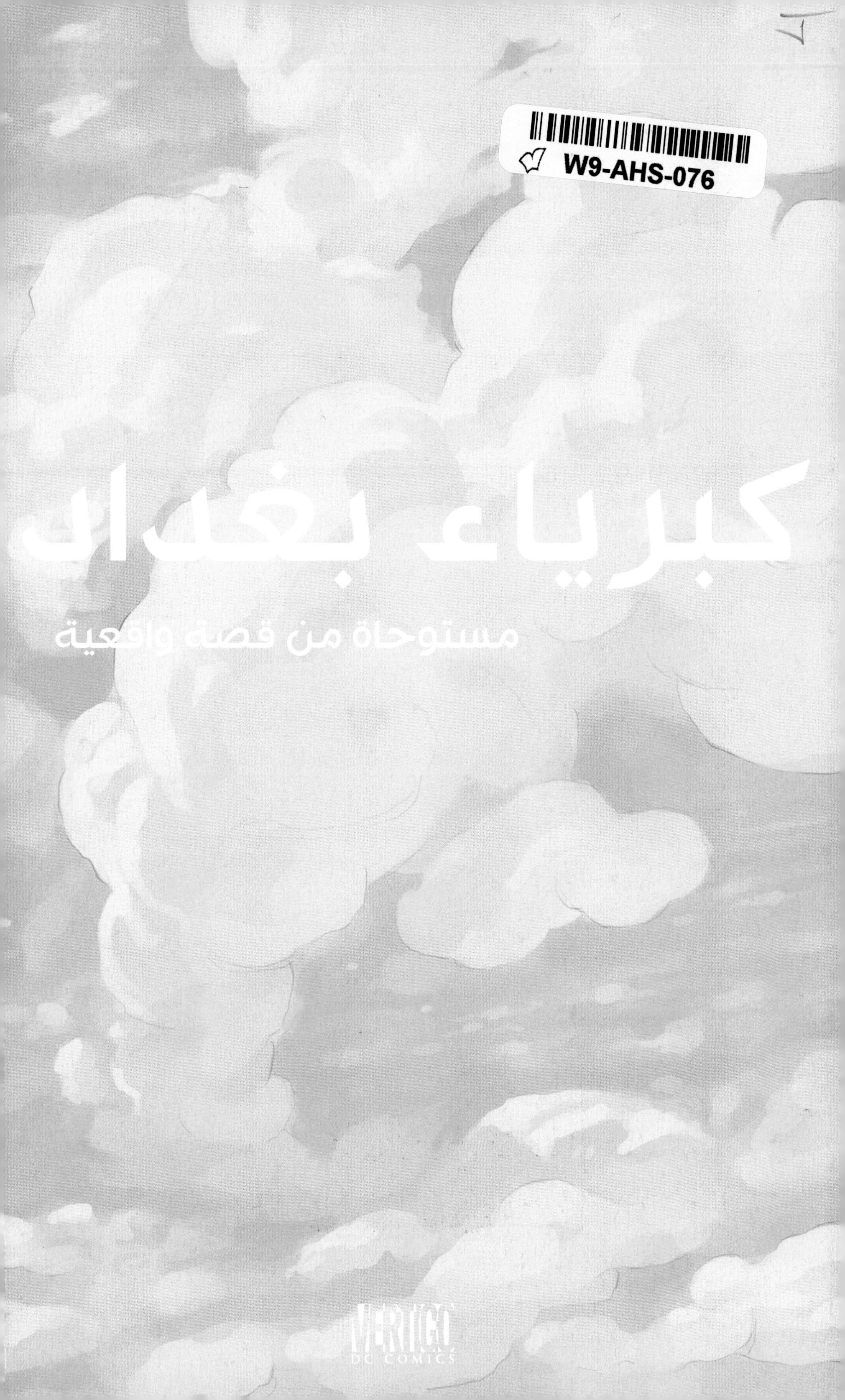

كبرياء بغداد

مستوحاة من قصة واقعية

VERTIGO
DC COMICS

بغداد

مستوحاة من قصة واقعية

للكاتب : بريان فوقـان

رسوم : نايكو هينريكون

طباعة : تـود كلـين

كبرياء

PRIDE OF BAGHDAD

INSPIRED BY A TRUE STORY

WRITTEN BY BRIAN K. VAUGHAN

ART BY NIKO HENRICHON

LETTERING BY TODD KLEIN

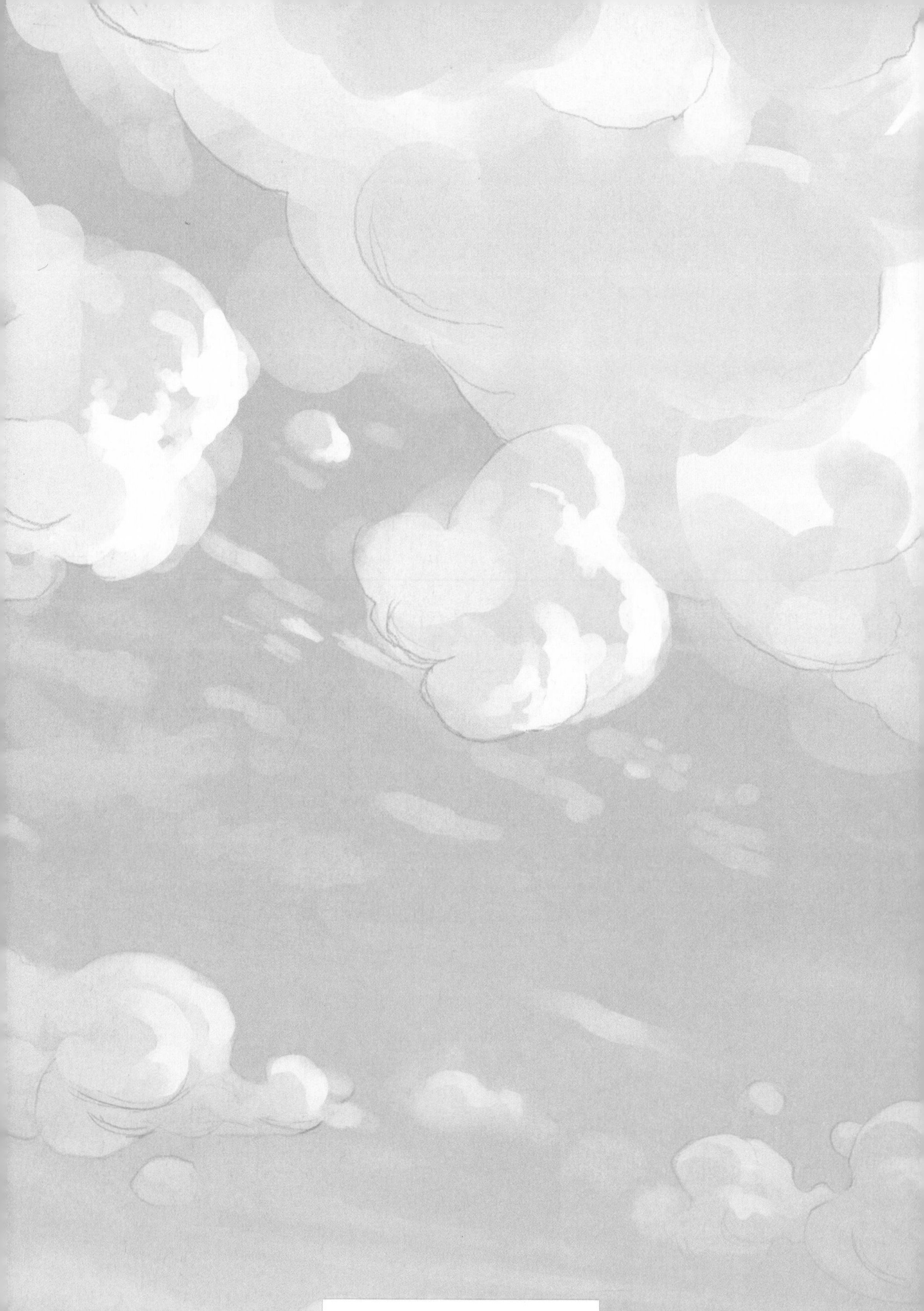

Logo design by Nessim Higson. Special thanks to Ihsan Alhammouri for Arabic lettering and translation.

PRIDE OF BAGHDAD Published by DC Comics, 1700 Broadway, New York, NY 10019.
ISBN: 978-1-4012-0315-3 Fourth Printing. Printed in the USA. DC Comics, a Warner Bros. Entertainment Company.

FOR DANIEL M. KANEMOTO
-BRIAN K. VAUGHAN

FOR LAËTITIA CASSAN
-NIKO HENRICHON

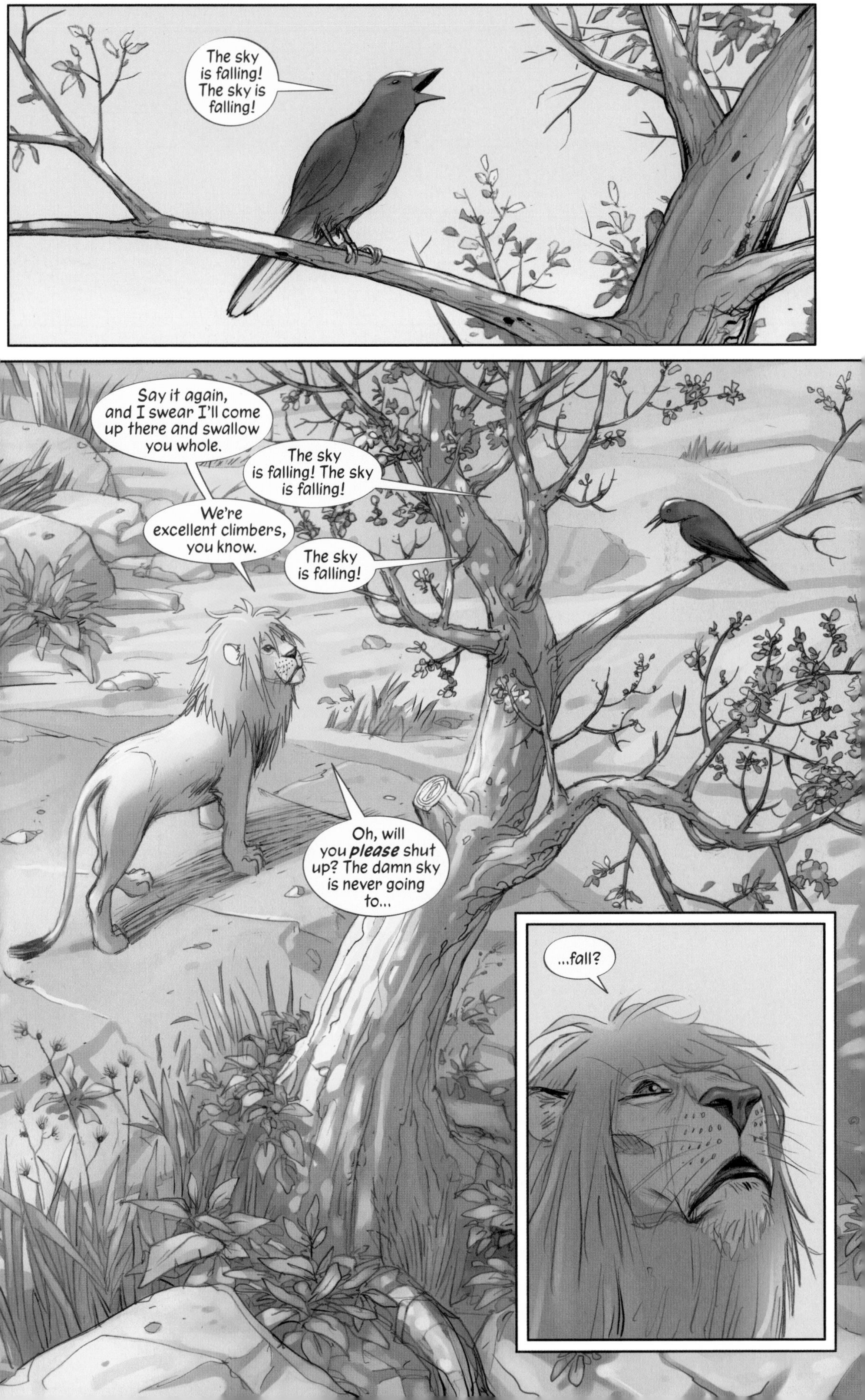
The sky is falling! The sky is falling!
Say it again, and I swear I'll come up there and swallow you whole.
The sky is falling! The sky is falling!
We're excellent climbers, you know.
The sky is falling!
Oh, will you *please* shut up? The damn sky is never going to...
...fall?

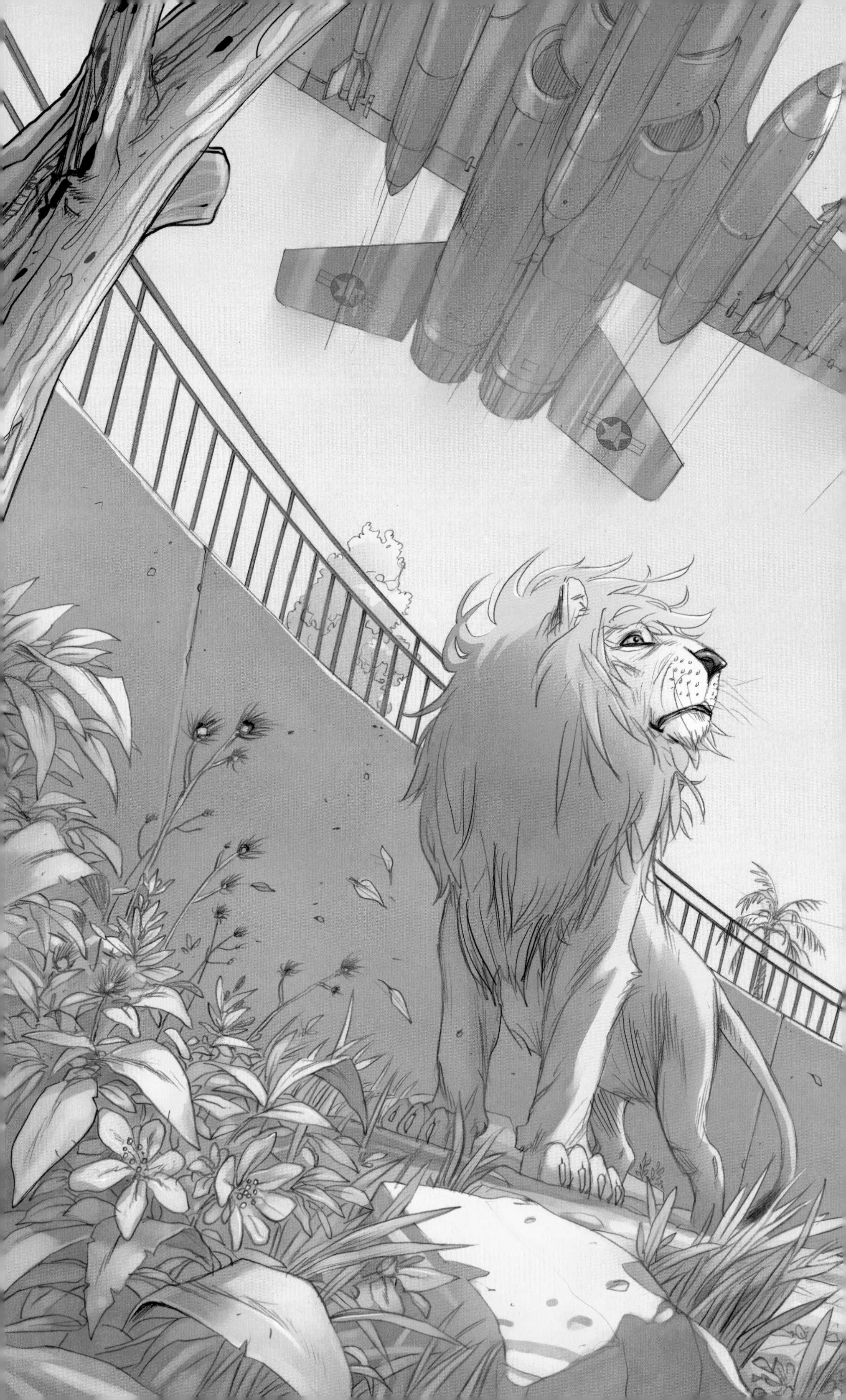

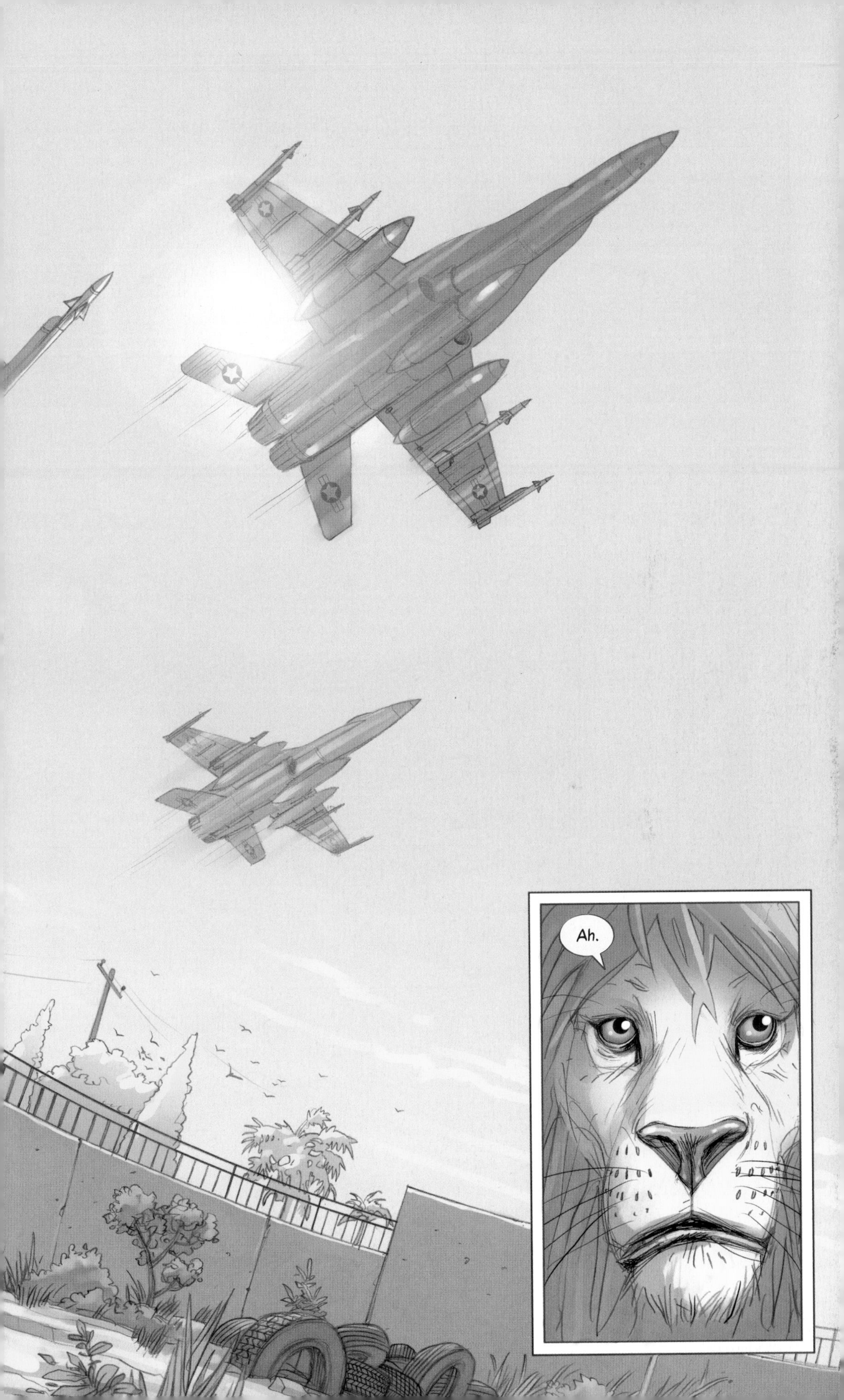
Ah.

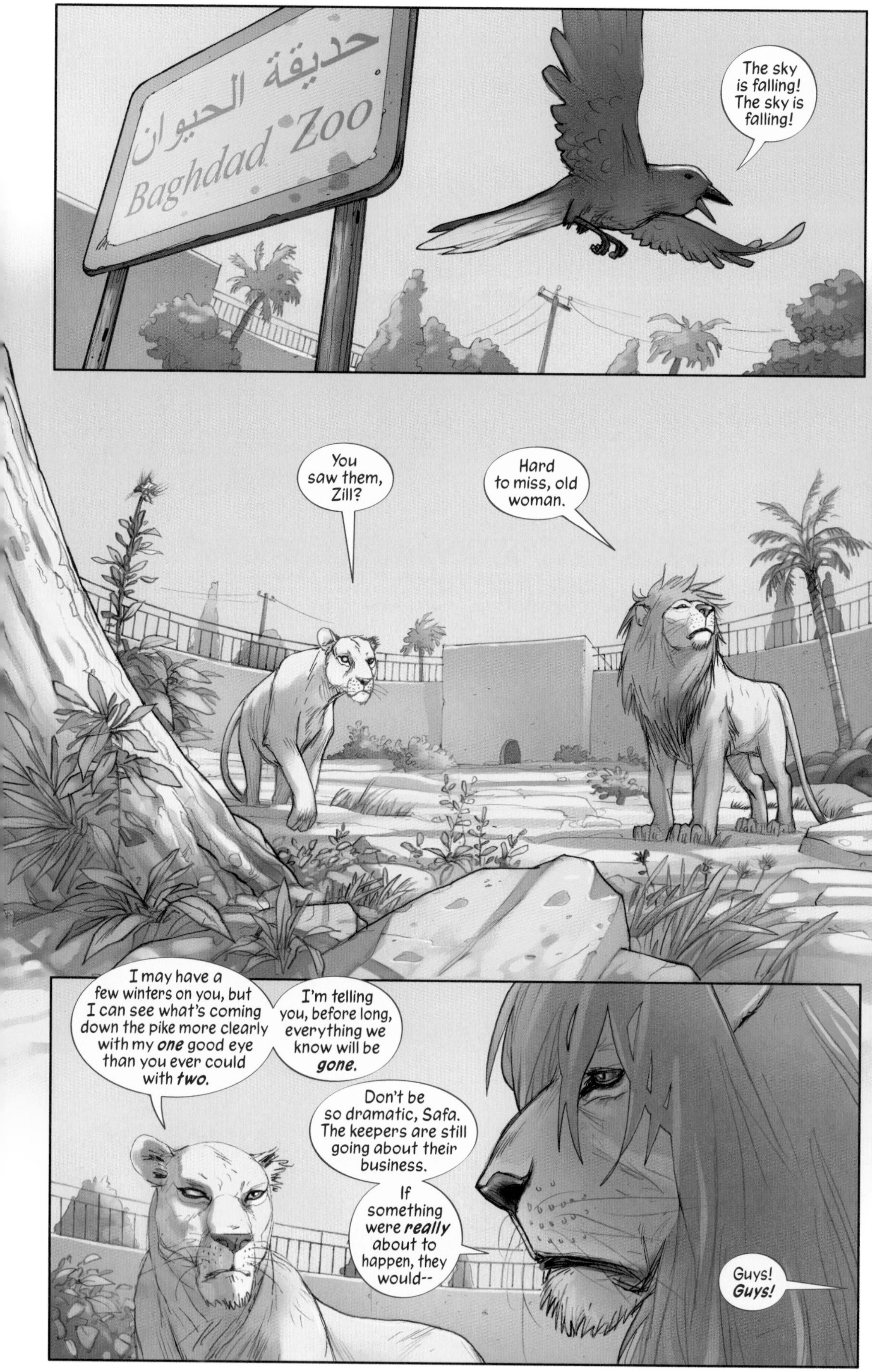

حديقة الحيوان
Baghdad Zoo
The sky is falling! The sky is falling!
You saw them, Zill?
Hard to miss, old woman.
I may have a few winters on you, but I can see what's coming down the pike more clearly with my *one* good eye than you ever could with *two*.
I'm telling you, before long, everything we know will be *gone*.
Don't be so dramatic, Safa. The keepers are still going about their business.
If something were *really* about to happen, they would--
Guys! *Guys!*

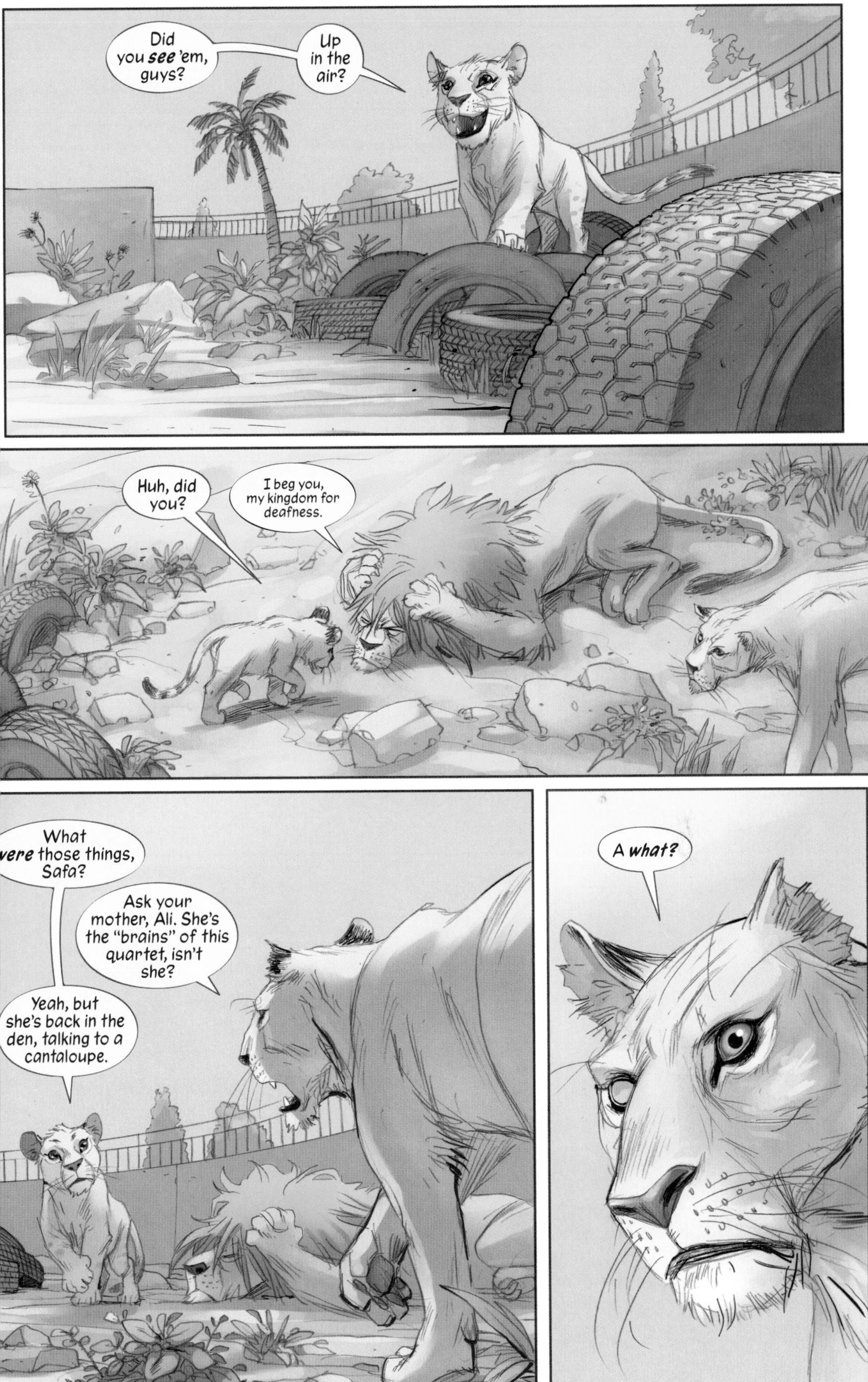
Did you *see* 'em, guys?
Up in the air?
Huh, did you?
I beg you, my kingdom for deafness.
What *were* those things, Safa?
Ask your mother, Ali. She's the "brains" of this quartet, isn't she?
Yeah, but she's back in the den, talking to a cantaloupe.
A *what?*

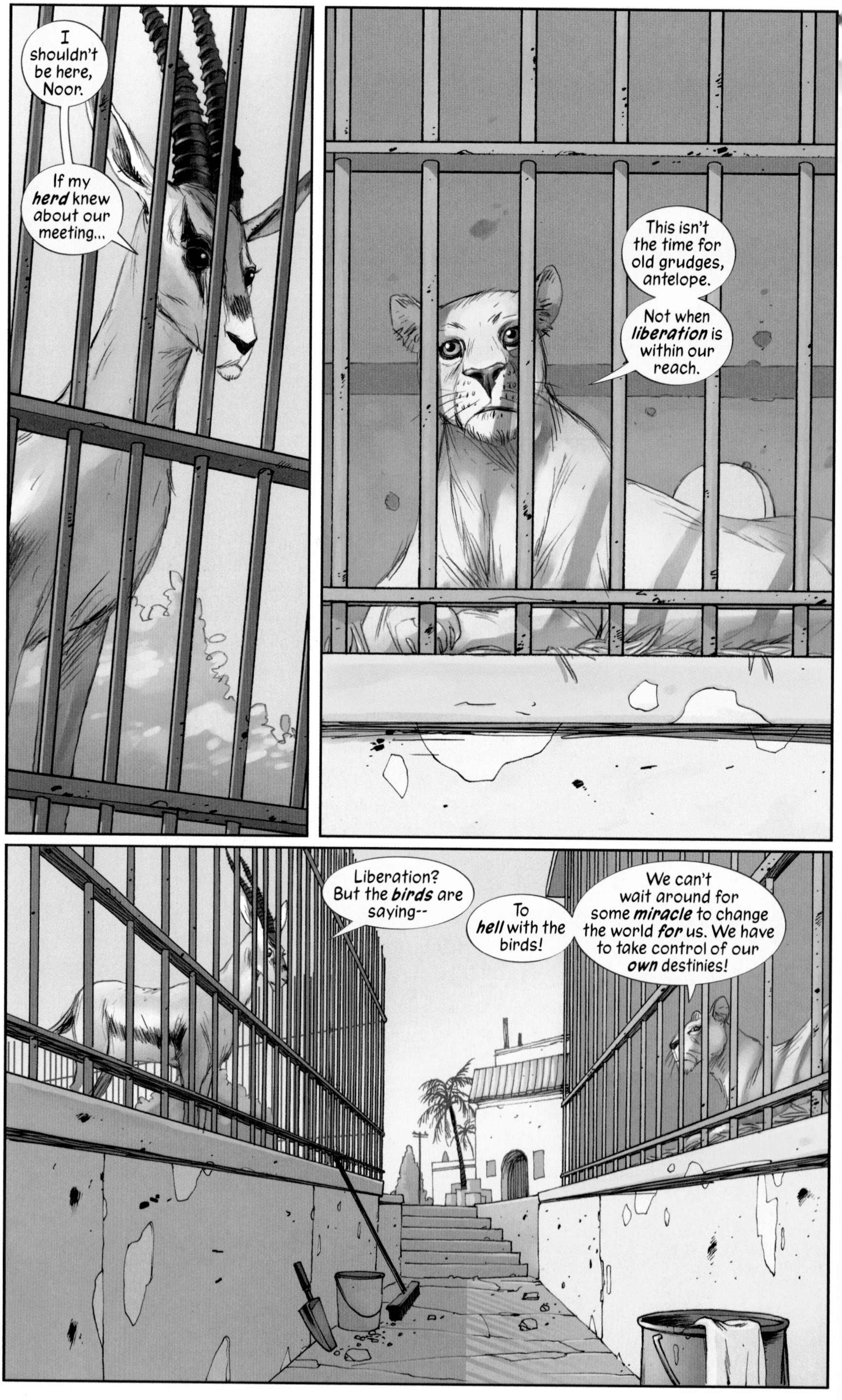
I shouldn't be here, Noor.
If my *herd* knew about our meeting...
This isn't the time for old grudges, antelope.
Not when *liberation* is within our reach.
Liberation? But the *birds* are saying--
To *hell* with the birds!
We can't wait around for some *miracle* to change the world *for* us. We have to take control of our *own* destinies!

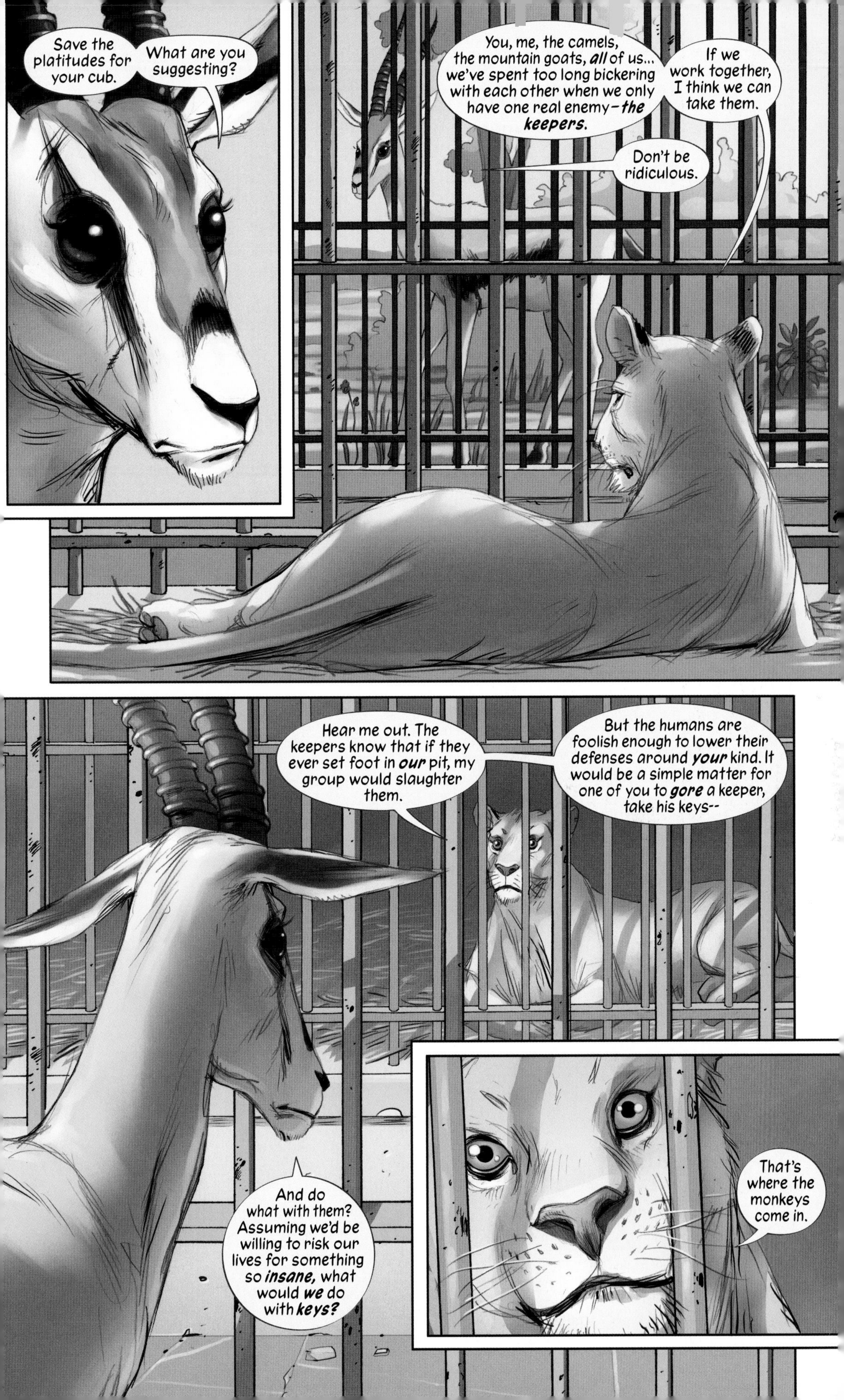
Save the platitudes for your cub.
What are you suggesting?
You, me, the camels, the mountain goats, *all* of us... we've spent too long bickering with each other when we only have one real enemy—*the keepers*.
If we work together, I think we can take them.
Don't be ridiculous.
Hear me out. The keepers know that if they ever set foot in *our* pit, my group would slaughter them.
But the humans are foolish enough to lower their defenses around *your* kind. It would be a simple matter for one of you to *gore* a keeper, take his keys--
And do what with them? Assuming we'd be willing to risk our lives for something so *insane*, what would *we* do with *keys?*
That's where the monkeys come in.

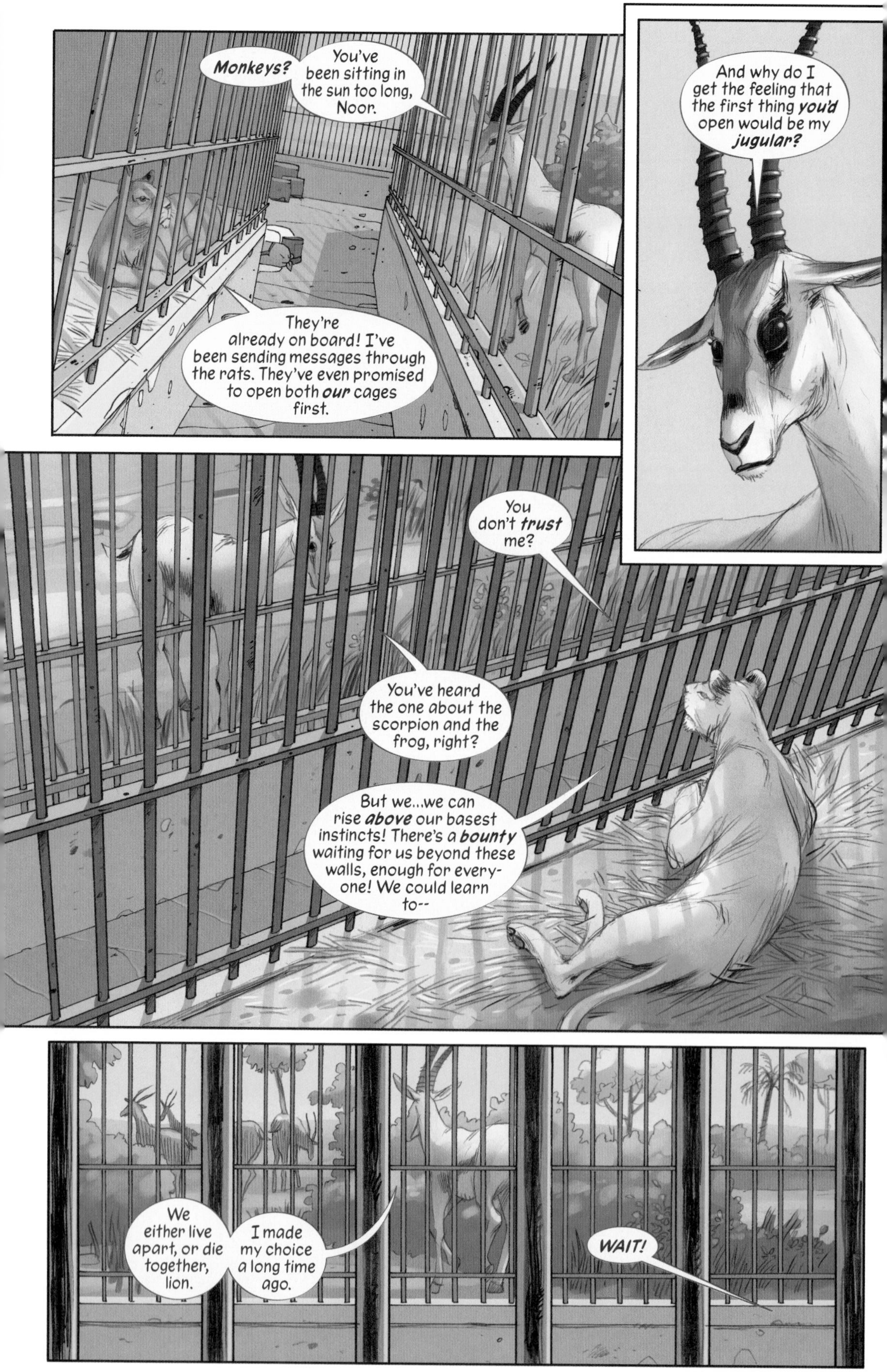
Monkeys?
You've been sitting in the sun too long, Noor.
They're already on board! I've been sending messages through the rats. They've even promised to open both our cages first.
And why do I get the feeling that the first thing you'd open would be my jugular?
You don't trust me?
You've heard the one about the scorpion and the frog, right?
But we...we can rise above our basest instincts! There's a bounty waiting for us beyond these walls, enough for every-one! We could learn to--
We either live apart, or die together, lion.
I made my choice a long time ago.
WAIT!

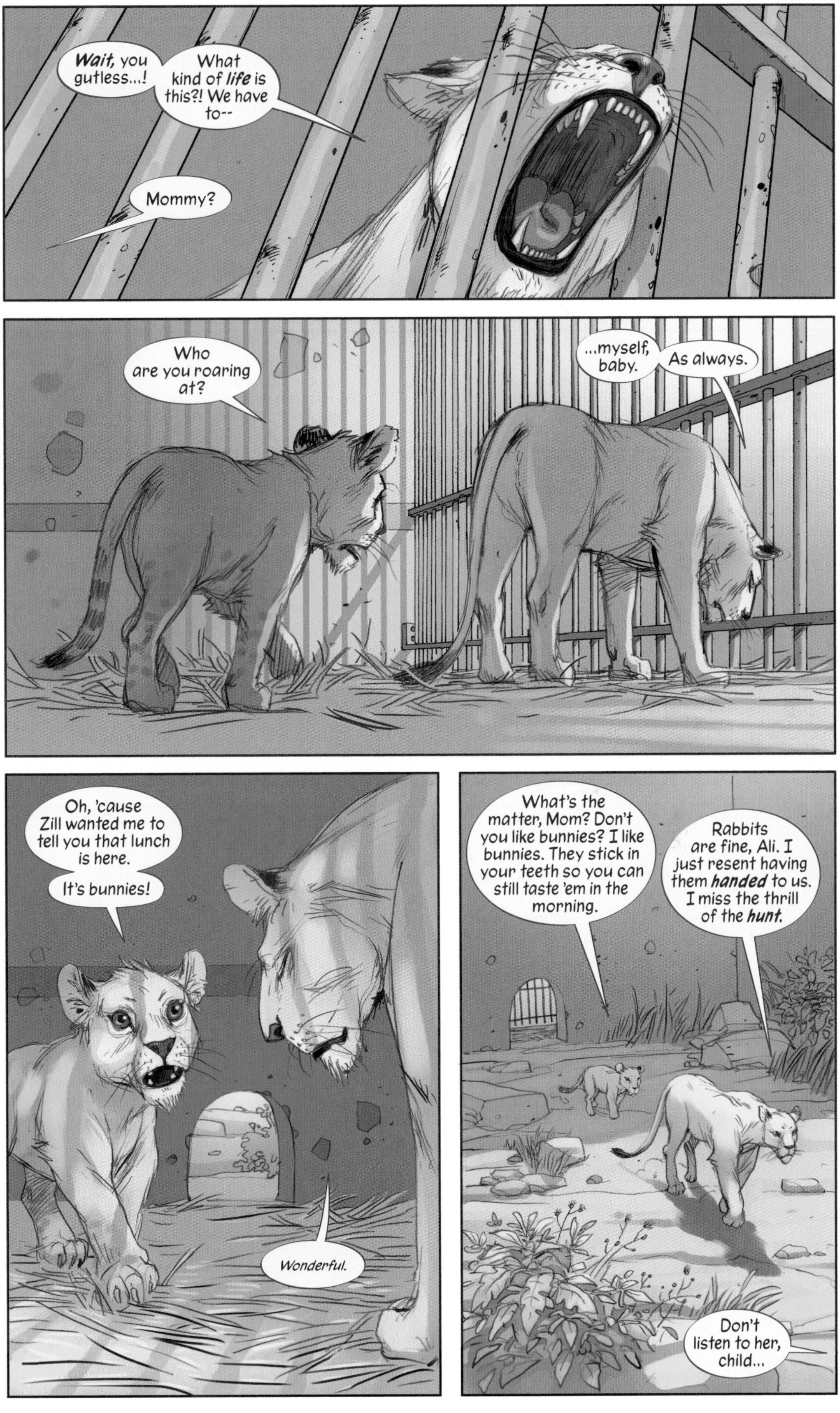

Wait, you gutless...!
What kind of *life* is this?! We have to--
Mommy?
Who are you roaring at?
...myself, baby.
As always.
Oh, 'cause Zill wanted me to tell you that lunch is here.
It's bunnies!
Wonderful.
What's the matter, Mom? Don't you like bunnies? I like bunnies. They stick in your teeth so you can still taste 'em in the morning.
Rabbits are fine, Ali. I just resent having them ***handed*** to us. I miss the thrill of the ***hunt.***
Don't listen to her, child...

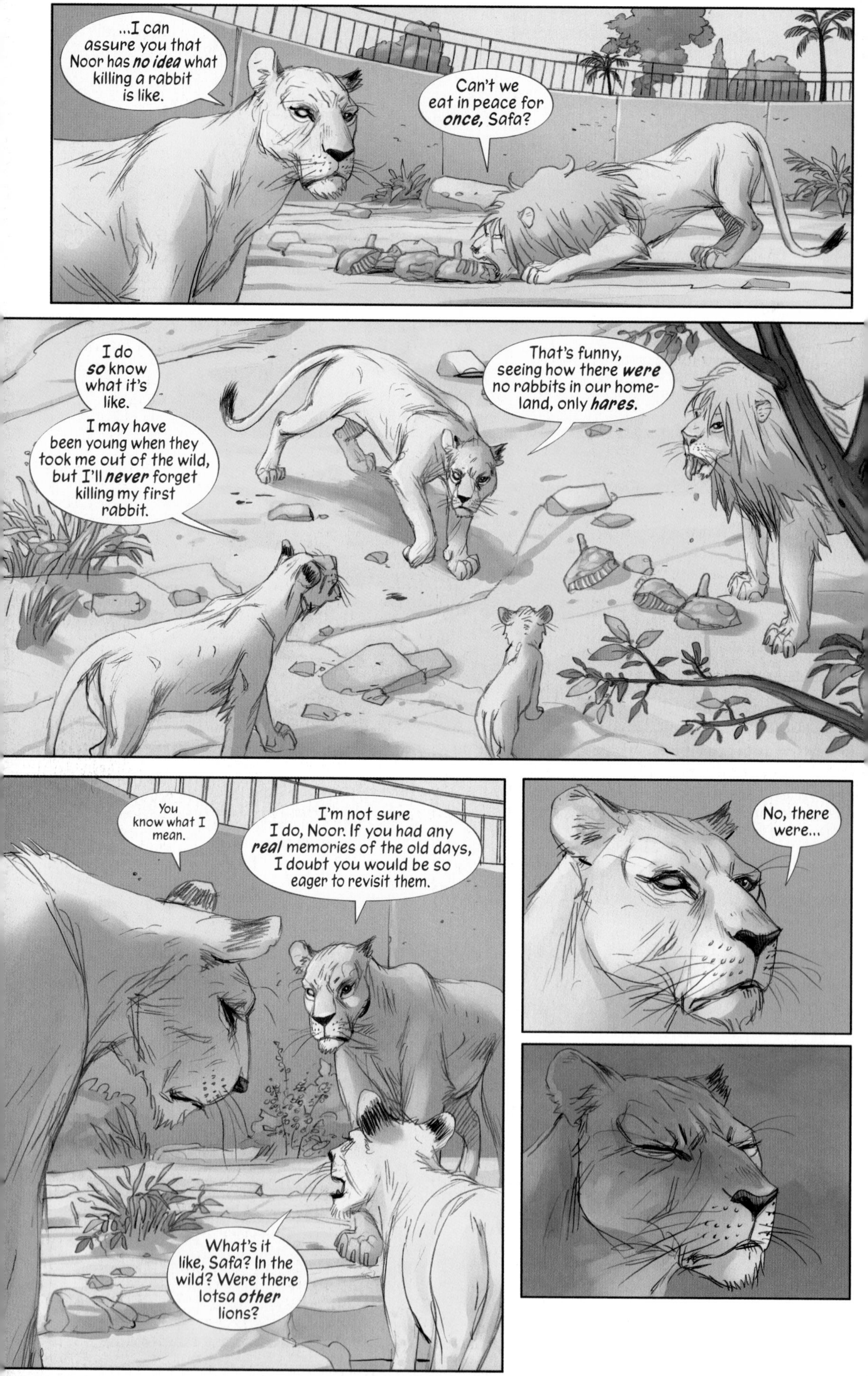
...I can assure you that Noor has *no idea* what killing a rabbit is like.
Can't we eat in peace for *once*, Safa?
I do *so* know what it's like.
I may have been young when they took me out of the wild, but I'll *never* forget killing my first rabbit.
That's funny, seeing how there *were* no rabbits in our homeland, only *hares*.
You know what I mean.
I'm not sure I do, Noor. If you had any *real* memories of the old days, I doubt you would be so eager to revisit them.
What's it like, Safa? In the wild? Were there lotsa *other* lions?
No, there were...

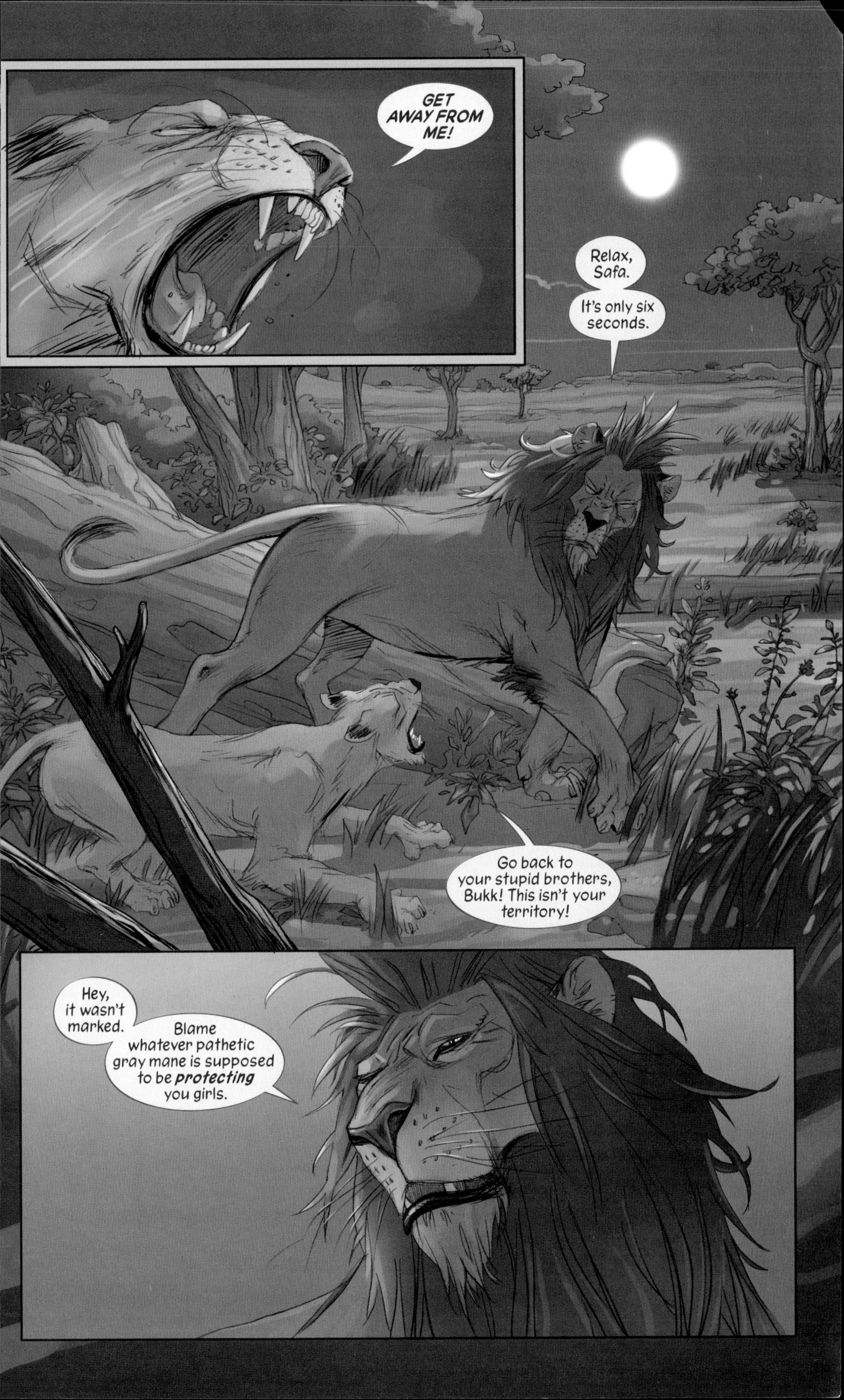
GET AWAY FROM ME!
Relax, Safa.
It's only six seconds.
Go back to your stupid brothers, Bukk! This isn't your territory!
Hey, it wasn't marked.
Blame whatever pathetic gray mane is supposed to be *protecting* you girls.

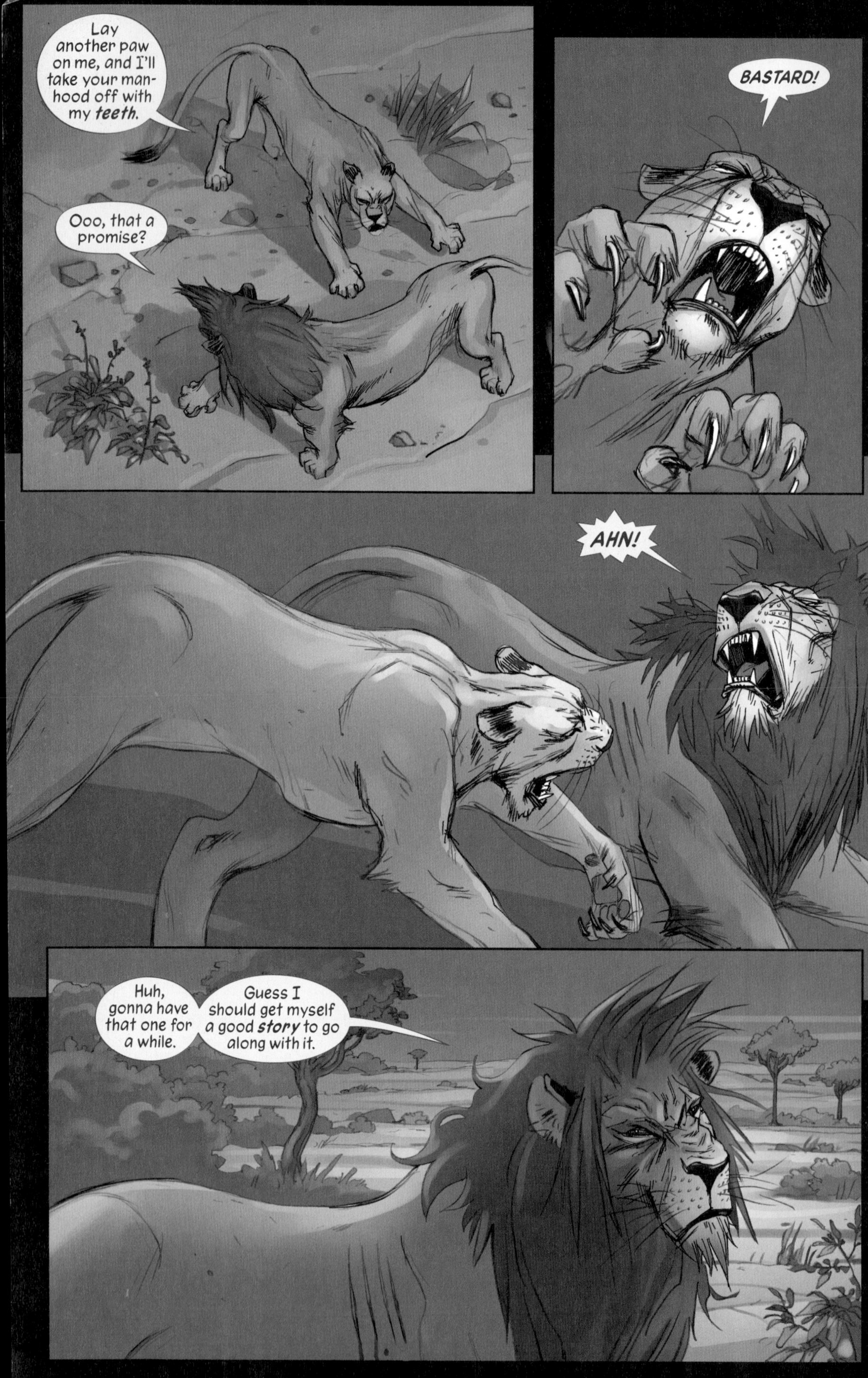
Lay another paw on me, and I'll take your manhood off with my *teeth*.
Ooo, that a promise?
BASTARD!
AHN!
Huh, gonna have that one for a while.
Guess I should get myself a good *story* to go along with it.

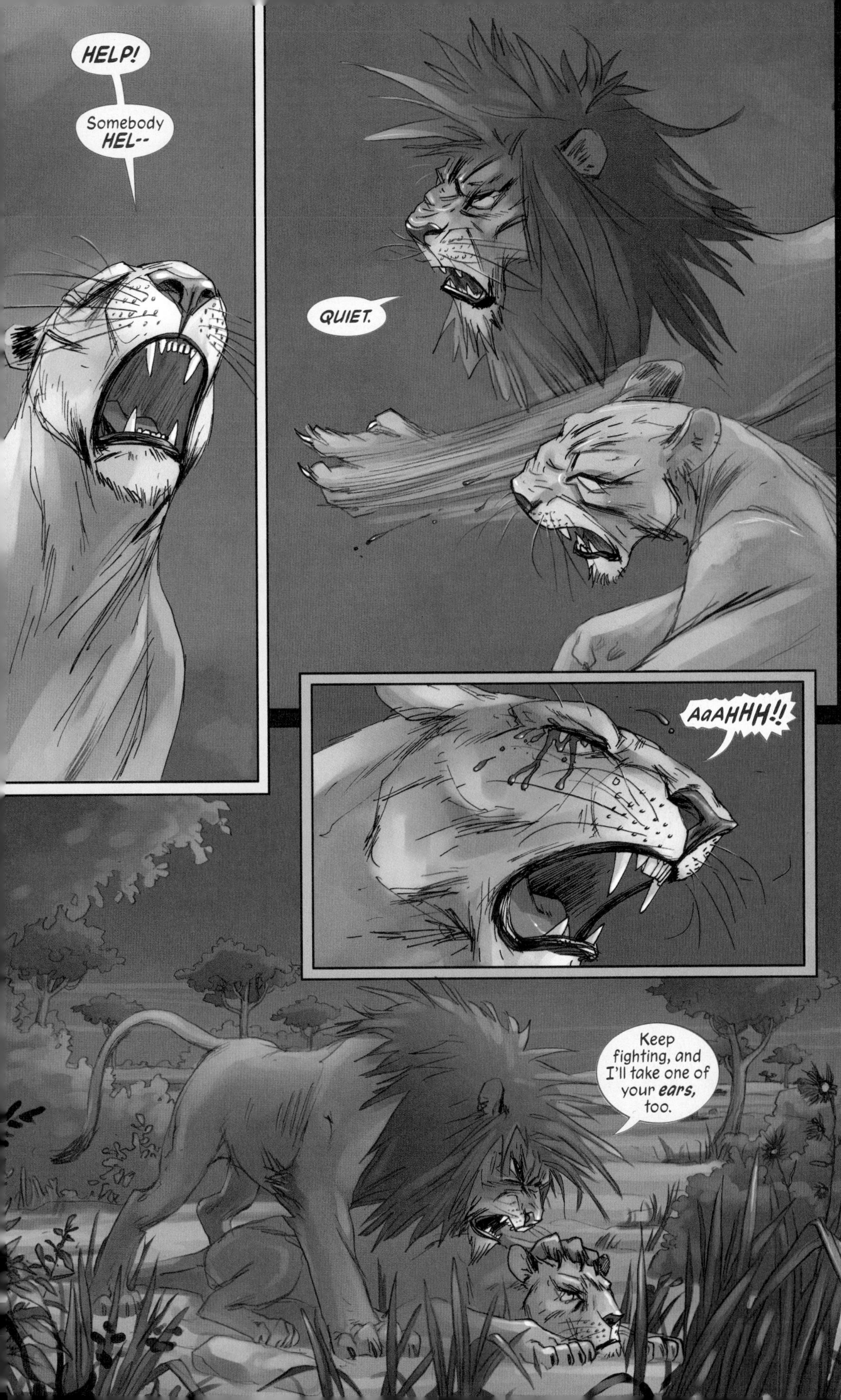
HELP!
Somebody HEL--
QUIET.
AaAHHH!!
Keep fighting, and I'll take one of your ears, too.

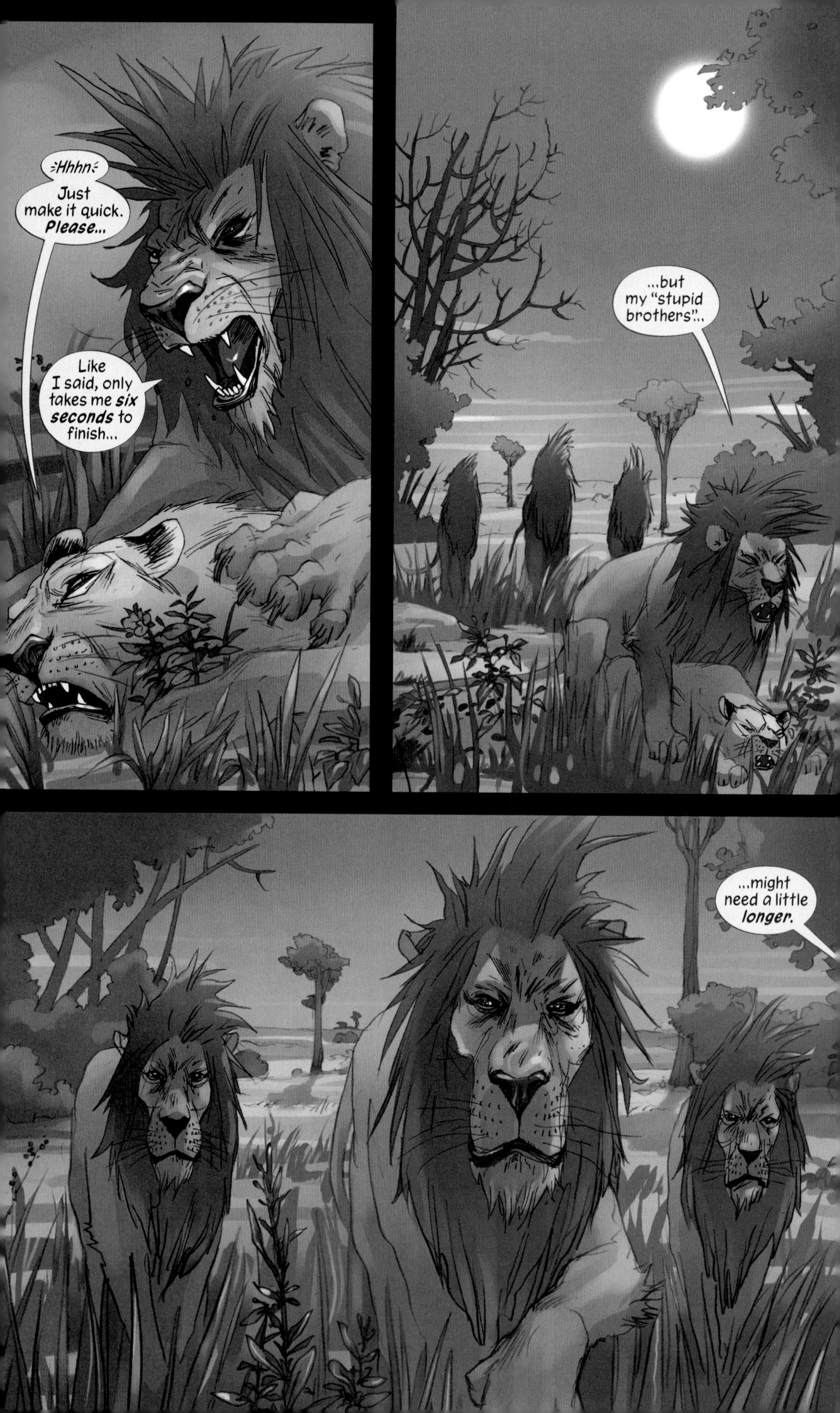
Hhhn
Just make it quick. Please...
Like I said, only takes me six seconds to finish...
...but my "stupid brothers"...
...might need a little longer.

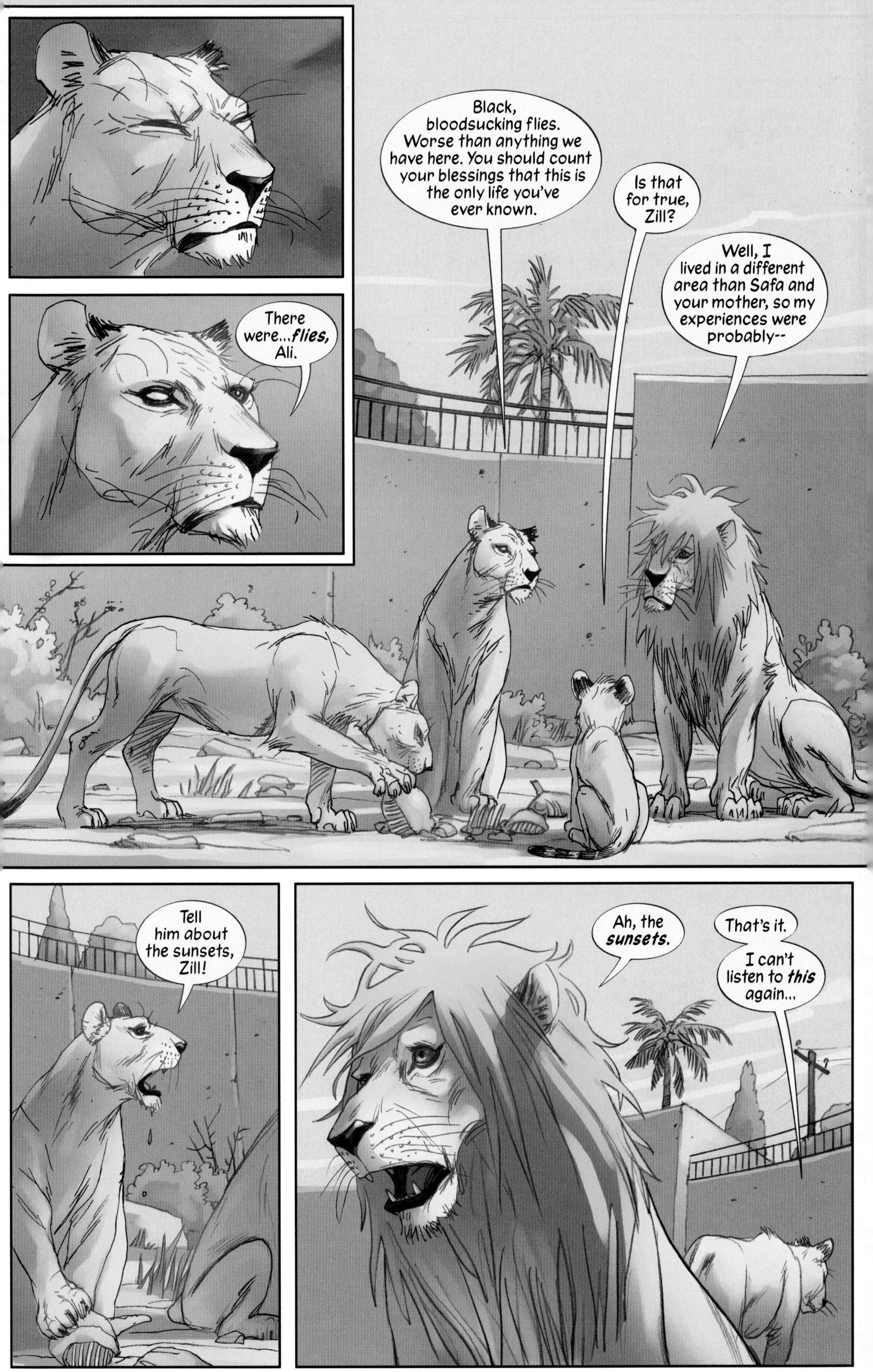
There were...*flies,* Ali.
Black, bloodsucking flies. Worse than anything we have here. You should count your blessings that this is the only life you've ever known.
Is that for true, Zill?
Well, I lived in a different area than Safa and your mother, so my experiences were probably--
Tell him about the sunsets, Zill!
Ah, the ***sunsets.***
That's it.
I can't listen to ***this*** again...

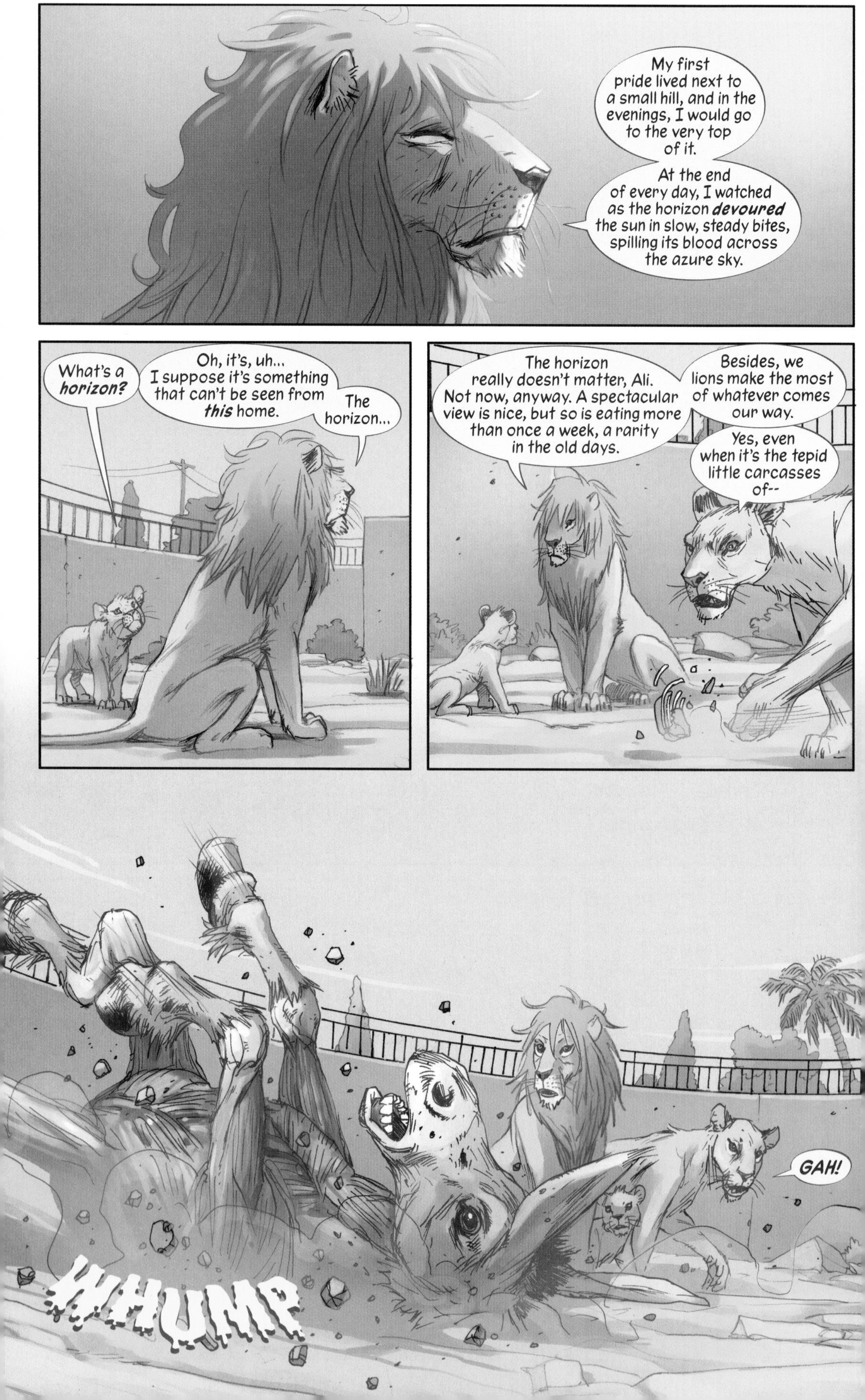
My first pride lived next to a small hill, and in the evenings, I would go to the very top of it.
At the end of every day, I watched as the horizon ***devoured*** the sun in slow, steady bites, spilling its blood across the azure sky.
The horizon...
What's a ***horizon?***
Oh, it's, uh... I suppose it's something that can't be seen from ***this*** home.
The horizon really doesn't matter, Ali. Not now, anyway. A spectacular view is nice, but so is eating more than once a week, a rarity in the old days.
Besides, we lions make the most of whatever comes our way.
Yes, even when it's the tepid little carcasses of--
WHUMP
GAH!

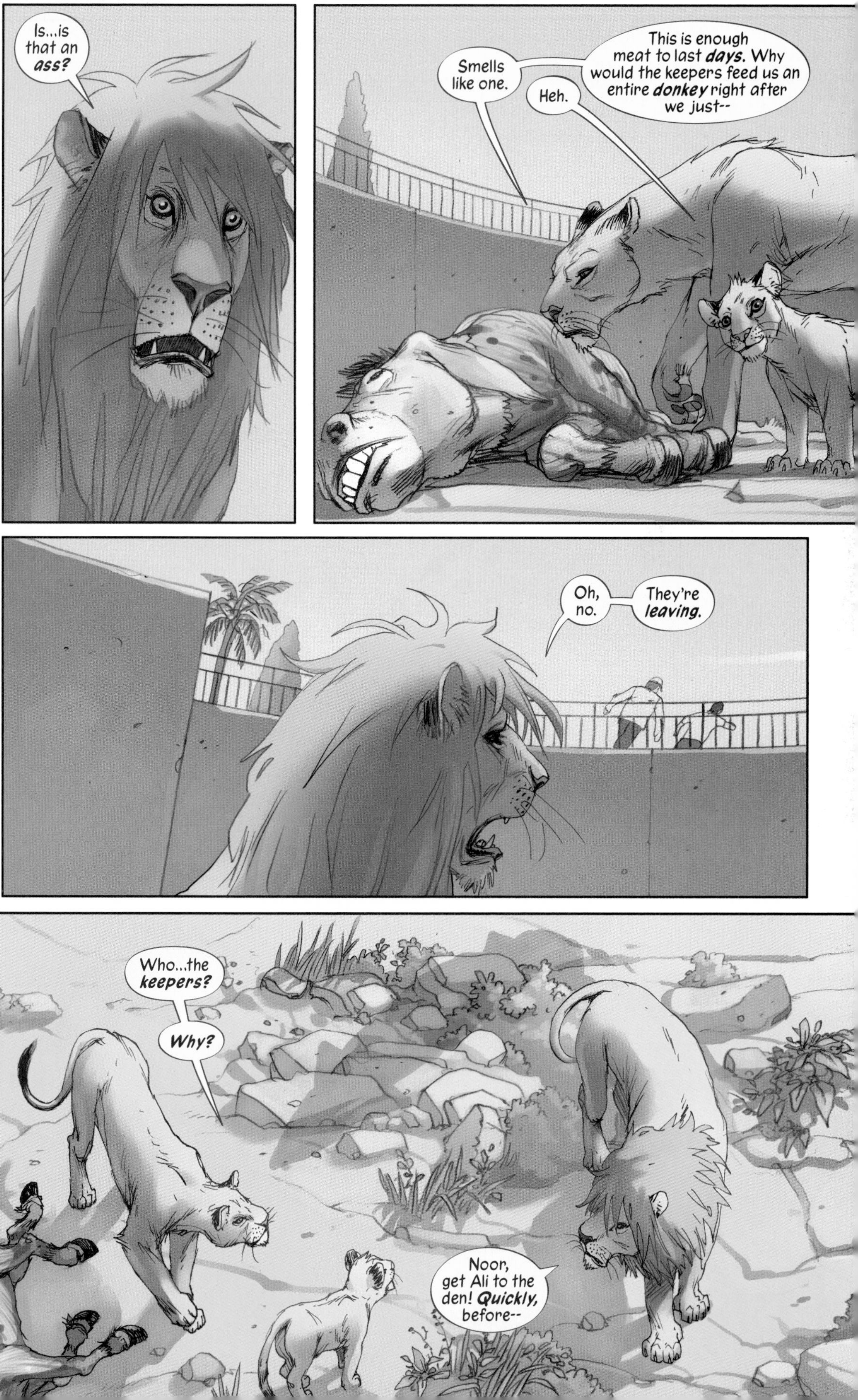
Is...is that an ***ass?***
Smells like one.
This is enough meat to last ***days.*** Why would the keepers feed us an entire ***donkey*** right after we just--
Heh.
Oh, no.
They're ***leaving.***
Who...the ***keepers?***
Why?
Noor, get Ali to the den! ***Quickly,*** before--

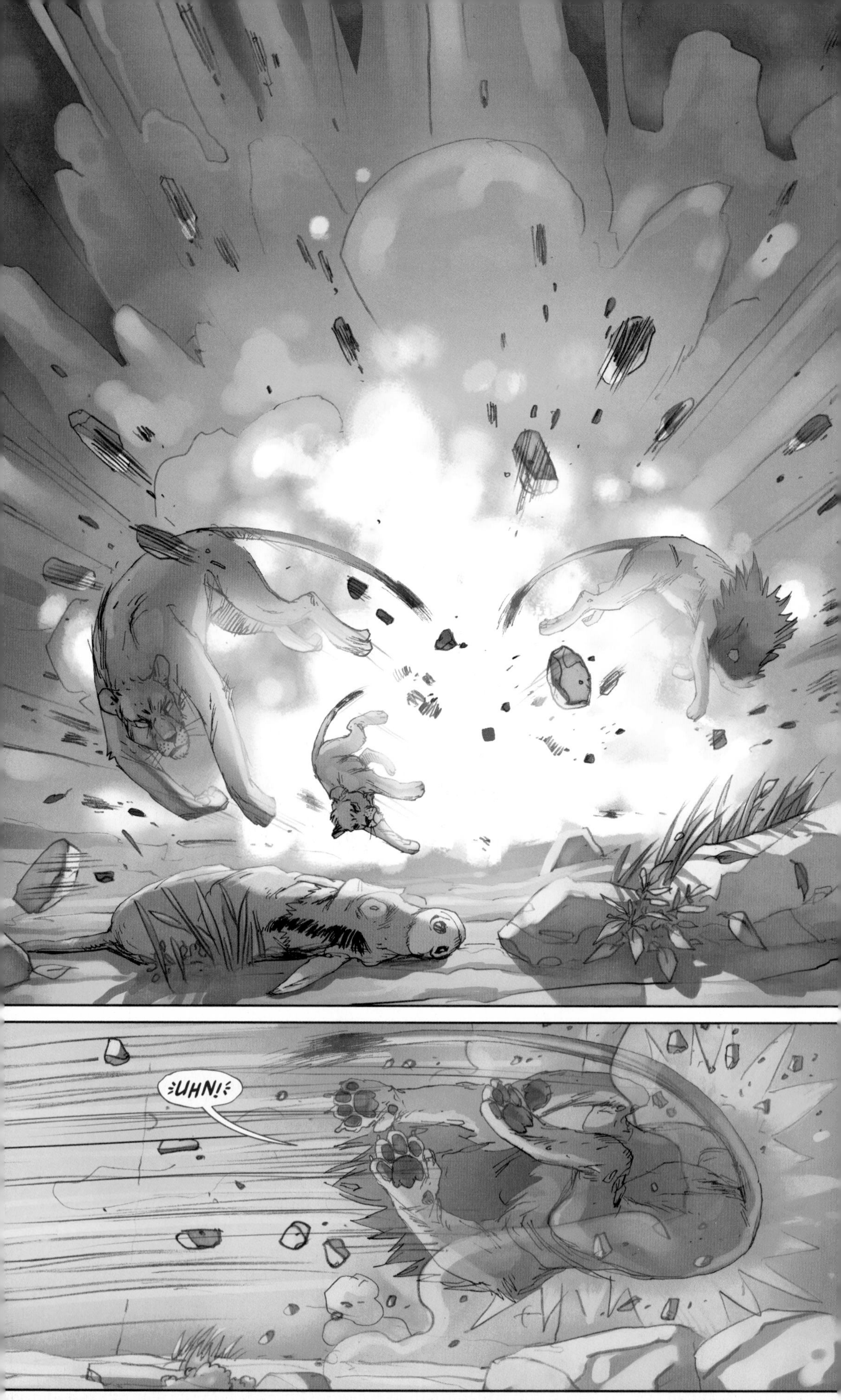
UHN!

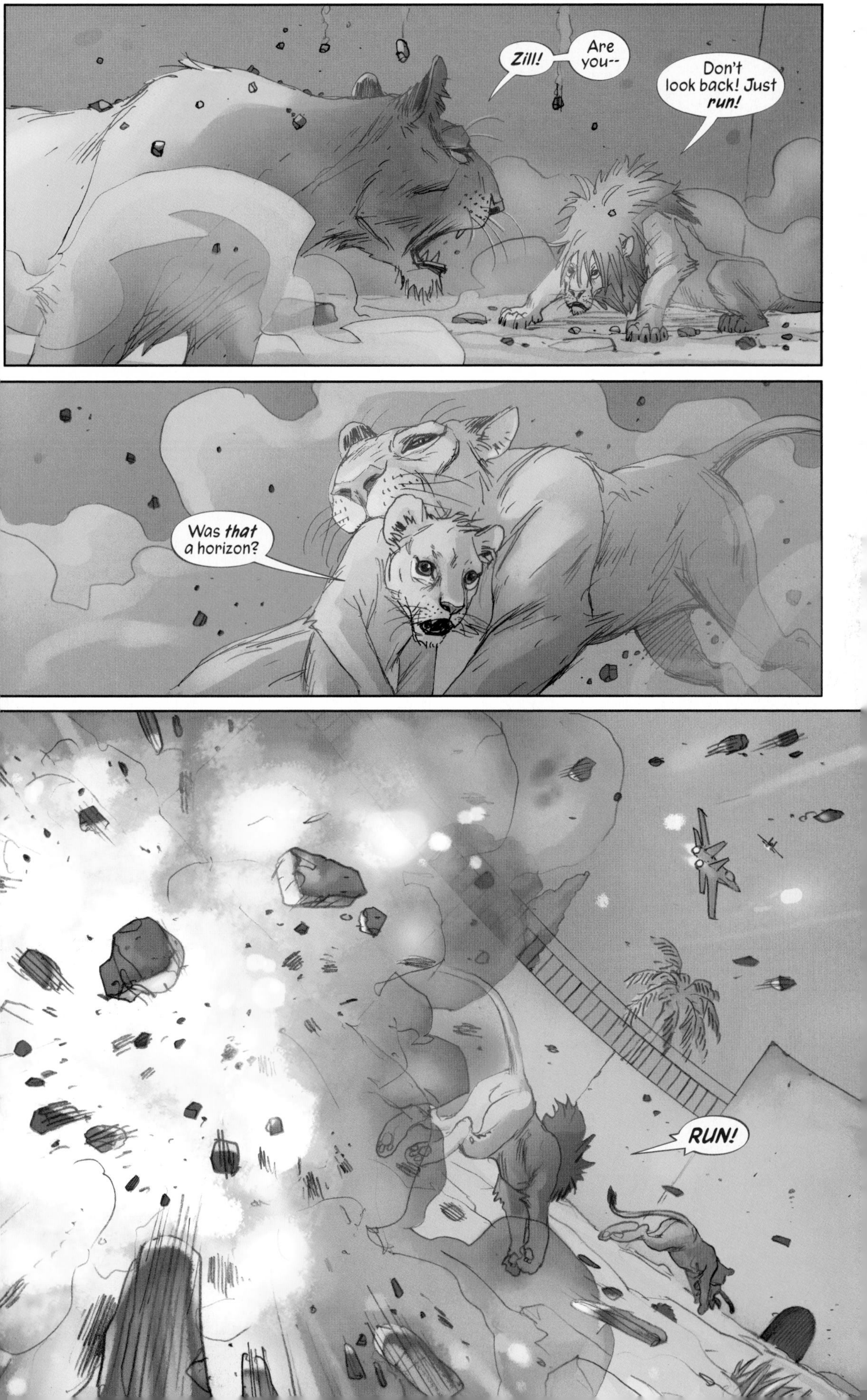
Zill!
Are you--
Don't look back! Just *run!*
Was *that* a horizon?
RUN!

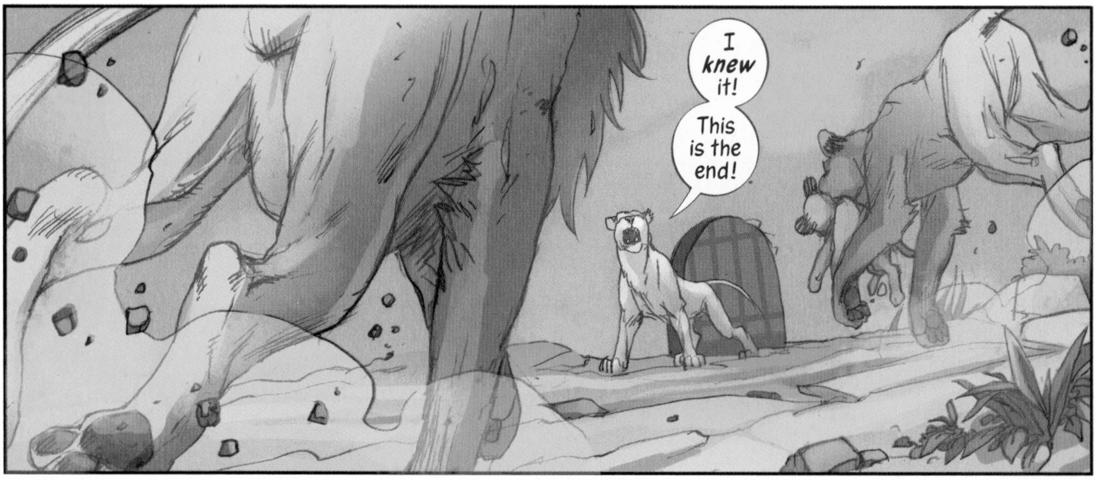

I *knew* it!
This is the end!

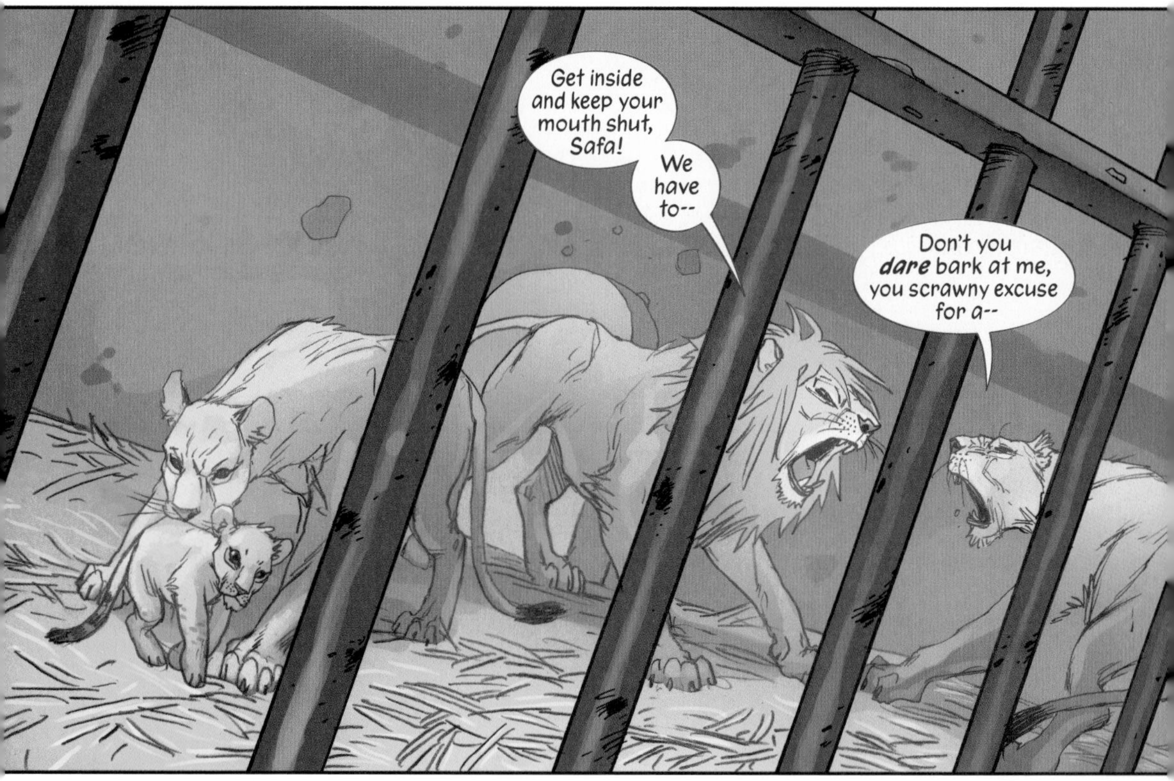

Get inside and keep your mouth shut, Safa!
We have to--
Don't you *dare* bark at me, you scrawny excuse for a--

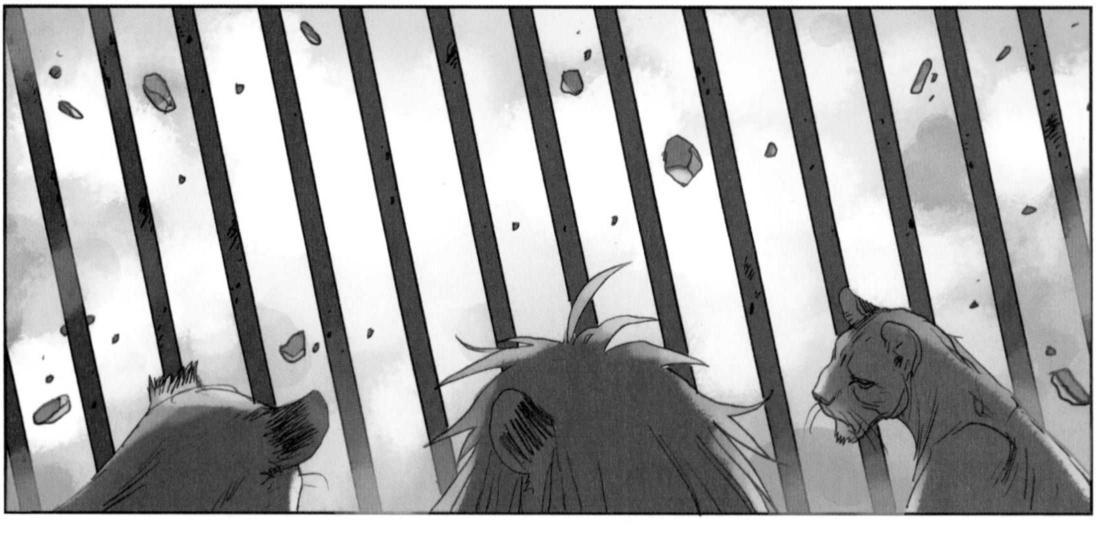

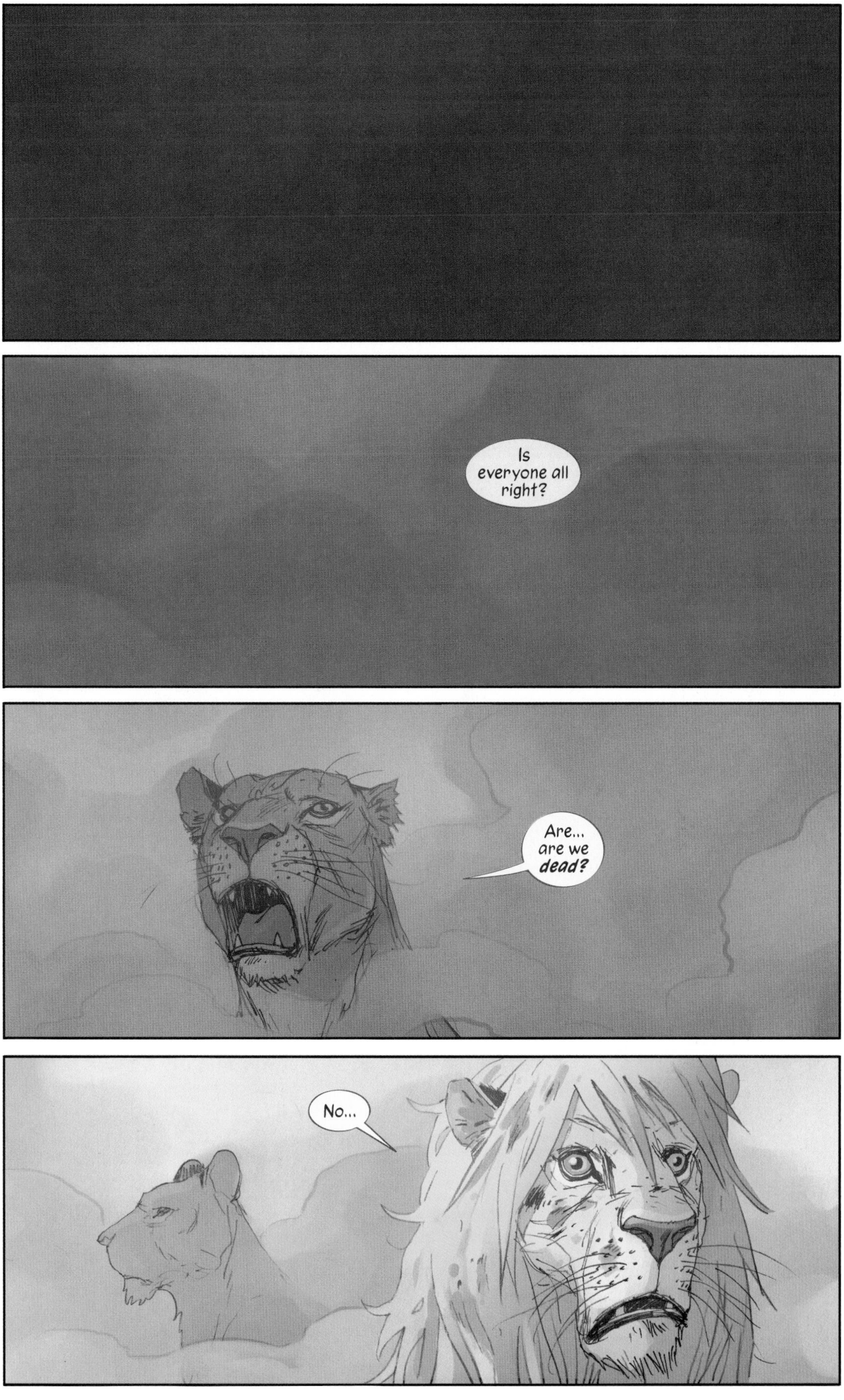
Is everyone all right?
Are... are we *dead?*
No...

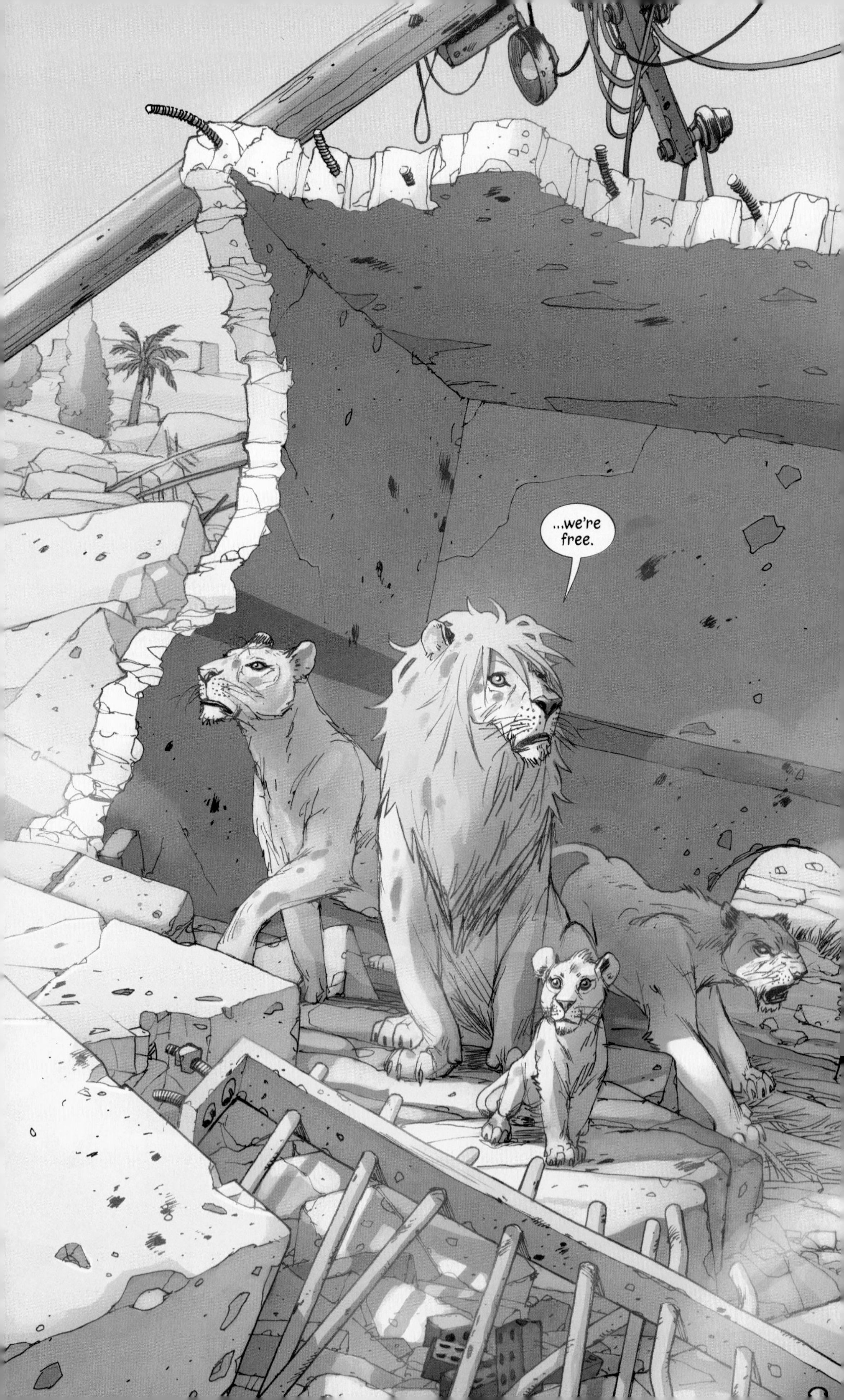
...we're free.

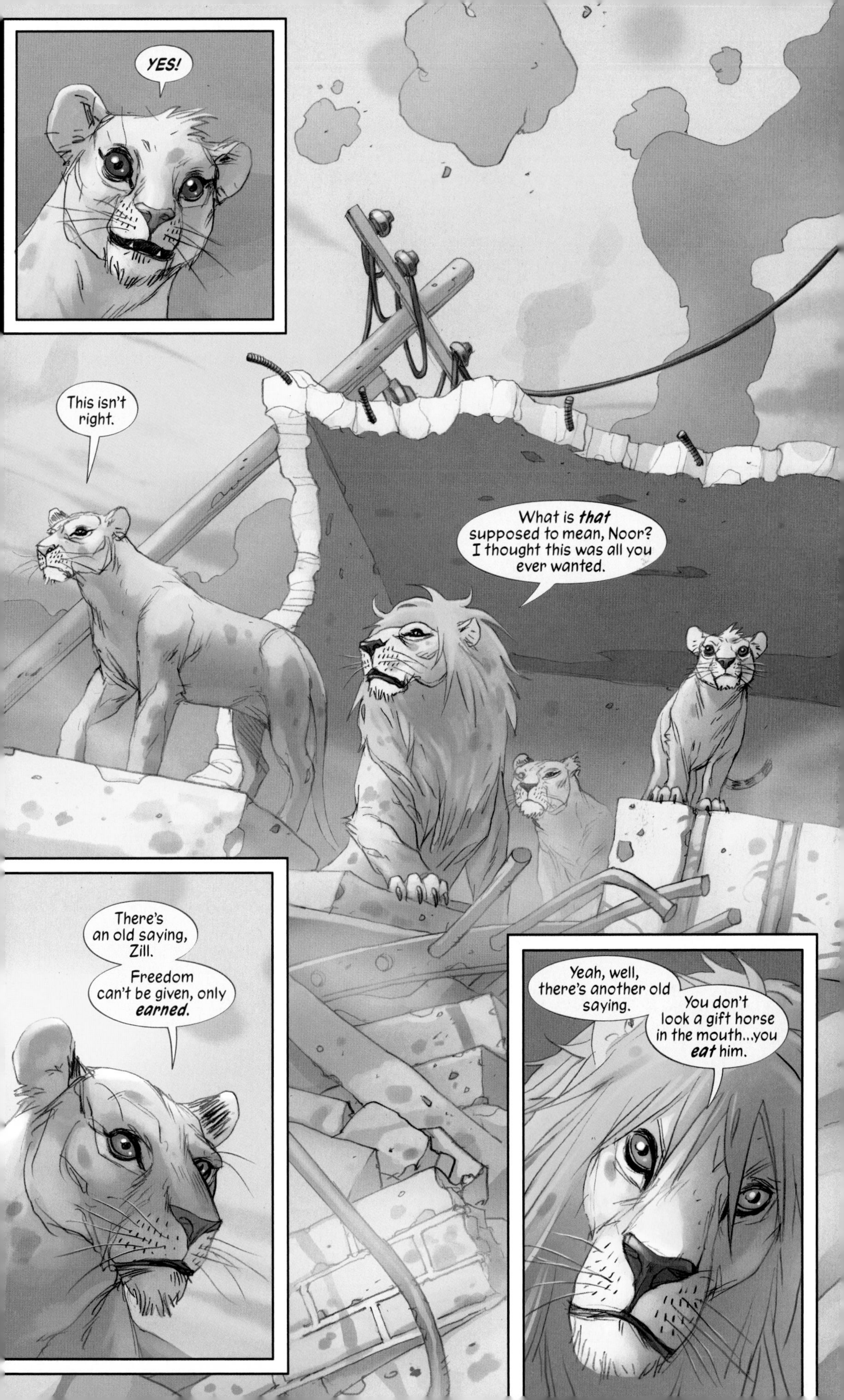
YES!
This isn't right.
What is that supposed to mean, Noor? I thought this was all you ever wanted.
There's an old saying, Zill.
Freedom can't be given, only earned.
Yeah, well, there's another old saying.
You don't look a gift horse in the mouth...you eat him.

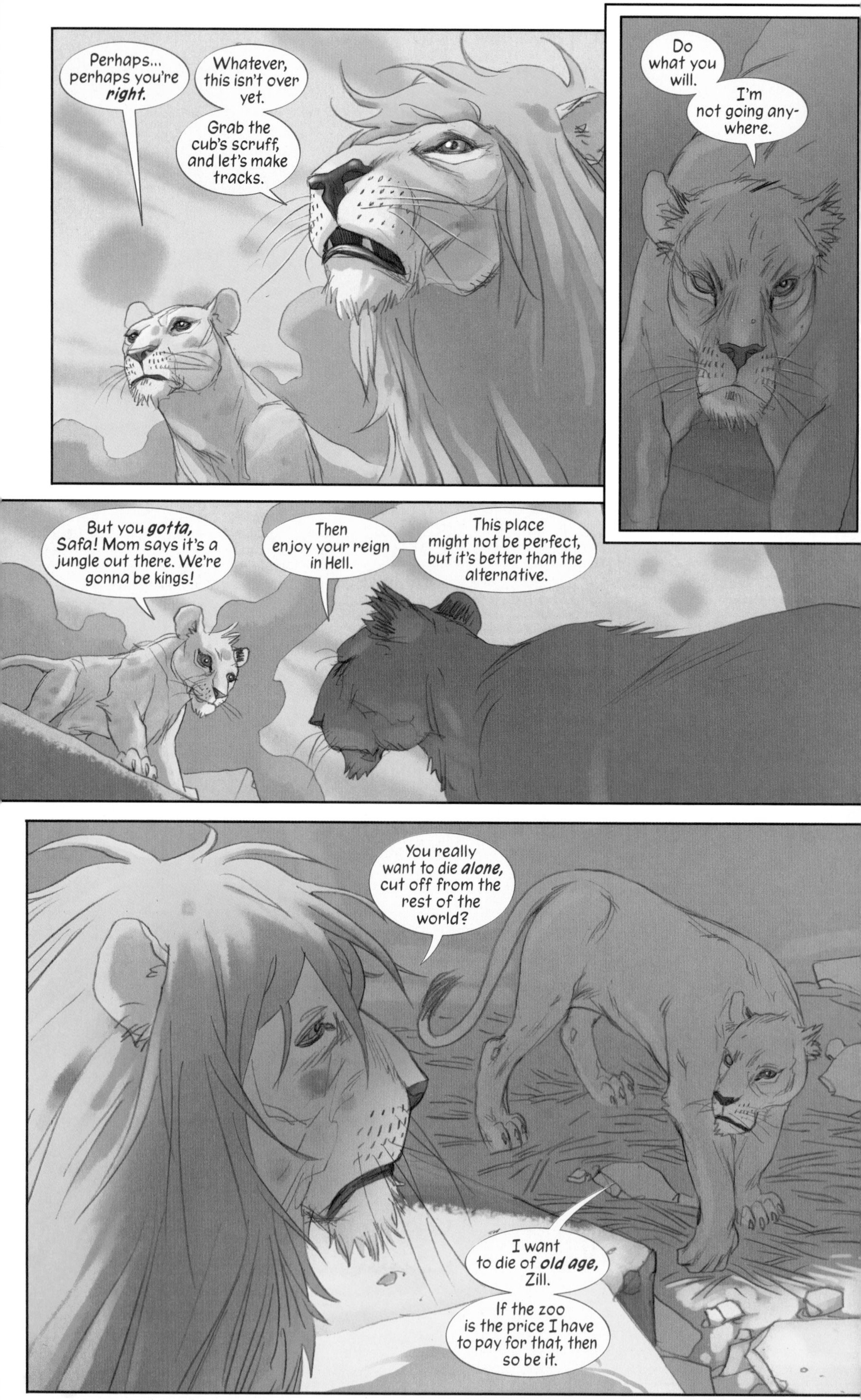
Perhaps... perhaps you're *right.*
Whatever, this isn't over yet.
Grab the cub's scruff, and let's make tracks.
Do what you will.
I'm not going any-where.
But you *gotta,* Safa! Mom says it's a jungle out there. We're gonna be kings!
Then enjoy your reign in Hell.
This place might not be perfect, but it's better than the alternative.
You really want to die *alone,* cut off from the rest of the world?
I want to die of *old age,* Zill.
If the zoo is the price I have to pay for that, then so be it.

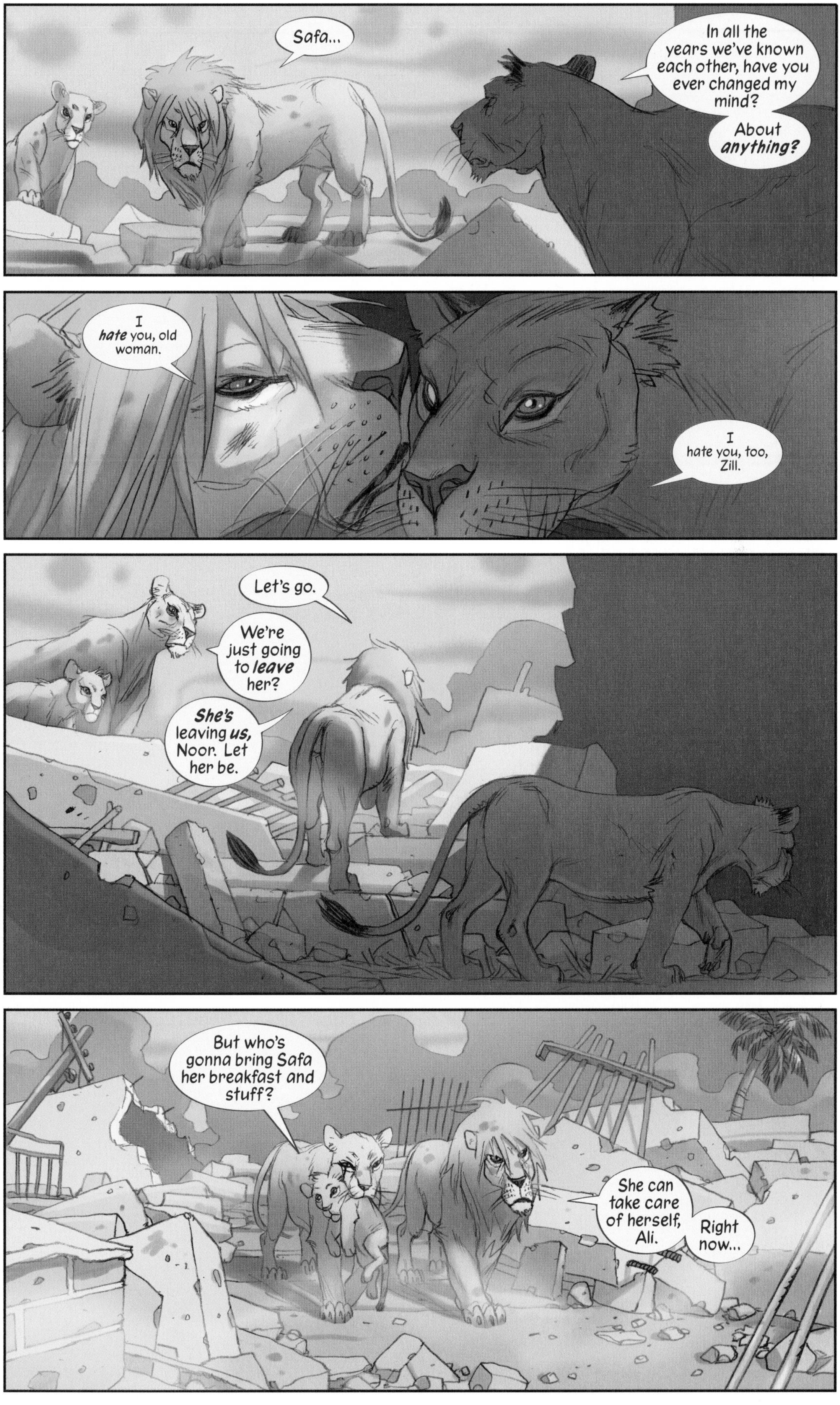
Safa...
In all the years we've known each other, have you ever changed my mind?
About *anything?*
I *hate* you, old woman.
I hate you, too, Zill.
Let's go.
We're just going to *leave* her?
She's leaving *us,* Noor. Let her be.
But who's gonna bring Safa her breakfast and stuff?
She can take care of herself, Ali.
Right now...

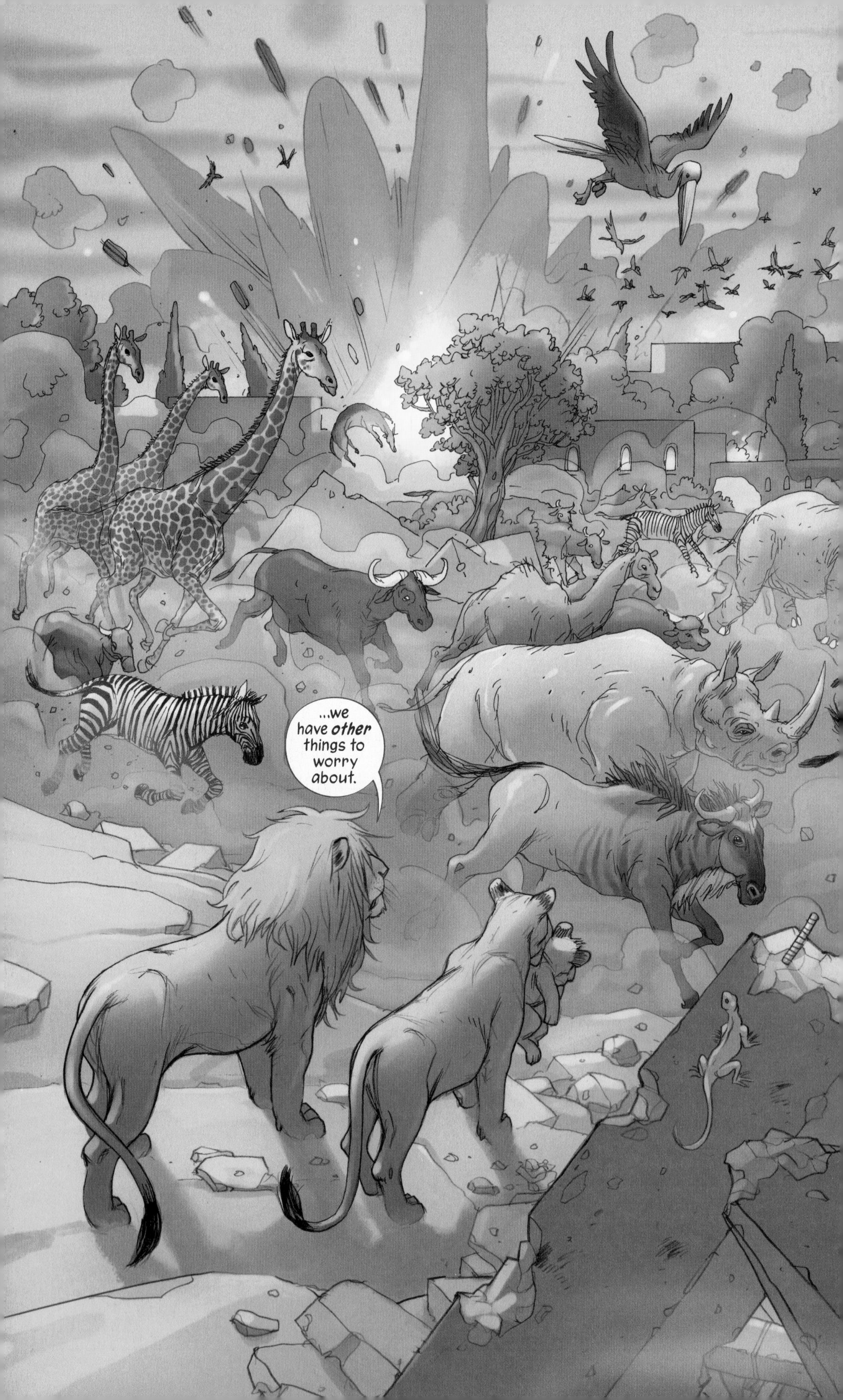
...we have *other* things to worry about.

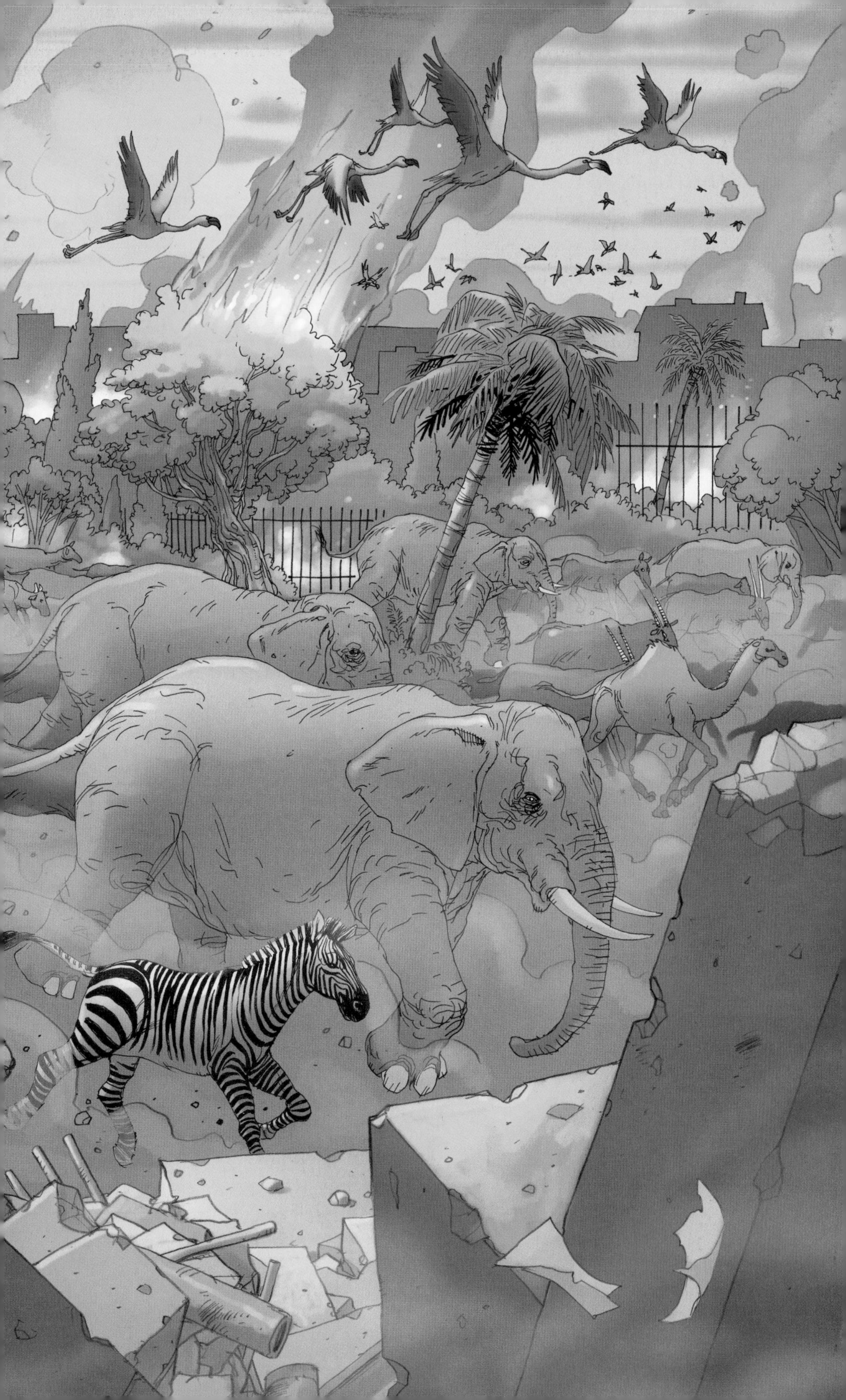

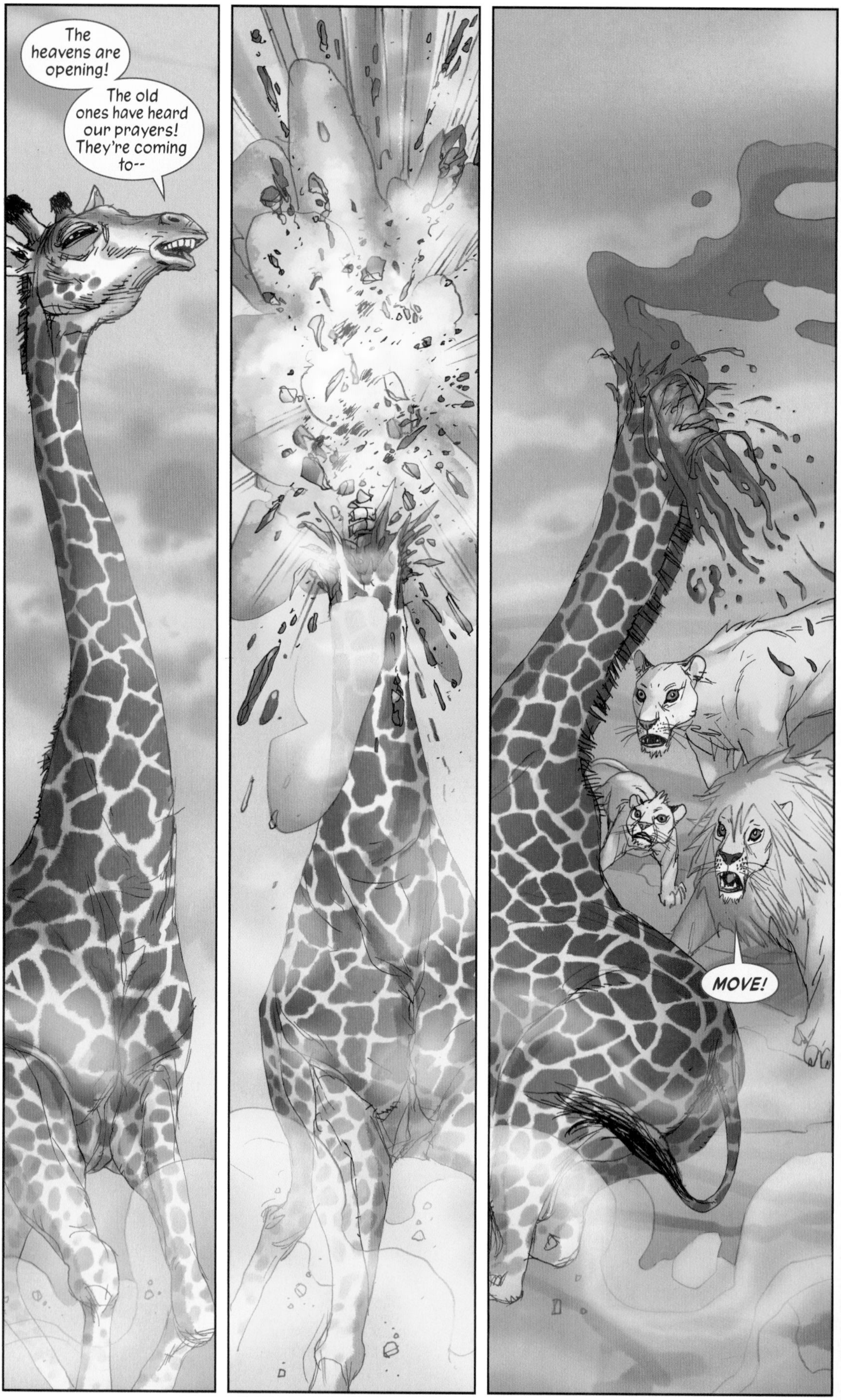
The heavens are opening!
The old ones have heard our prayers! They're coming to--
MOVE!

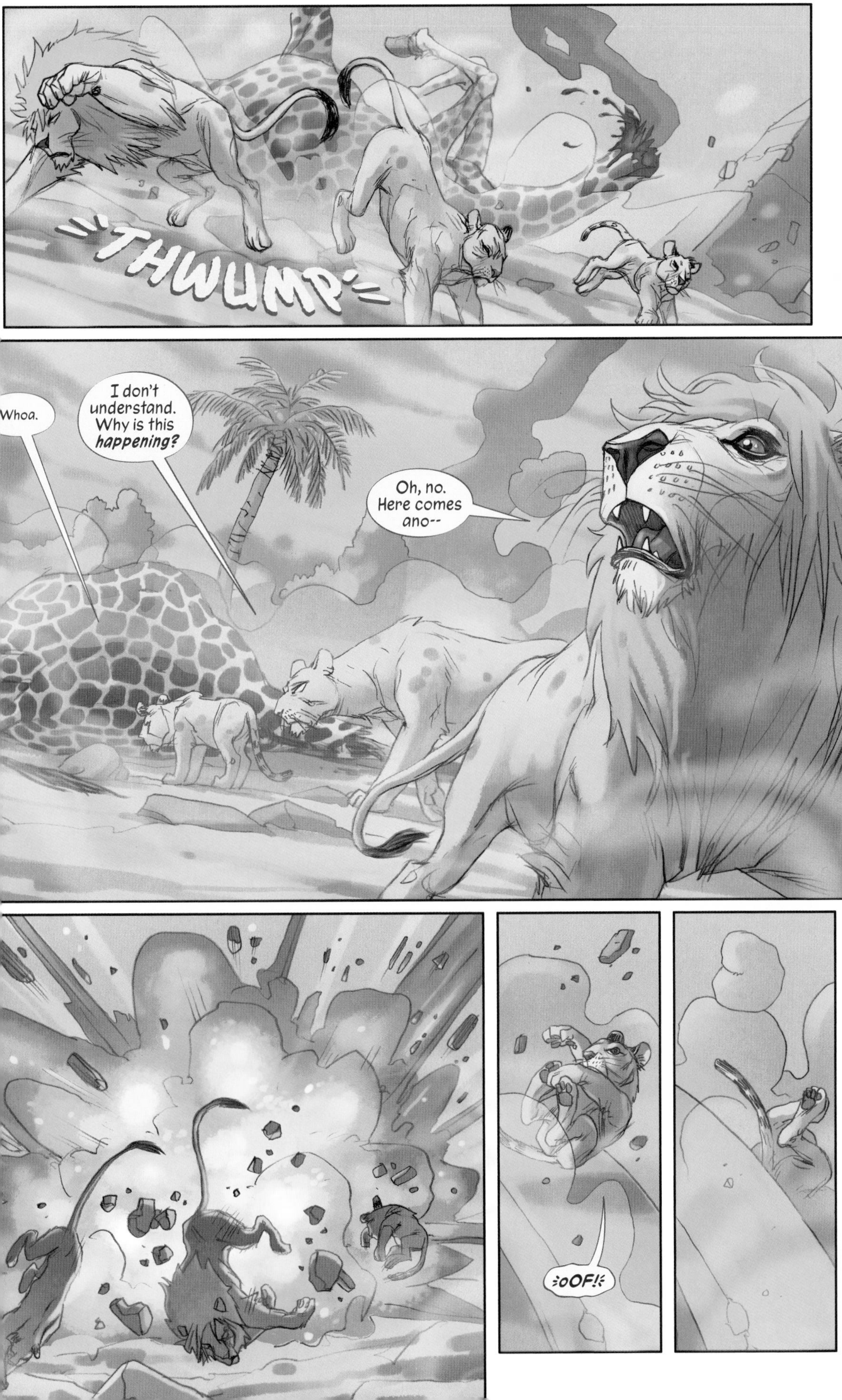
THWUMP
Whoa.
I don't understand. Why is this *happening?*
Oh, no. Here comes ano--
OOF!

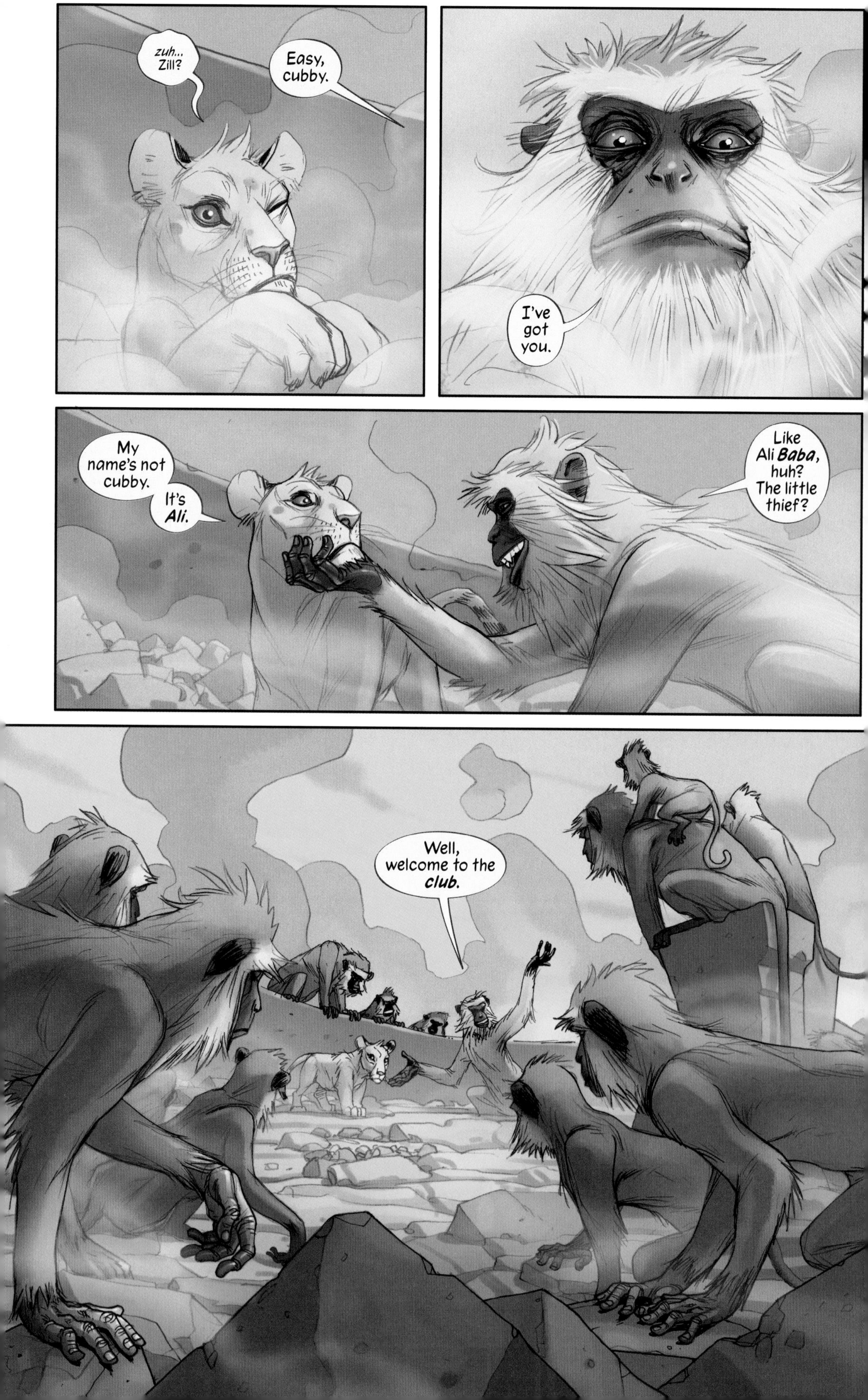
zuh... Zill?
Easy, cubby.
I've got you.
My name's not cubby.
It's Ali.
Like Ali Baba, huh? The little thief?
Well, welcome to the club.

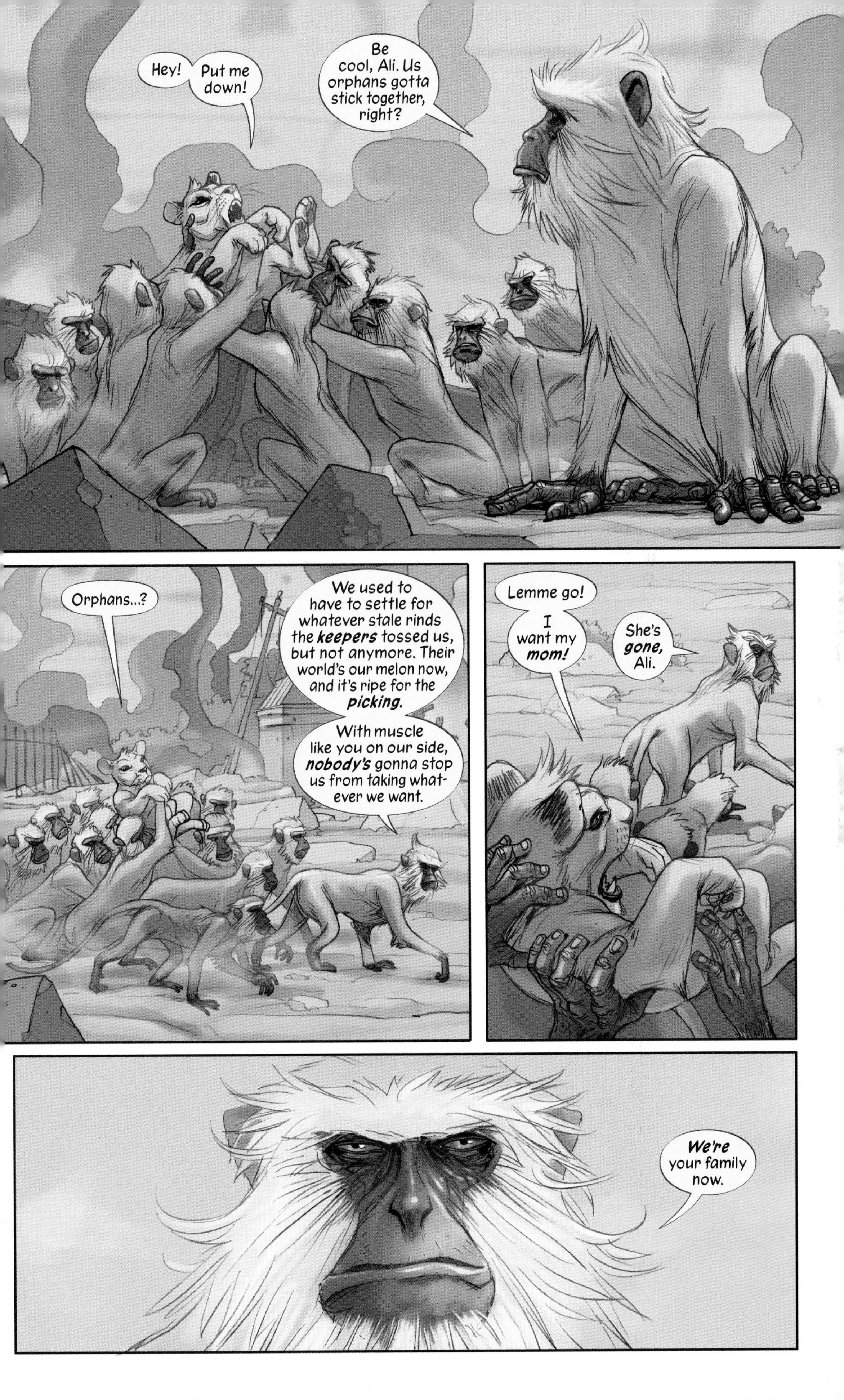
Hey!
Put me down!
Be cool, Ali. Us orphans gotta stick together, right?
Orphans...?
We used to have to settle for whatever stale rinds the **keepers** tossed us, but not anymore. Their world's our melon now, and it's ripe for the **picking**.
With muscle like you on our side, **nobody's** gonna stop us from taking whatever we want.
Lemme go!
I want my **mom!**
She's **gone,** Ali.
We're your family now.

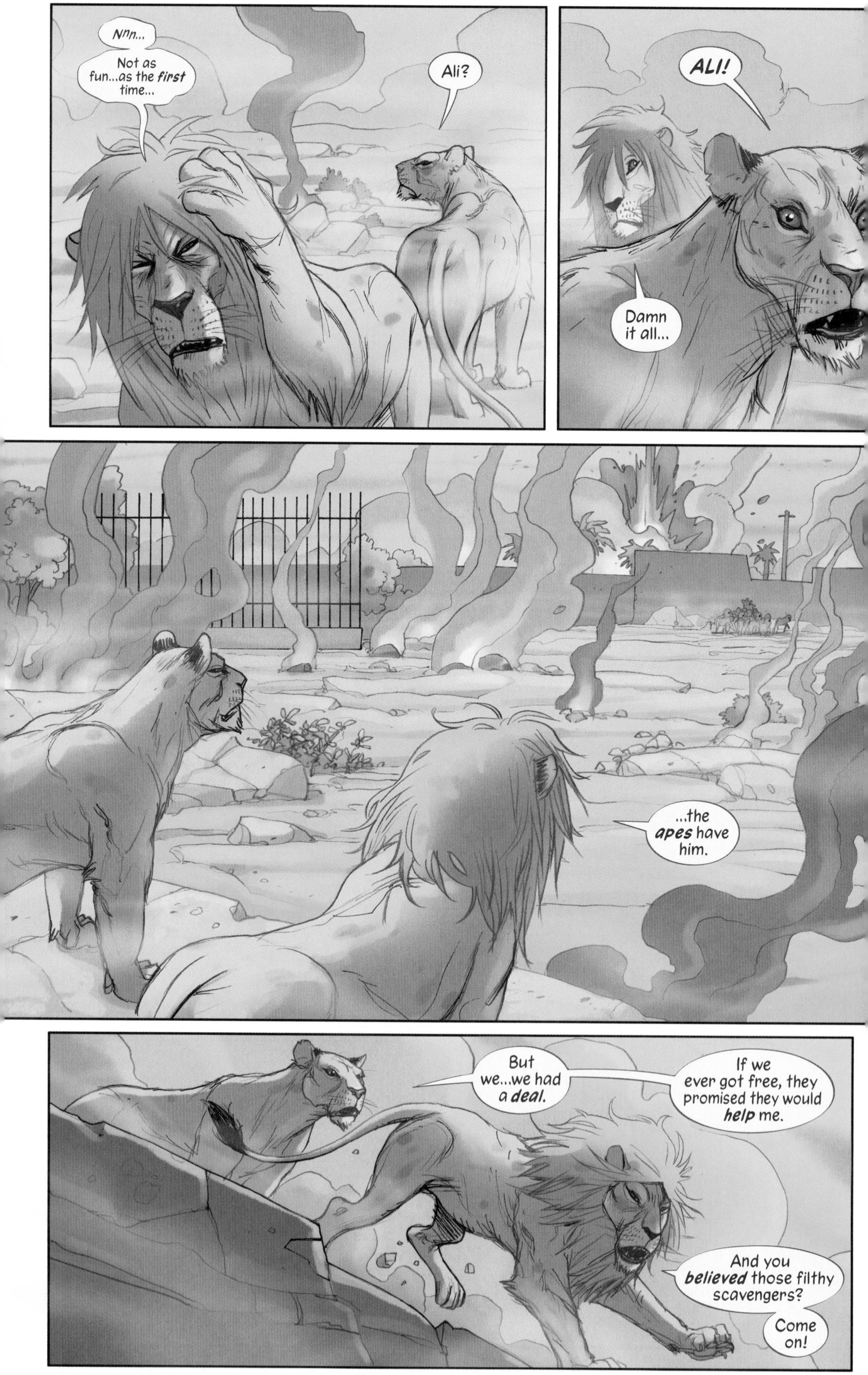

Nnn...
Not as fun...as the *first* time...
Ali?
ALI!
Damn it all...
...the *apes* have him.
But we...we had a *deal*.
If we ever got free, they promised they would *help* me.
And you *believed* those filthy scavengers?
Come on!

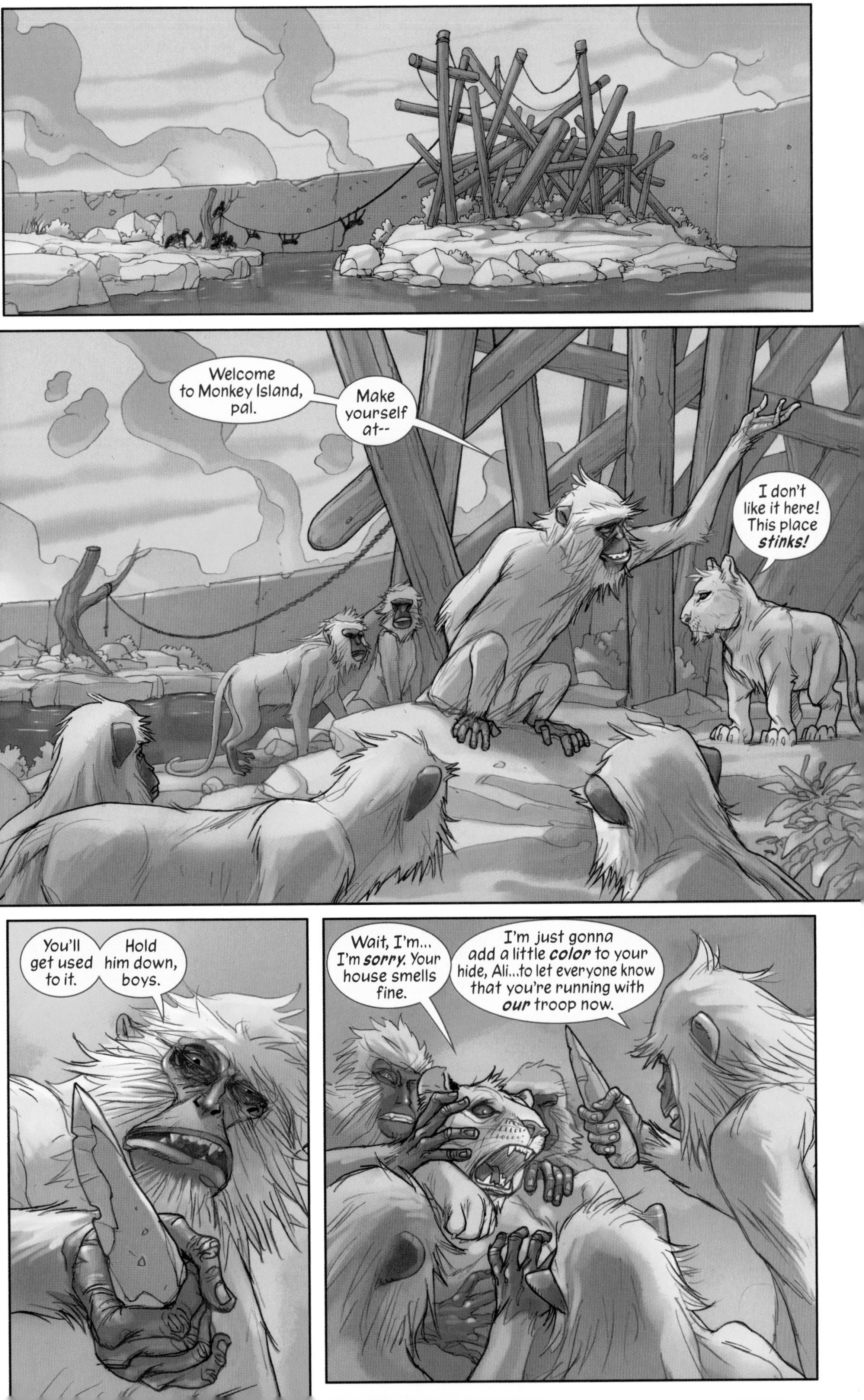
Welcome to Monkey Island, pal.
Make yourself at--
I don't like it here! This place stinks!
You'll get used to it.
Hold him down, boys.
Wait, I'm... I'm sorry. Your house smells fine.
I'm just gonna add a little color to your hide, Ali...to let everyone know that you're running with our troop now.

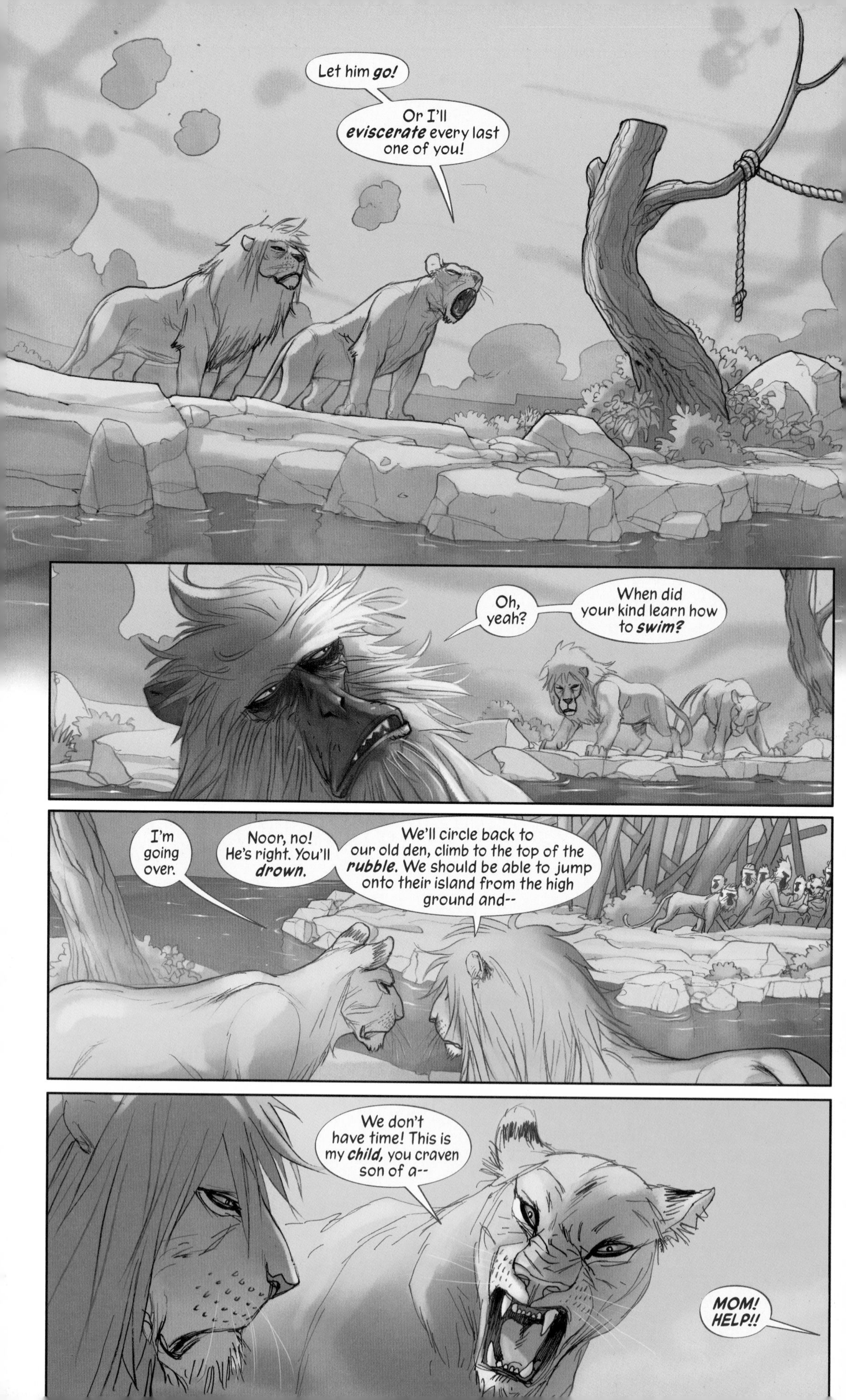
Let him go!
Or I'll eviscerate every last one of you!
Oh, yeah?
When did your kind learn how to swim?
I'm going over.
Noor, no! He's right. You'll drown.
We'll circle back to our old den, climb to the top of the rubble. We should be able to jump onto their island from the high ground and--
We don't have time! This is my child, you craven son of a--
MOM! HELP!!

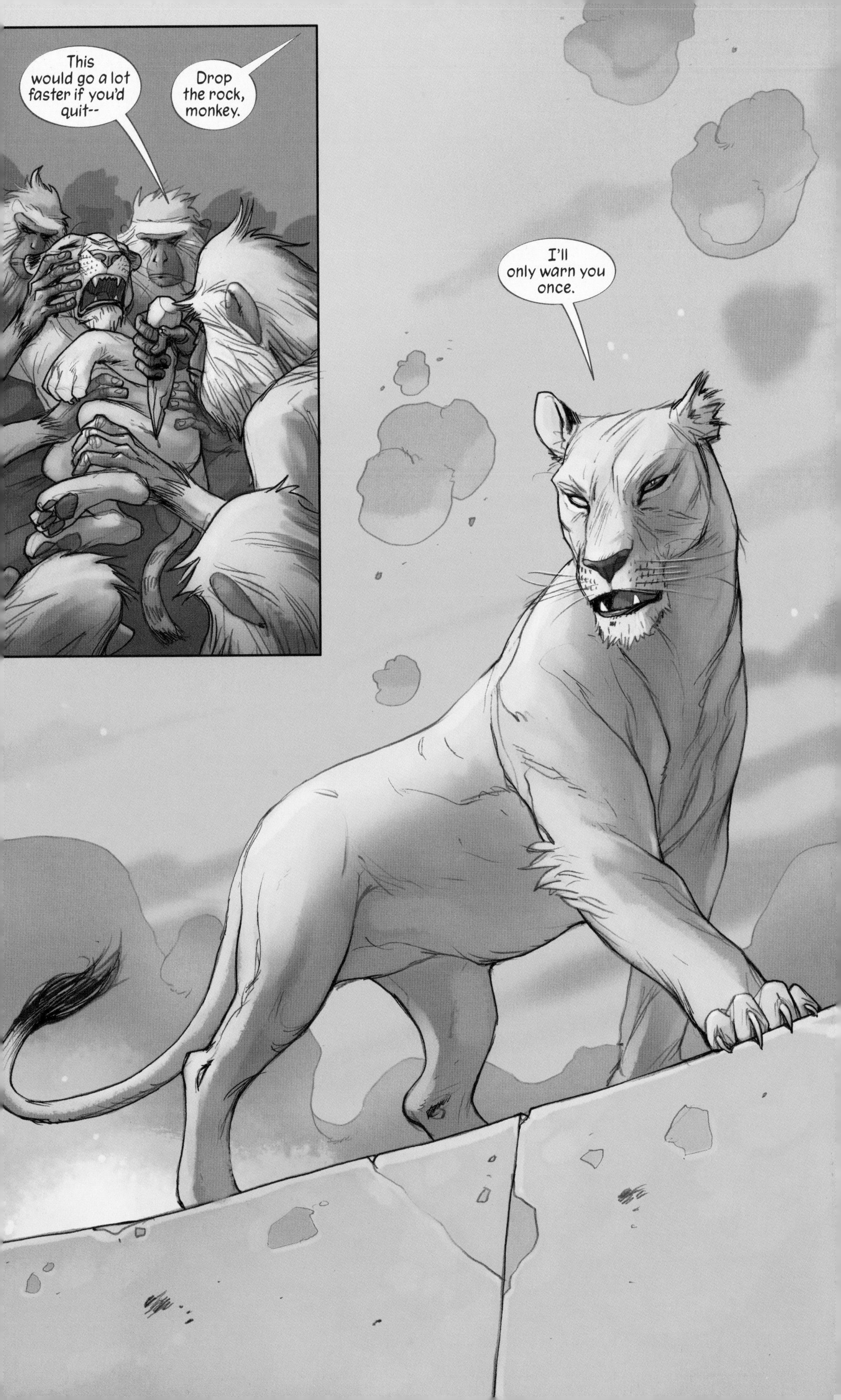
This would go a lot faster if you'd quit--
Drop the rock, monkey.
I'll only warn you once.

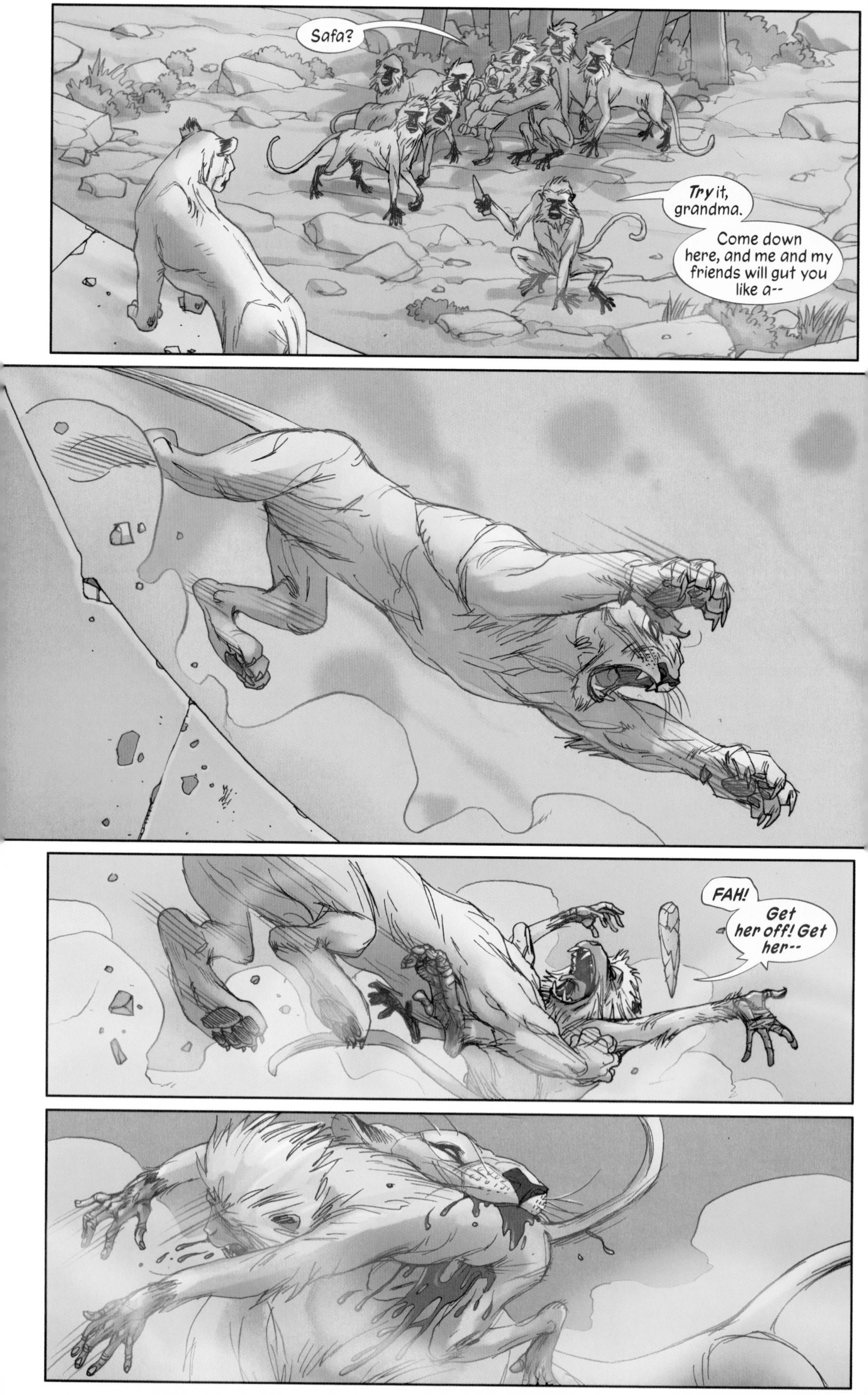
Safa?
Try it, grandma.
Come down here, and me and my friends will gut you like a--
FAH!
Get her off! Get her--

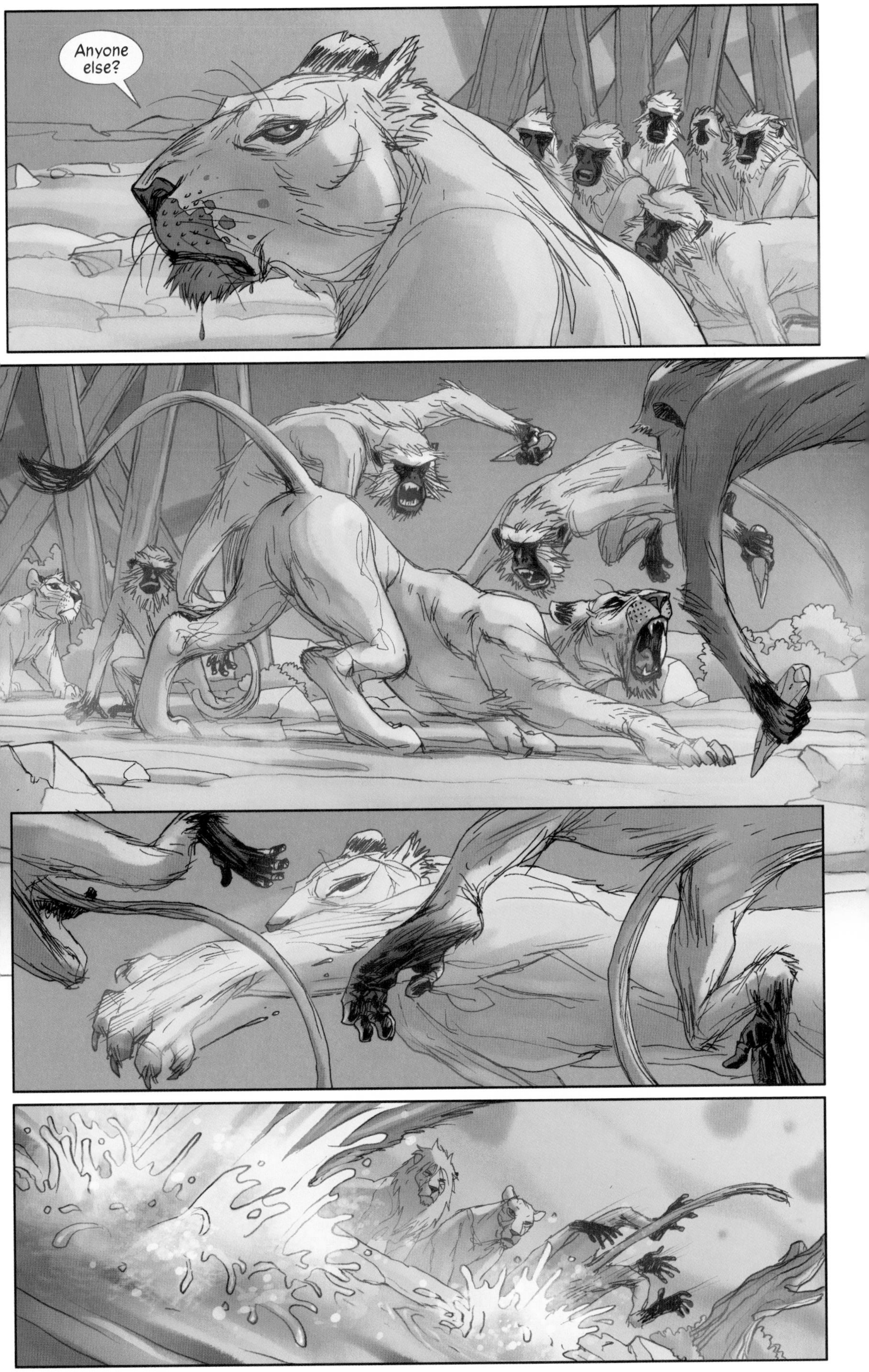
Anyone else?

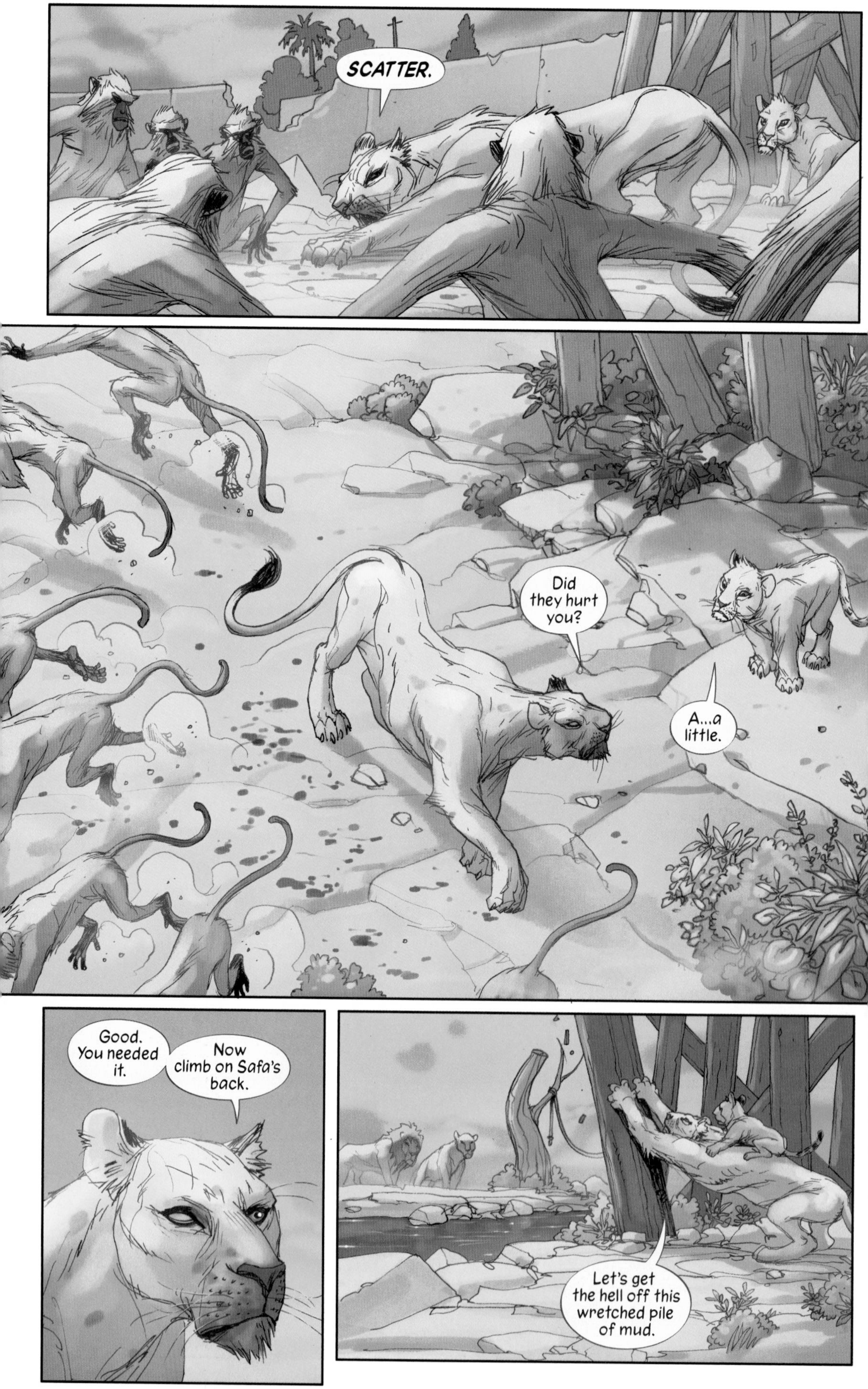
SCATTER.
Did they hurt you?
A...a little.
Good. You needed it.
Now climb on Safa's back.
Let's get the hell off this wretched pile of mud.

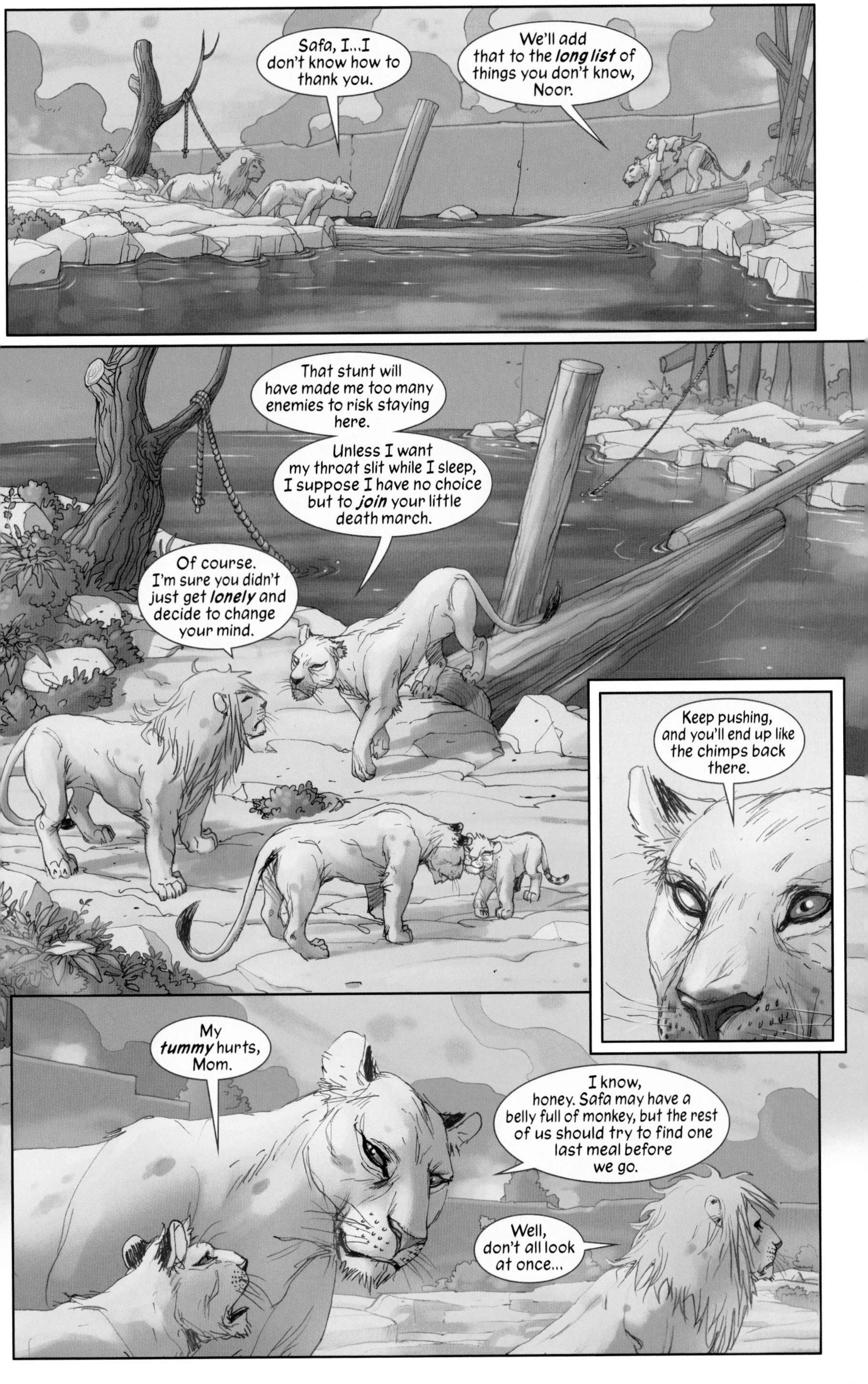
Safa, I...I don't know how to thank you.
We'll add that to the *long list* of things you don't know, Noor.
That stunt will have made me too many enemies to risk staying here.
Unless I want my throat slit while I sleep, I suppose I have no choice but to *join* your little death march.
Of course. I'm sure you didn't just get *lonely* and decide to change your mind.
Keep pushing, and you'll end up like the chimps back there.
My *tummy* hurts, Mom.
I know, honey. Safa may have a belly full of monkey, but the rest of us should try to find one last meal before we go.
Well, don't all look at once...

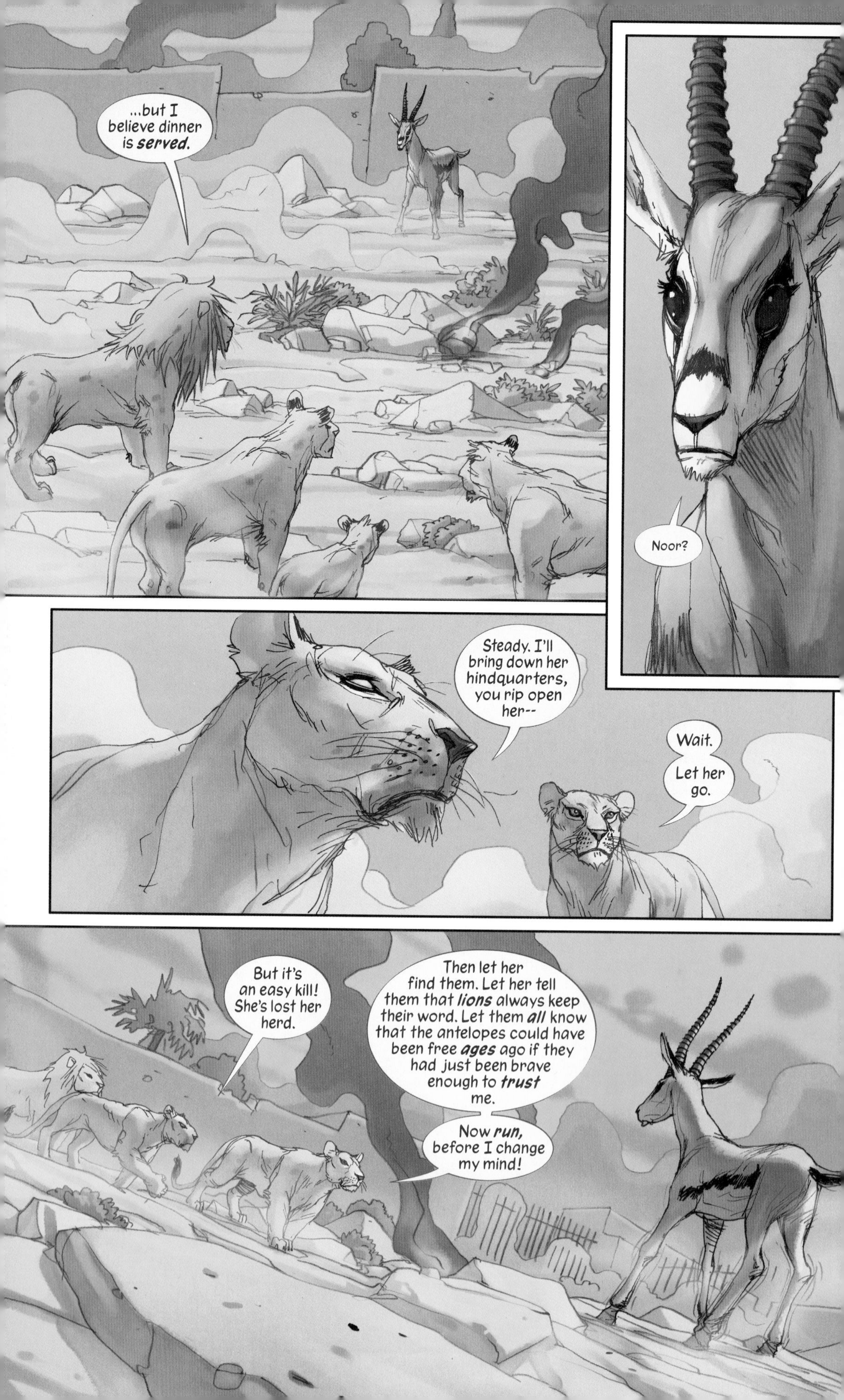
...but I believe dinner is *served.*
Noor?
Steady. I'll bring down her hindquarters, you rip open her--
Wait.
Let her go.
But it's an easy kill! She's lost her herd.
Then let her find them. Let her tell them that *lions* always keep their word. Let them *all* know that the antelopes could have been free *ages* ago if they had just been brave enough to *trust* me.
Now *run,* before I change my mind!

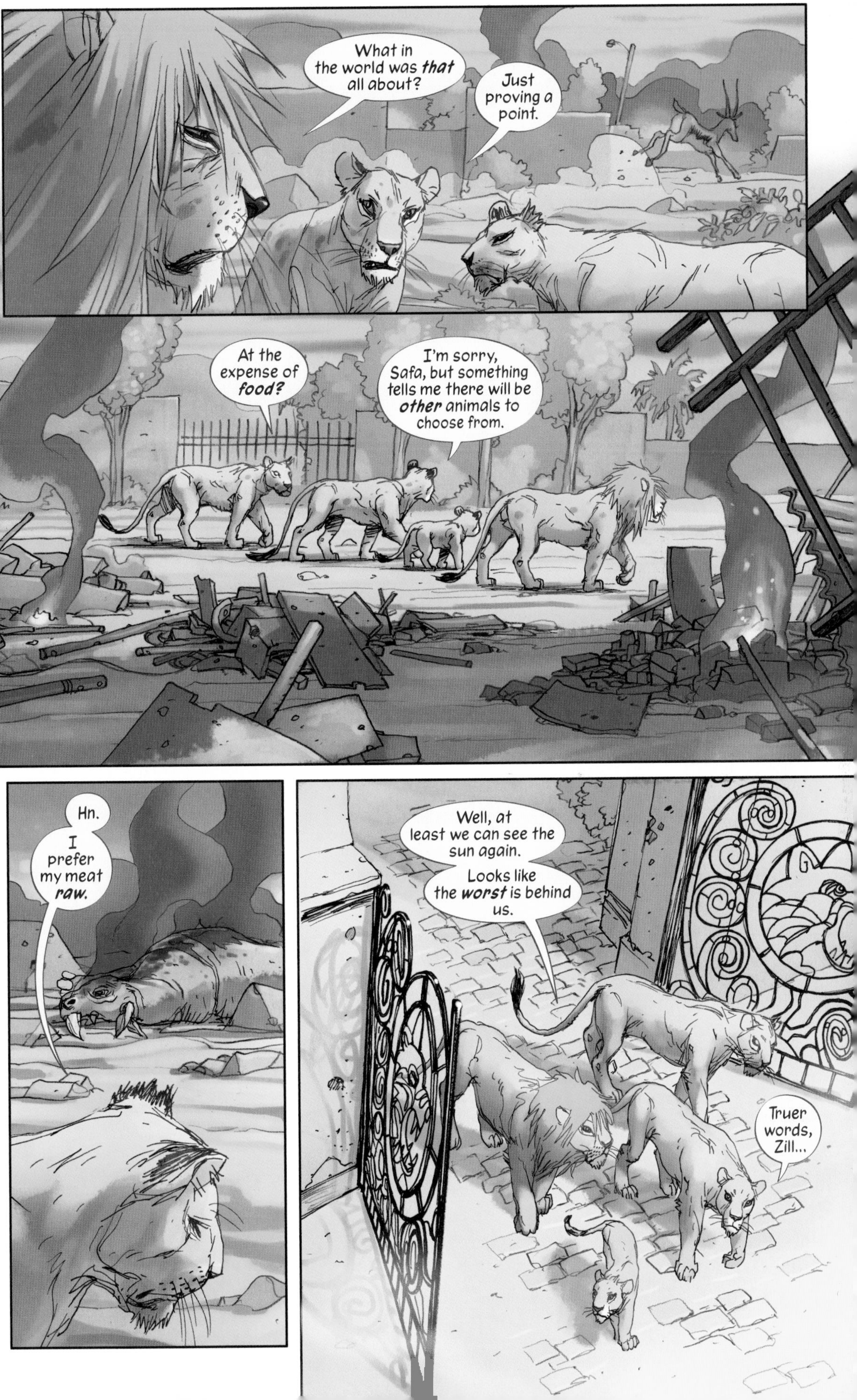

What in the world was *that* all about?
Just proving a point.
At the expense of *food?*
I'm sorry, Safa, but something tells me there will be *other* animals to choose from.
Hn.
I prefer my meat *raw.*
Well, at least we can see the sun again.
Looks like the *worst* is behind us.
Truer words, Zill...

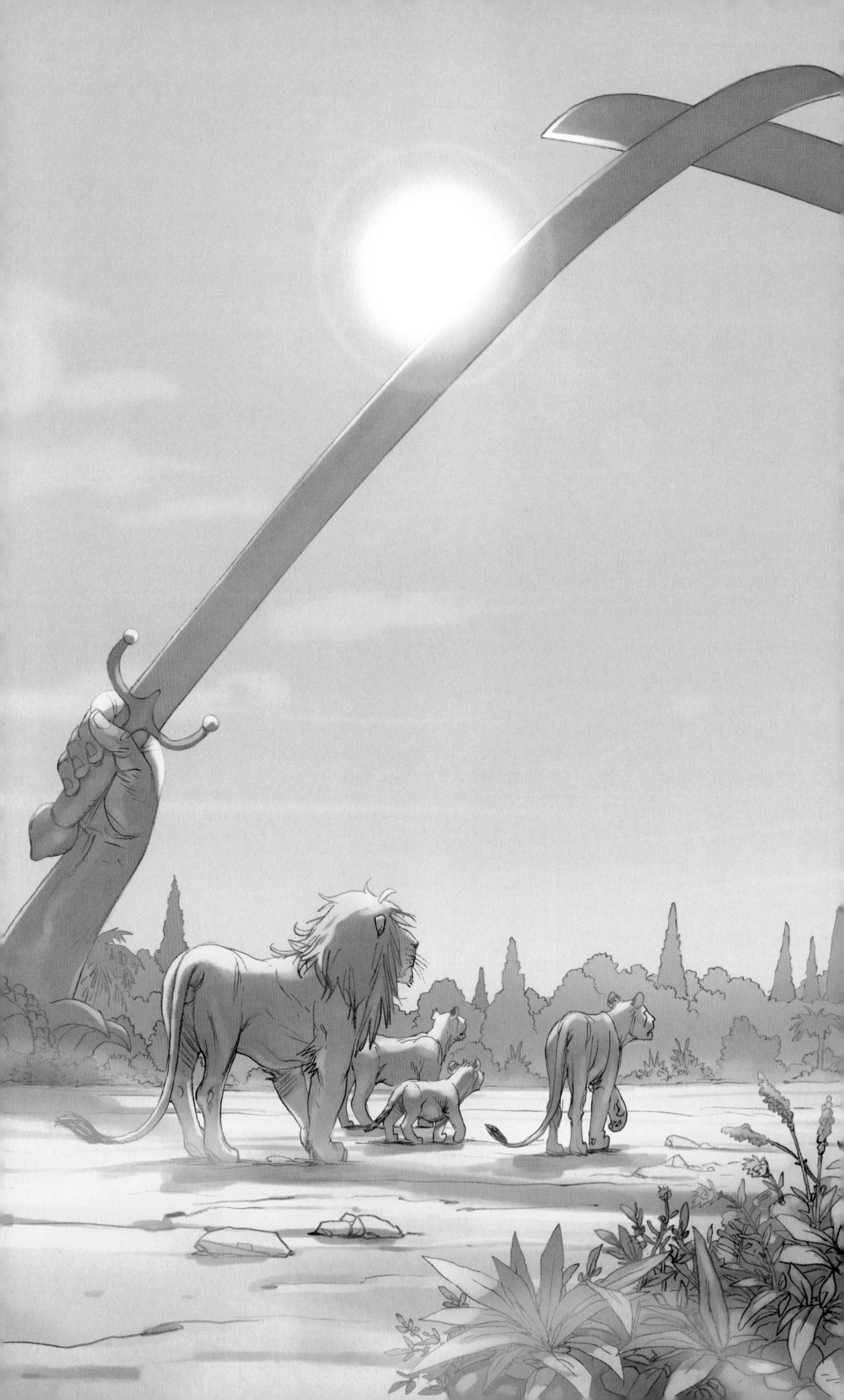

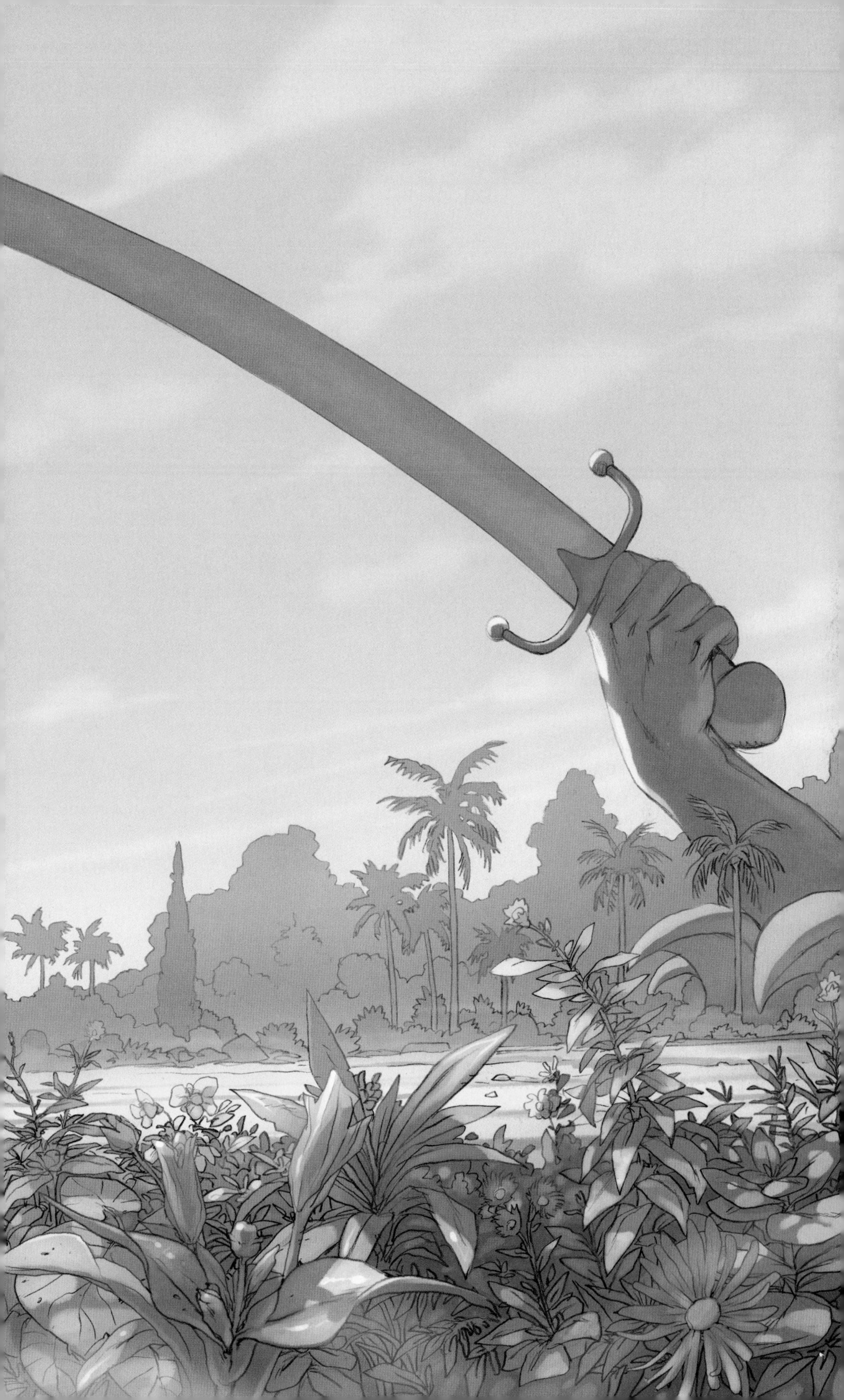

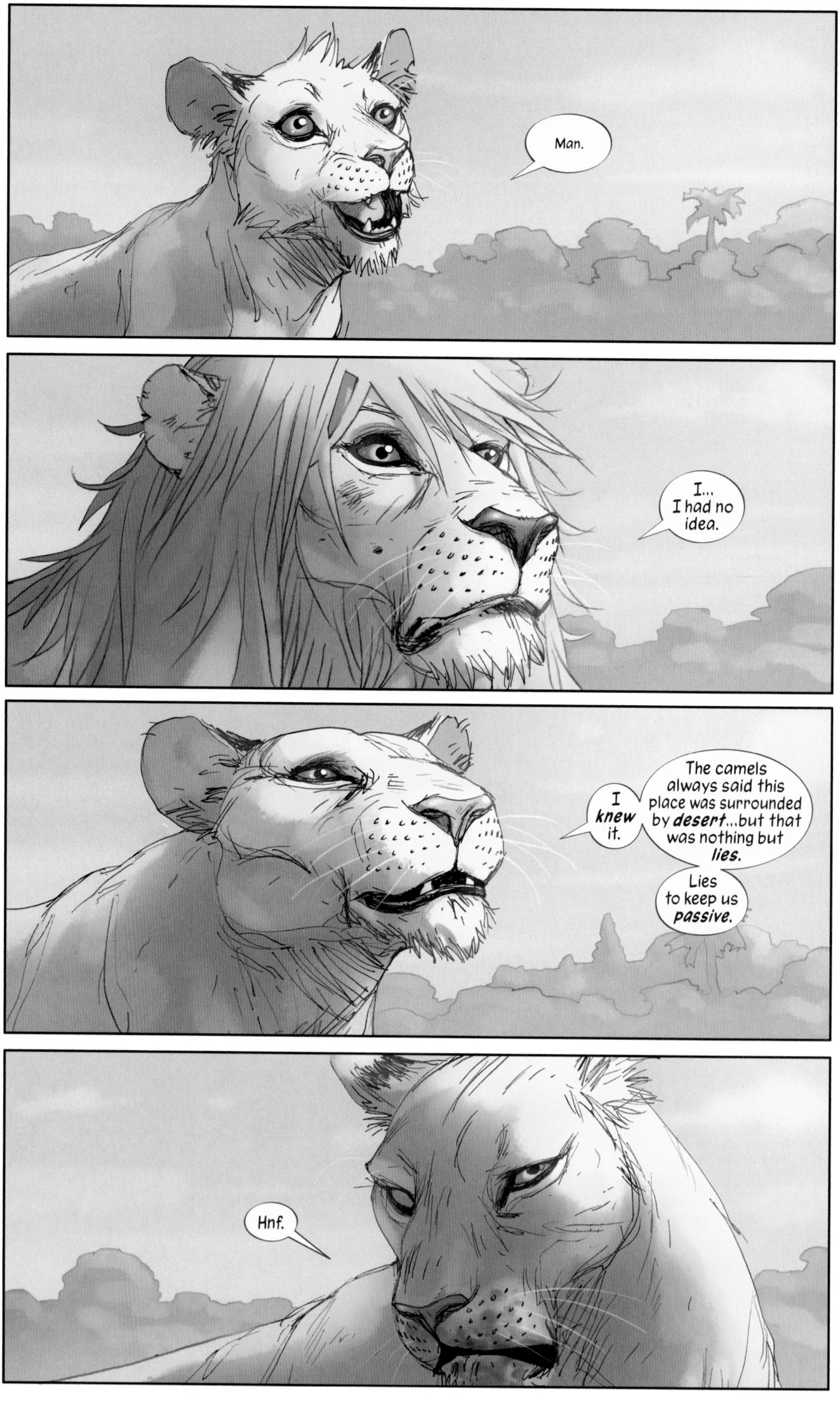
Man.
I... I had no idea.
I *knew* it.
The camels always said this place was surrounded by *desert*...but that was nothing but *lies.*
Lies to keep us *passive.*
Hnf.

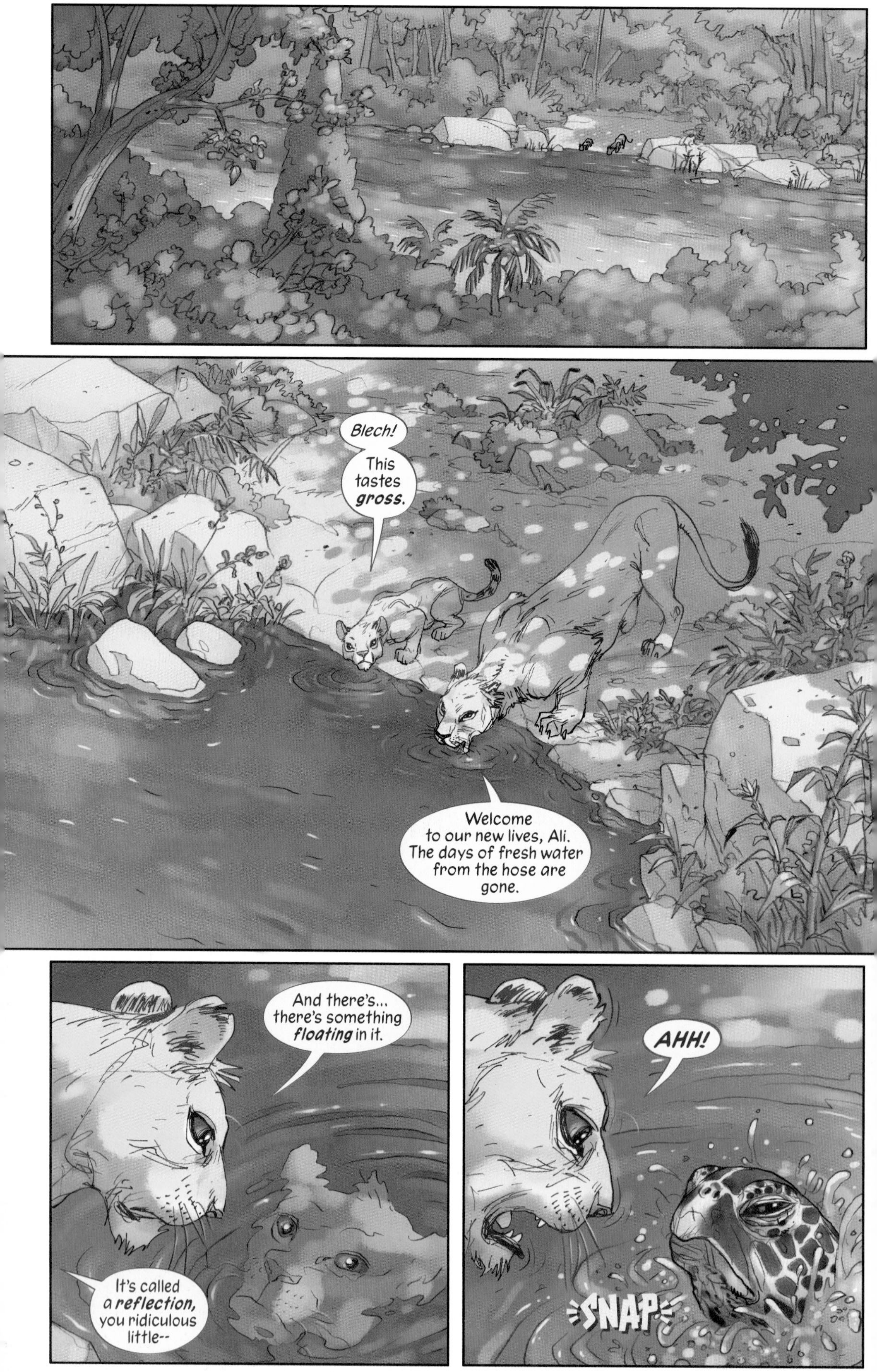
Blech!
This tastes gross.
Welcome to our new lives, Ali. The days of fresh water from the hose are gone.
And there's... there's something floating in it.
It's called a reflection, you ridiculous little--
AHH!
SNAP

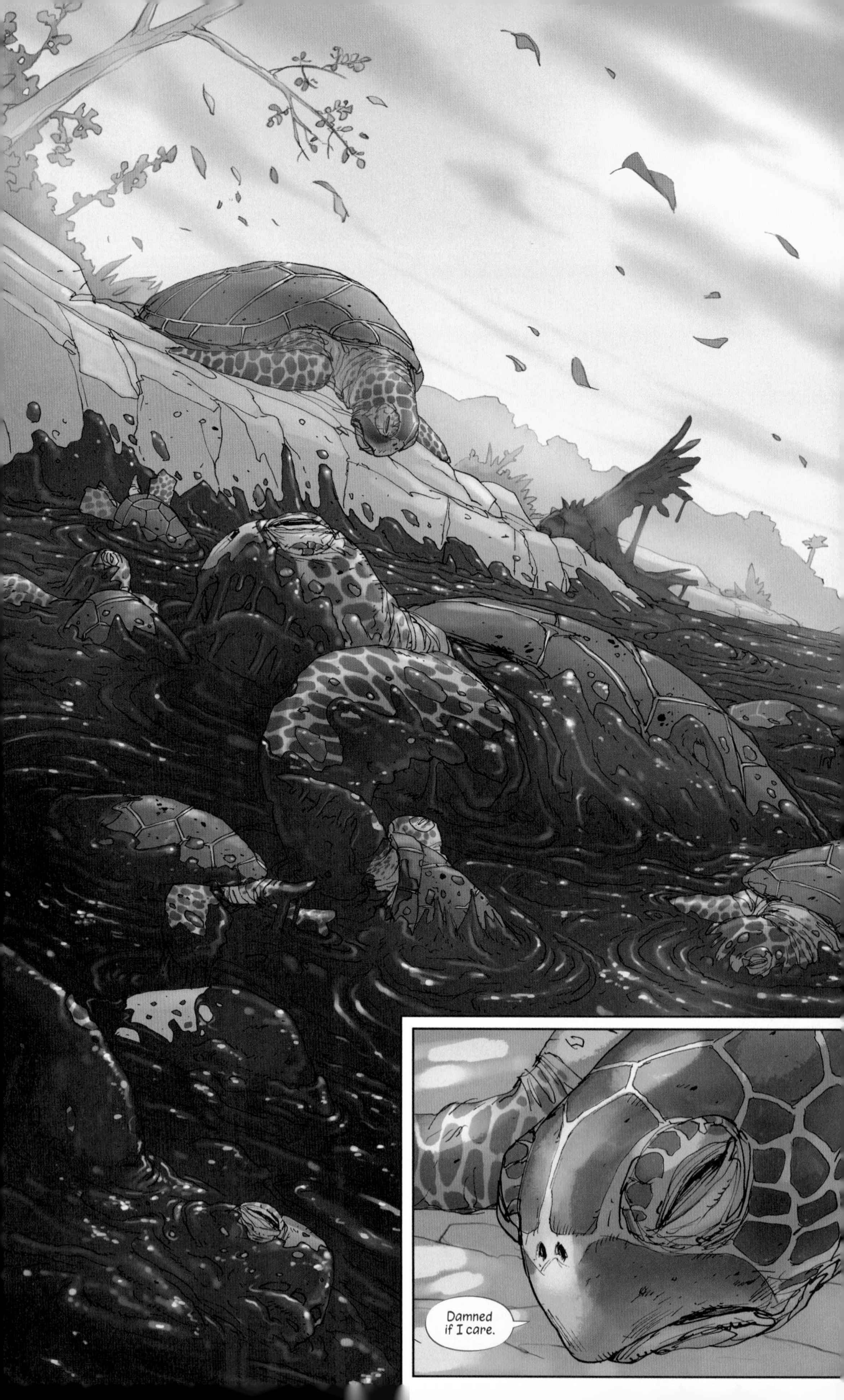
Damned
if I care.

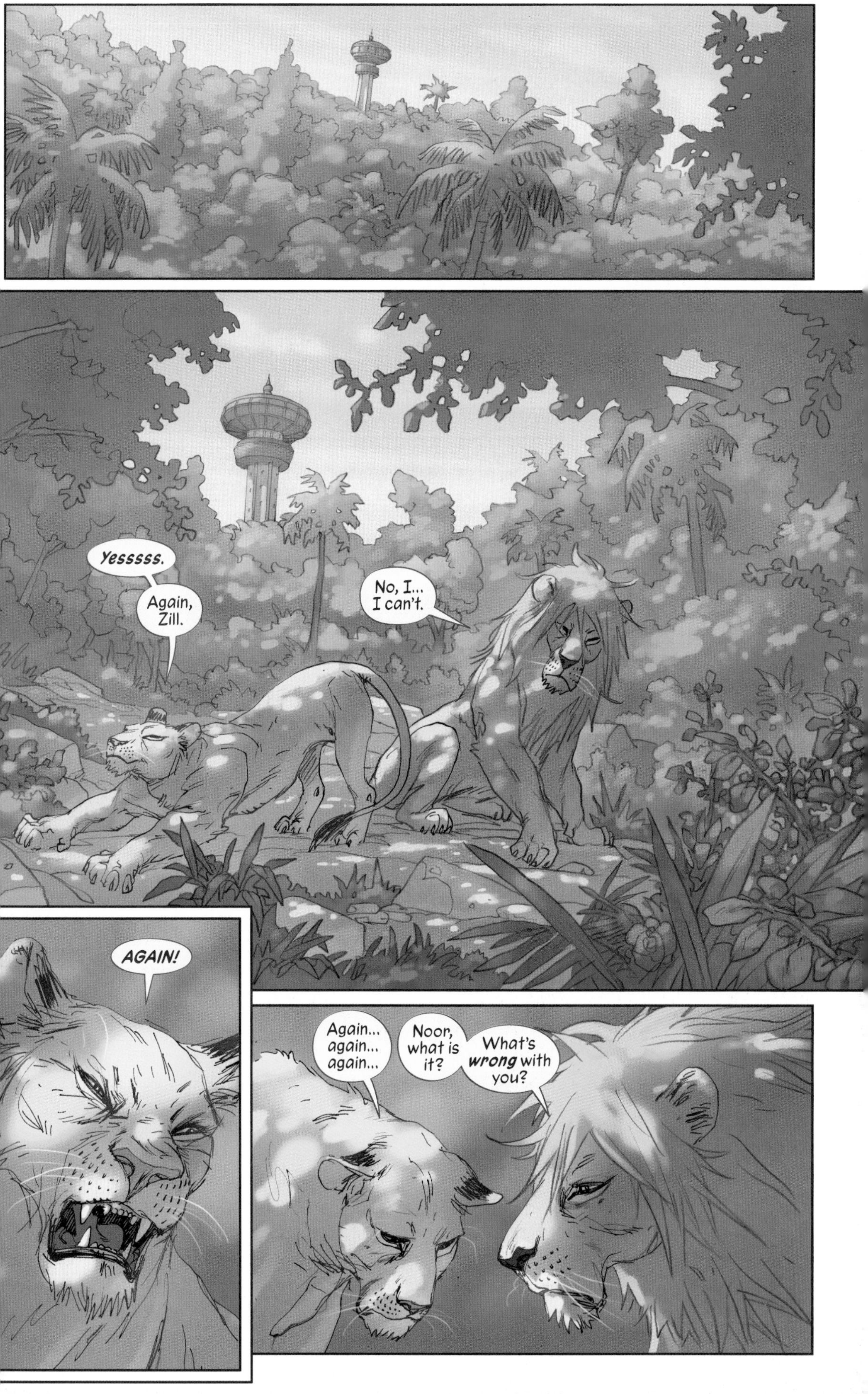
Yesssss.
Again, Zill.
No, I... I can't.
AGAIN!
Again... again... again...
Noor, what is it?
What's wrong with you?

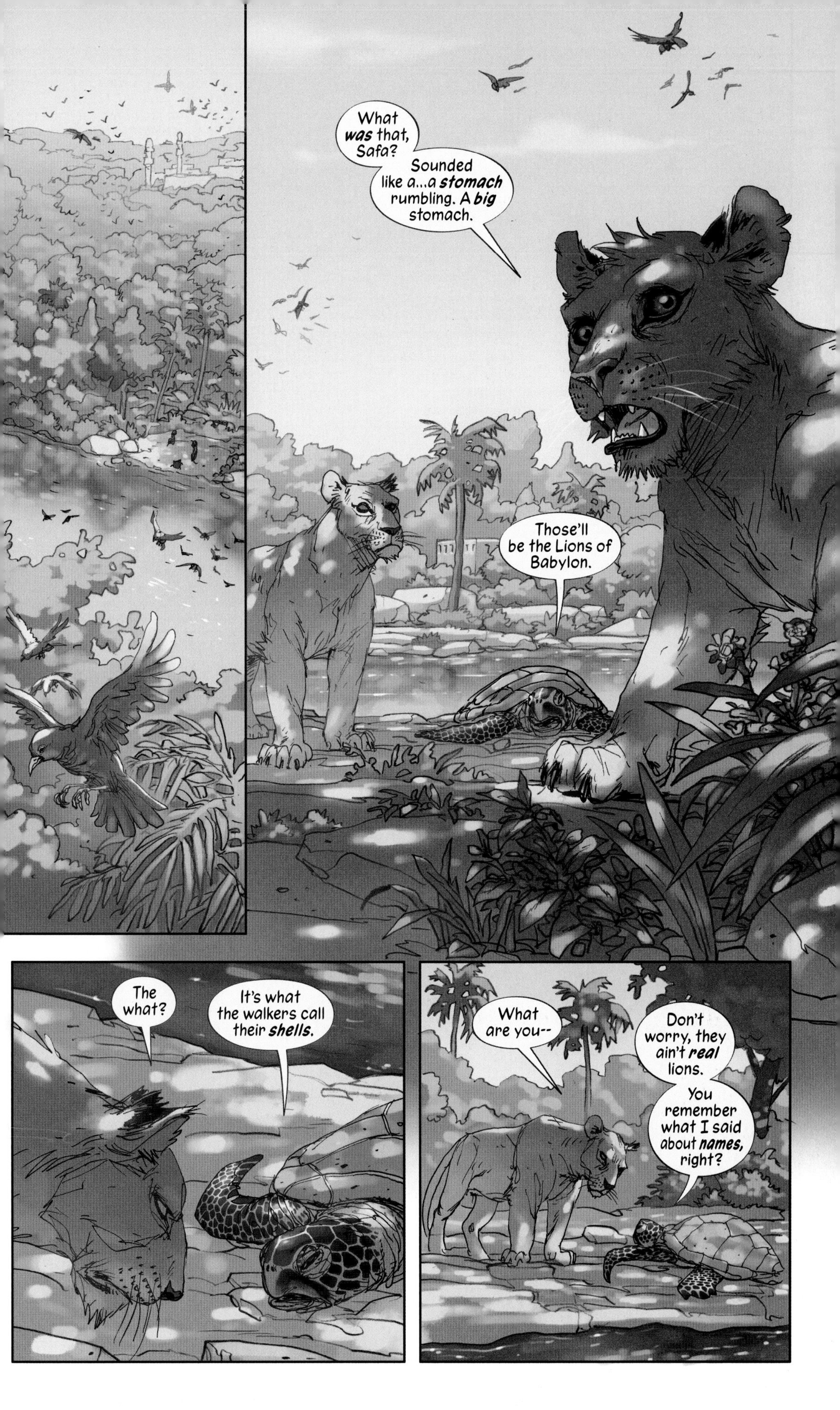
What was that, Safa?
Sounded like a...a stomach rumbling. A big stomach.
Those'll be the Lions of Babylon.
The what?
It's what the walkers call their shells.
What are you--
Don't worry, they ain't real lions.
You remember what I said about names, right?

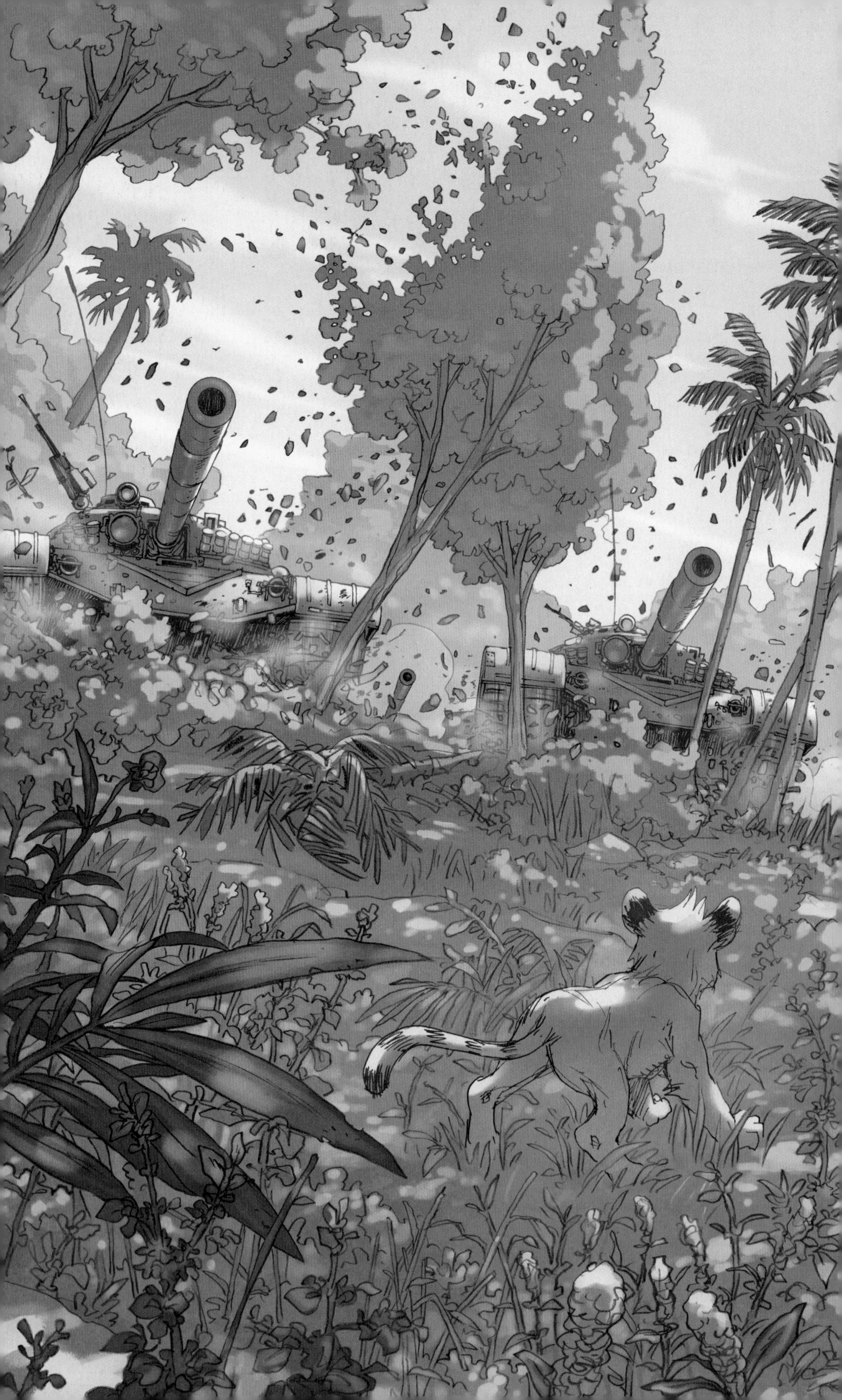

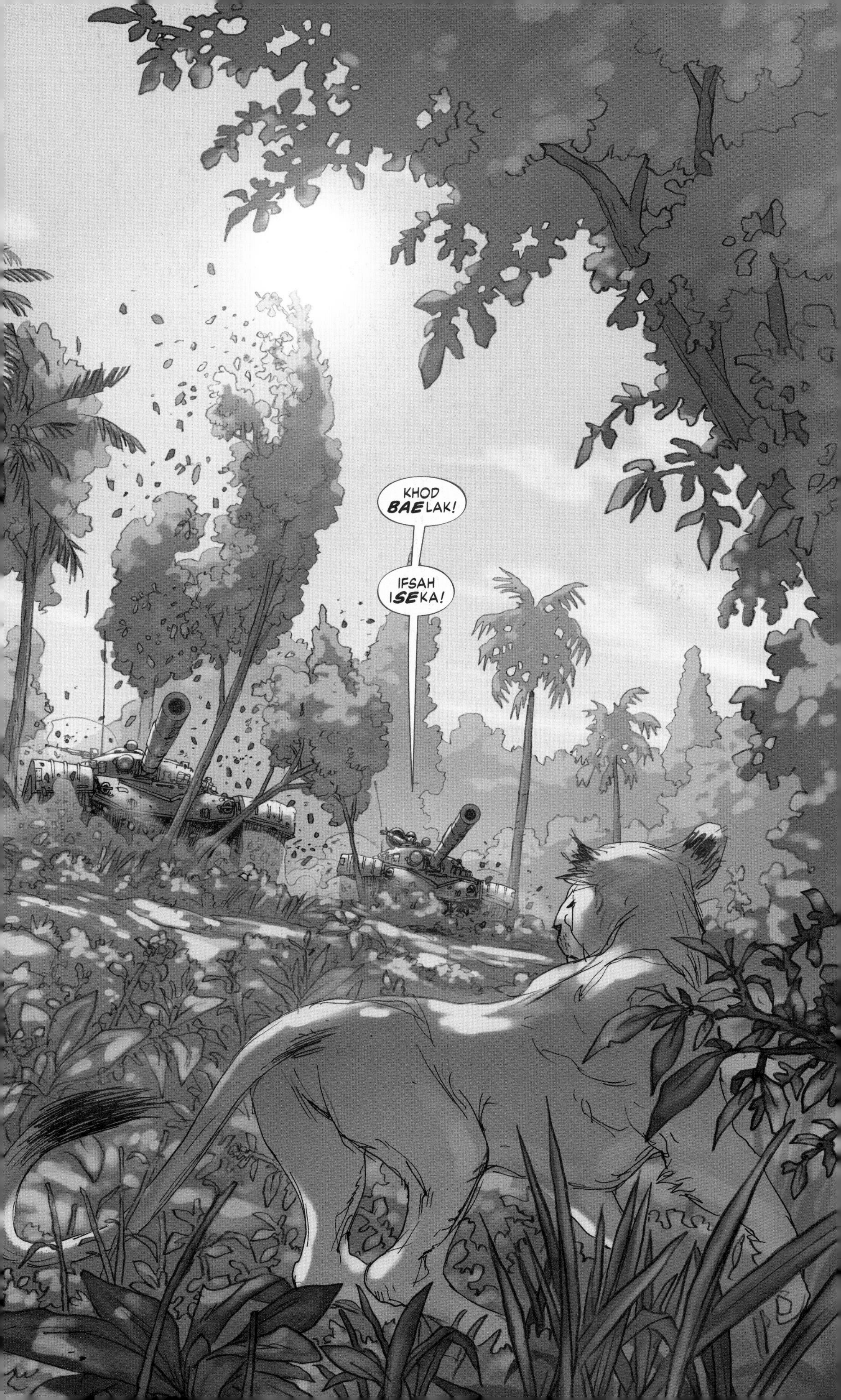
KHOD BAE LAK!
IFSAH ISE KA!

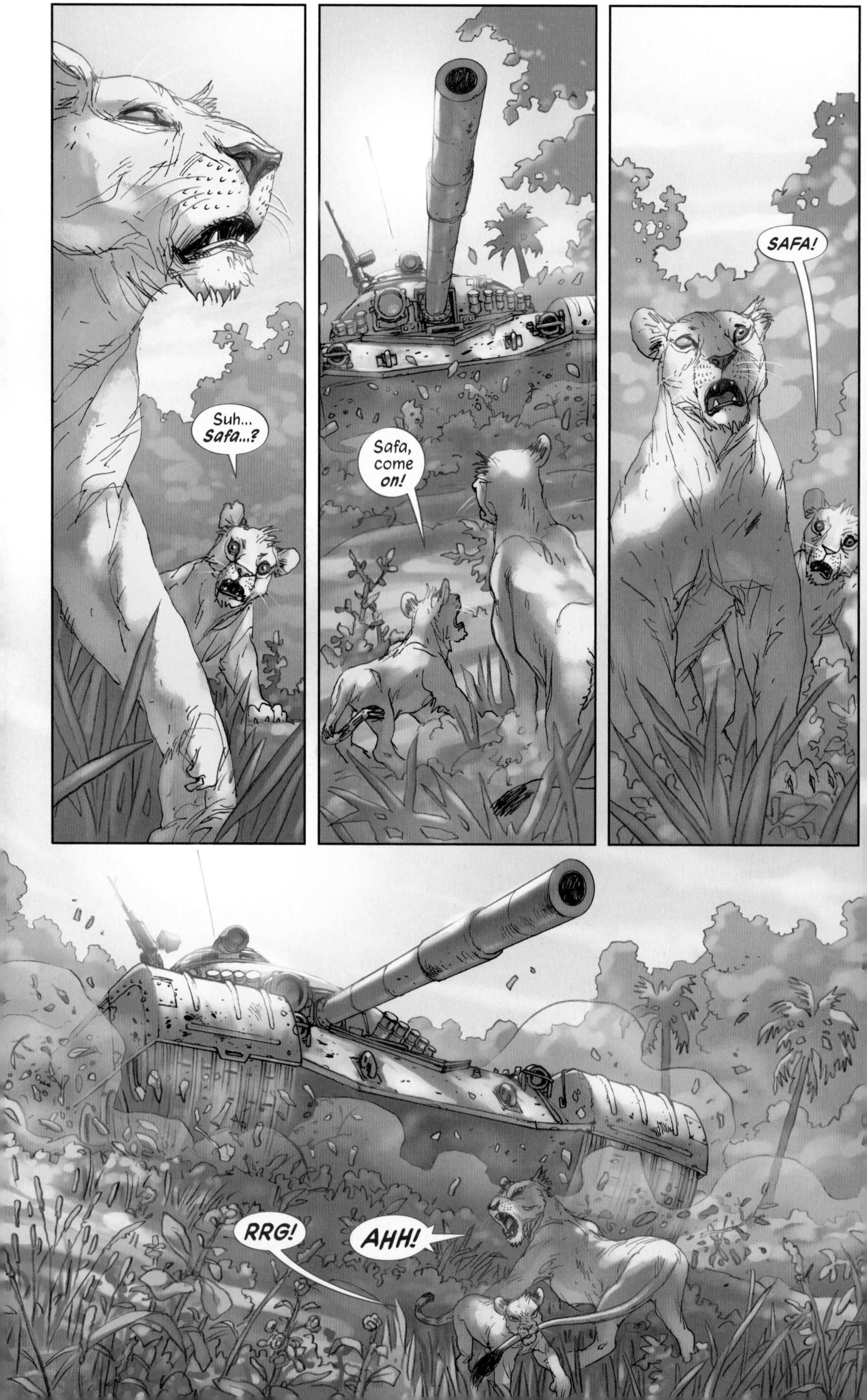
Suh...
Safa...?
Safa, come on!
SAFA!
RRG!
AHH!

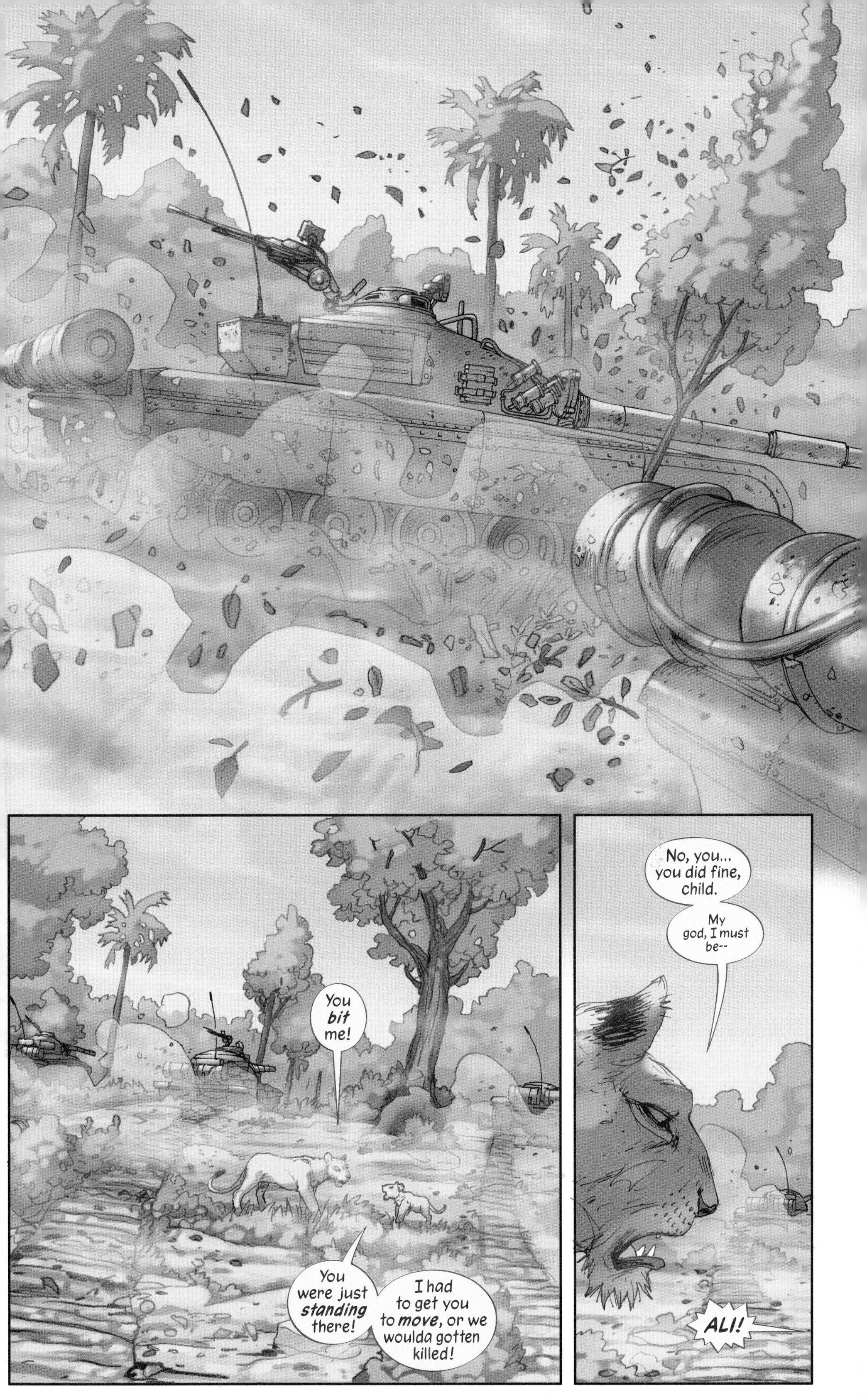
You bit me!
You were just standing there!
I had to get you to move, or we woulda gotten killed!
No, you... you did fine, child.
My god, I must be--
ALI!

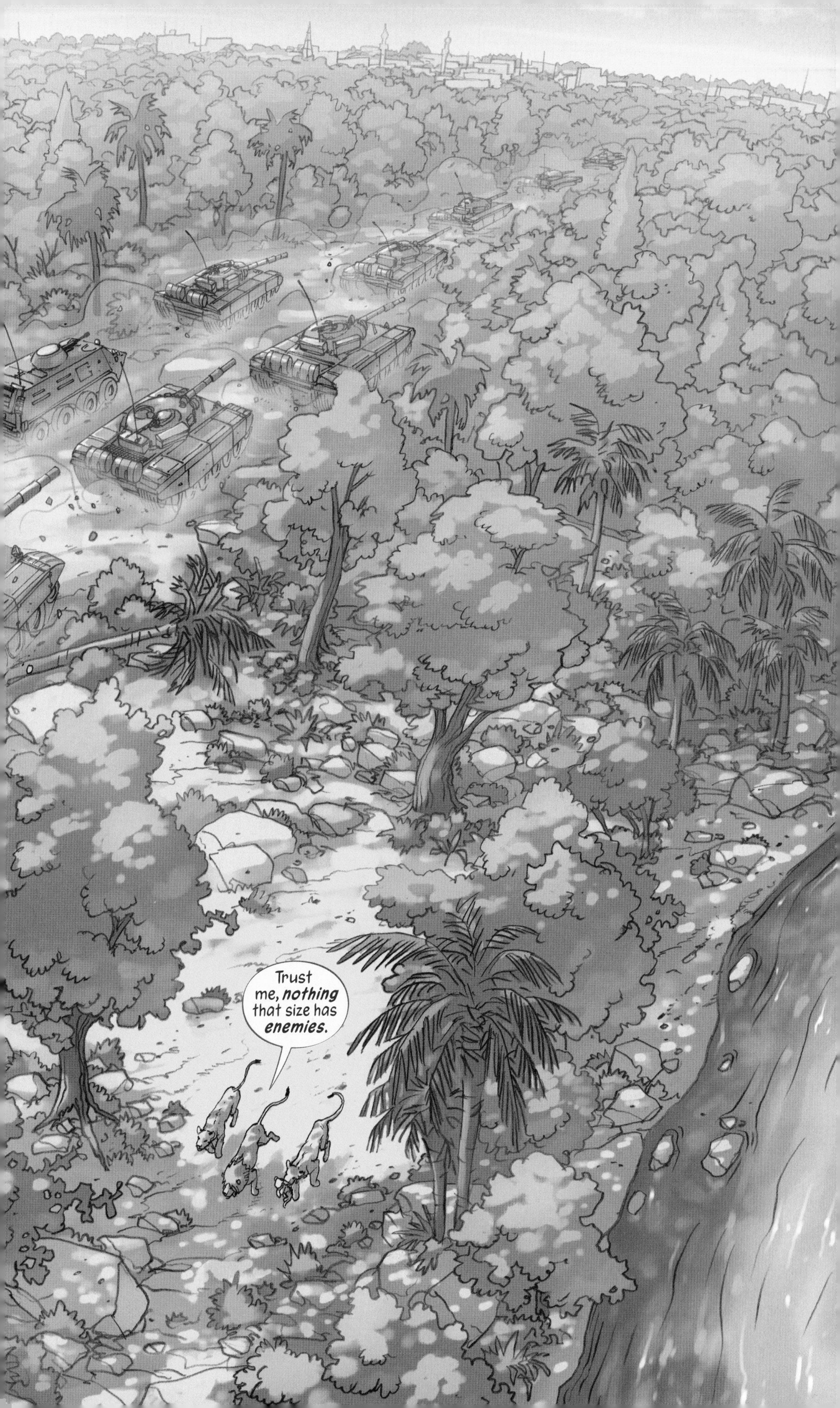
Trust me, *nothing* that size has *enemies*.

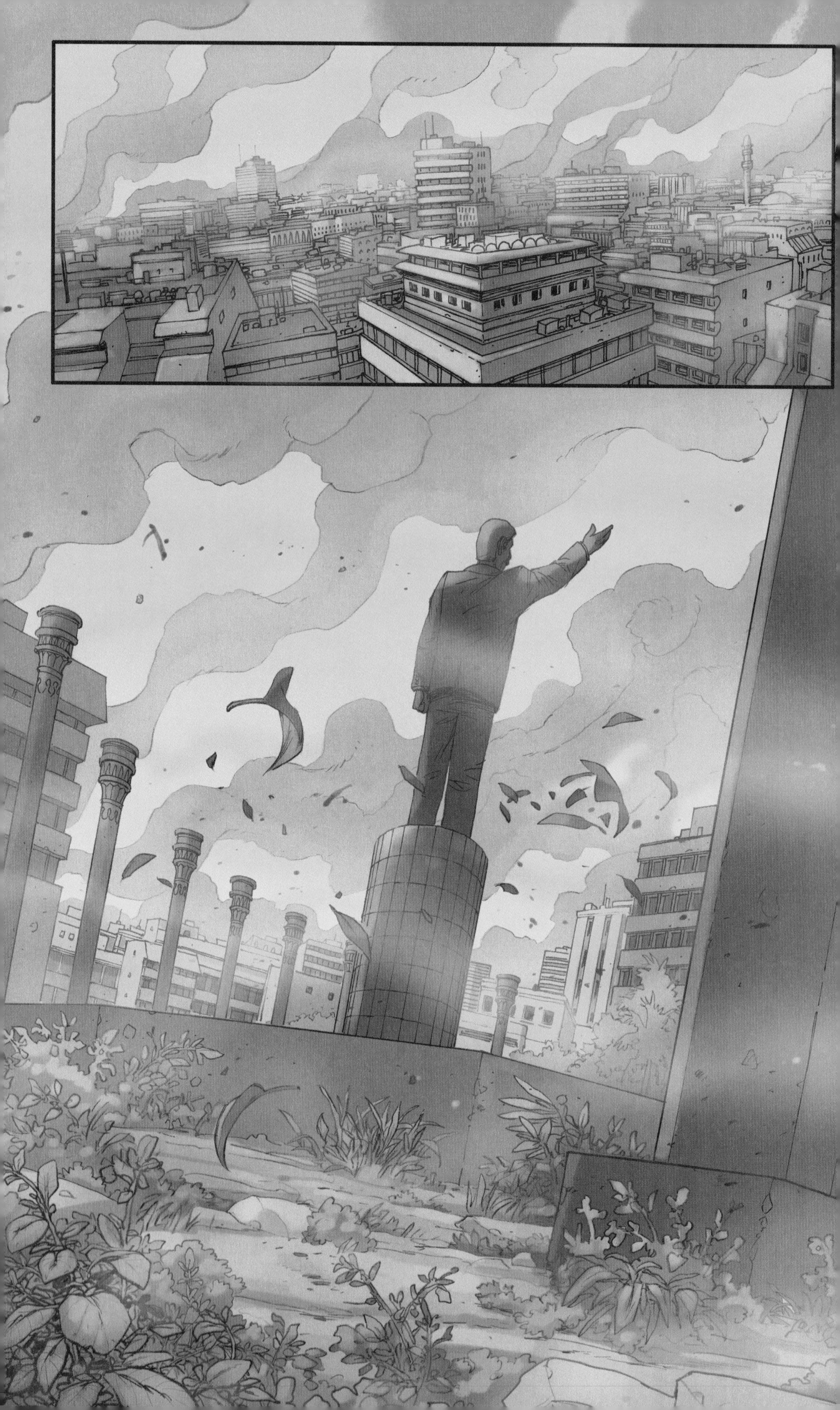

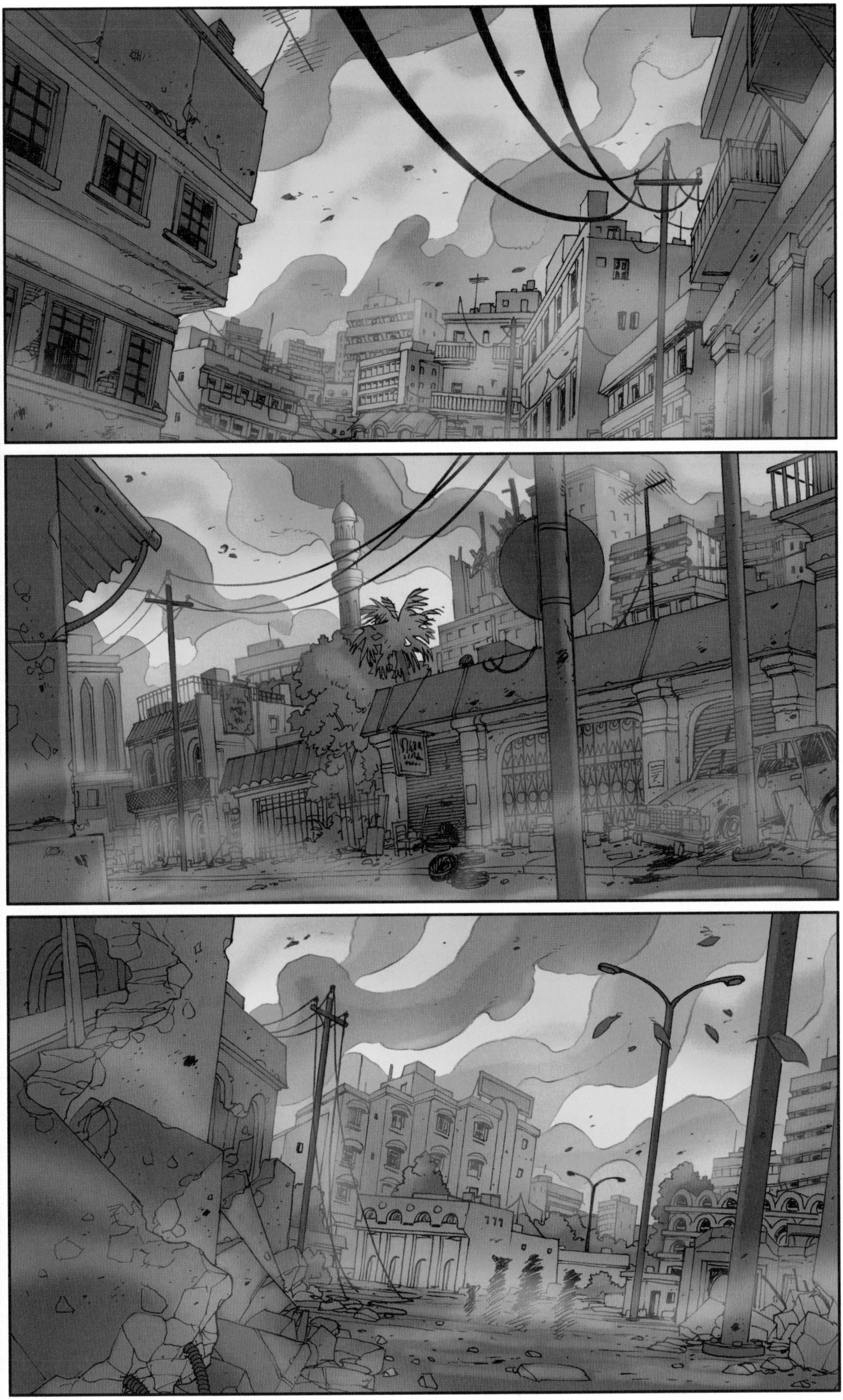

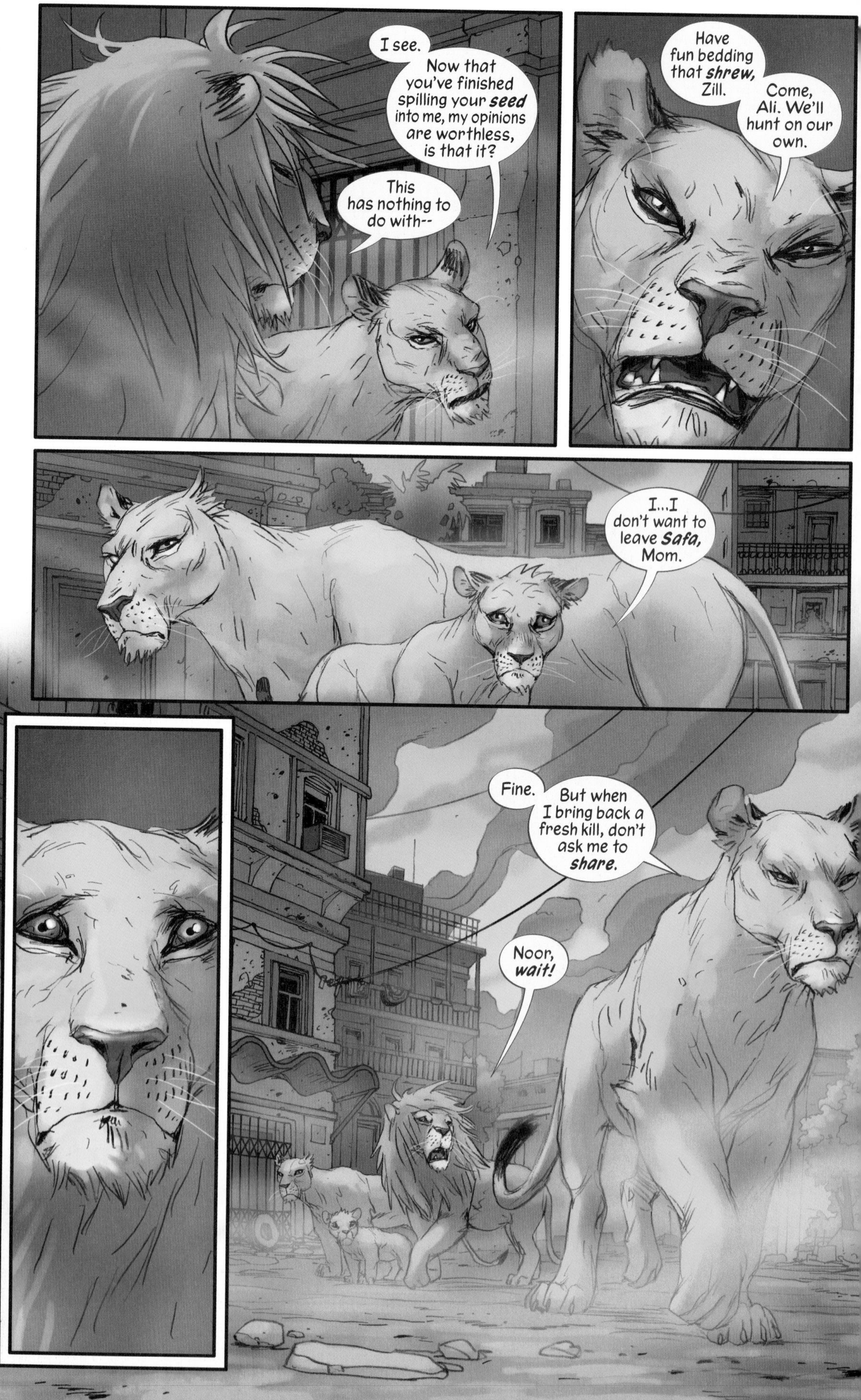
I see.
Now that you've finished spilling your *seed* into me, my opinions are worthless, is that it?
This has nothing to do with--
Have fun bedding that *shrew,* Zill.
Come, Ali. We'll hunt on our own.
I...I don't want to leave *Safa,* Mom.
Fine.
But when I bring back a fresh kill, don't ask me to *share.*
Noor, *wait!*

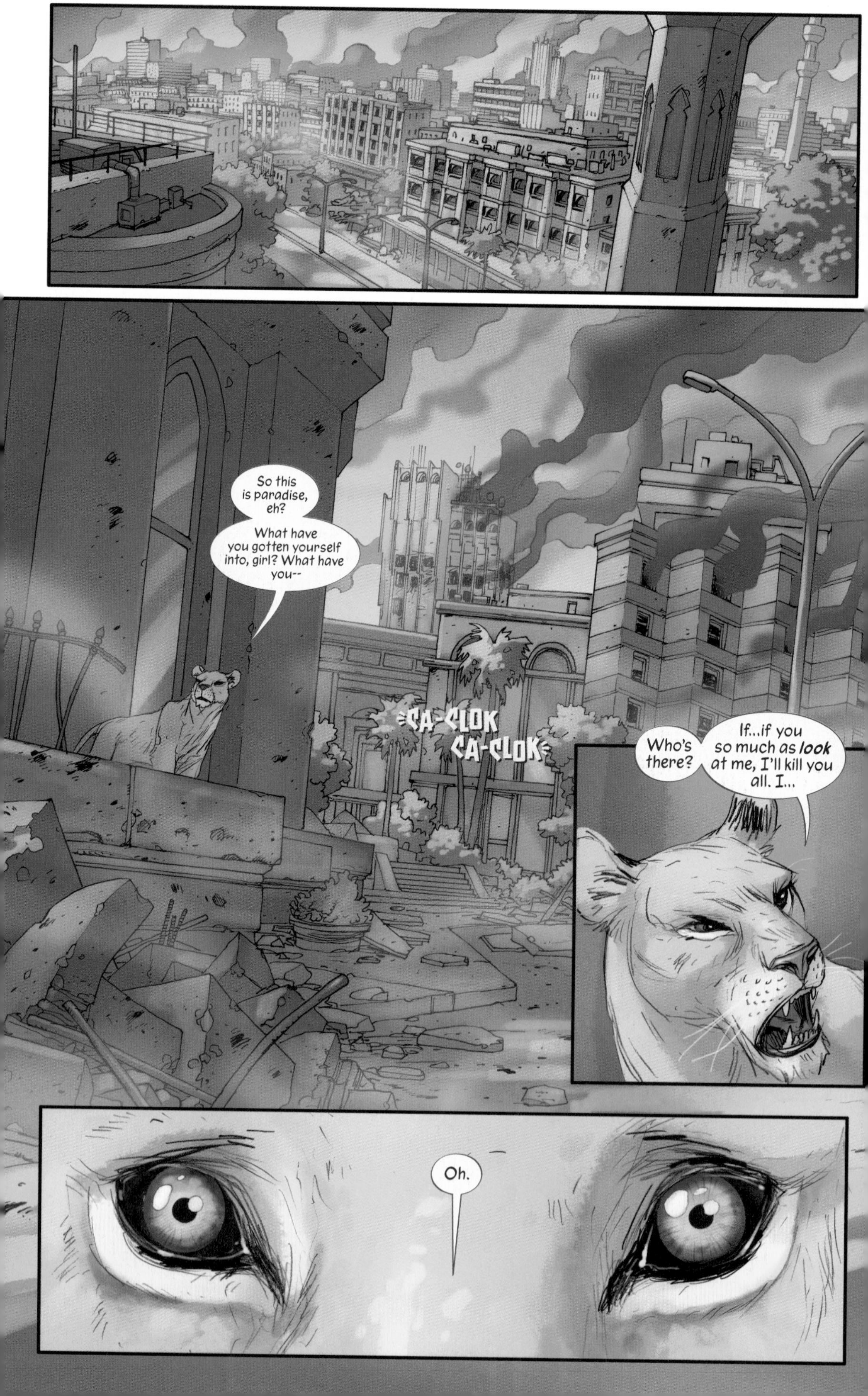
So this is paradise, eh?
What have you gotten yourself into, girl? What have you--
CA-CLOK
CA-CLOK
Who's there?
If...if you so much as *look* at me, I'll kill you all. I...
Oh.

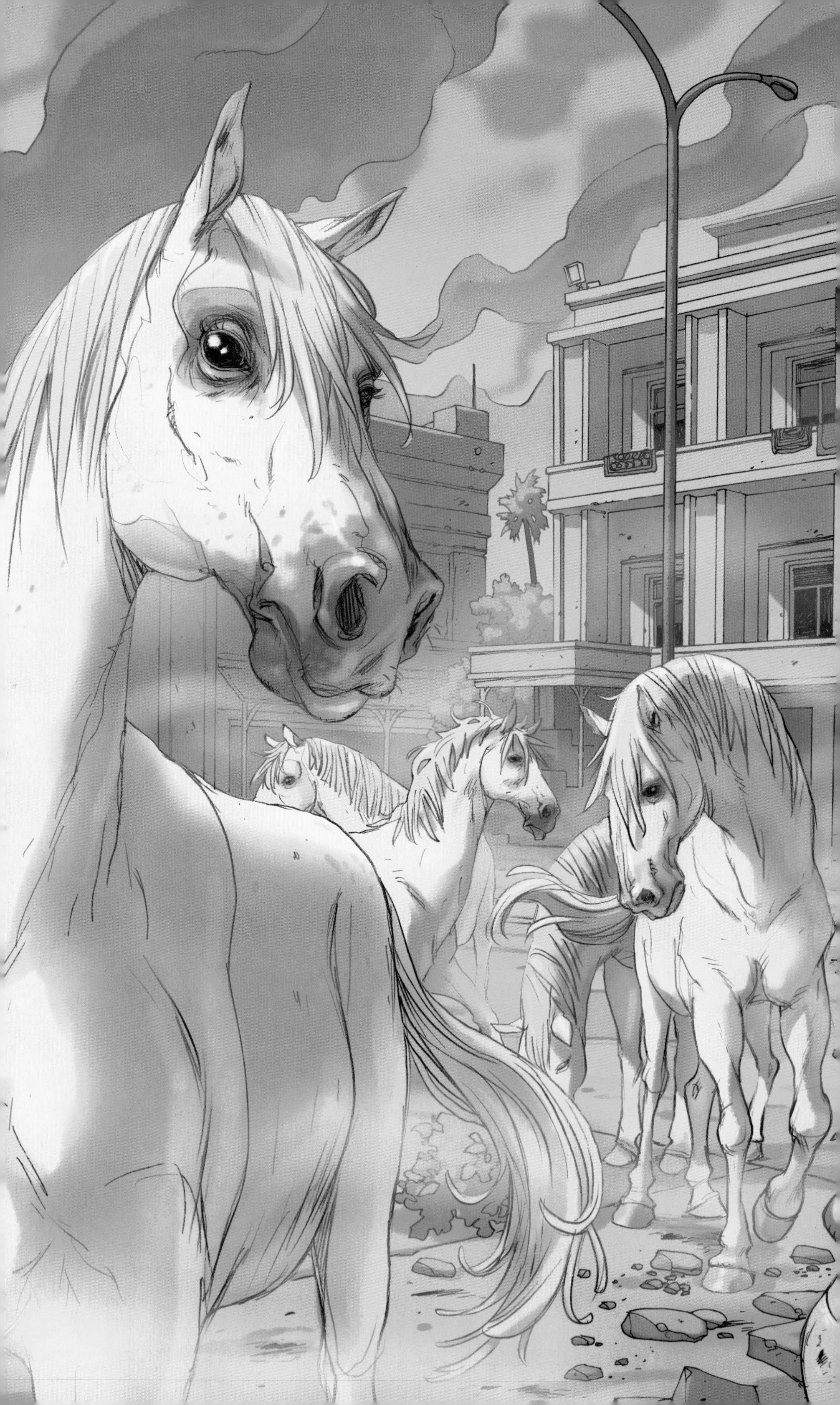

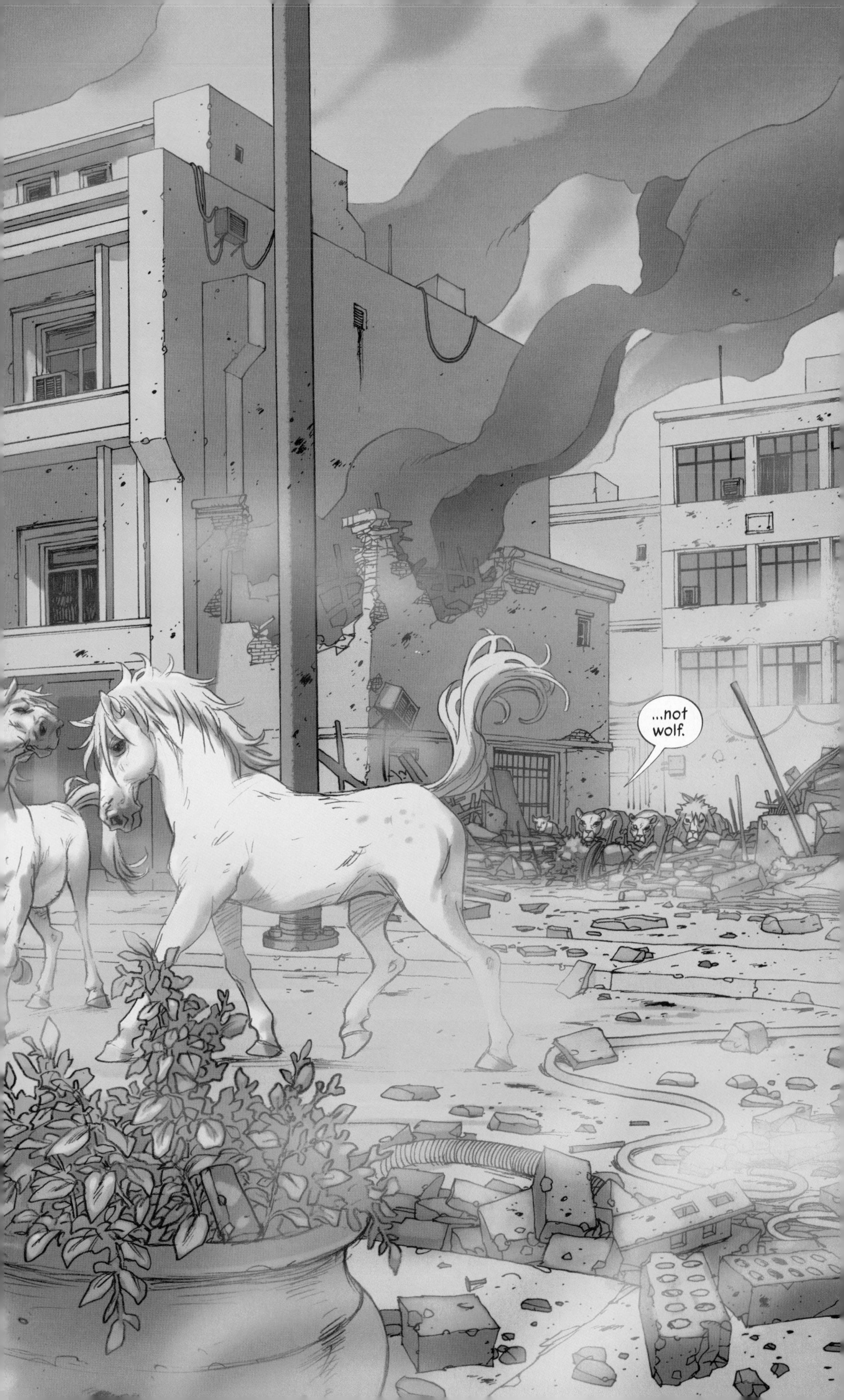
...not wolf.

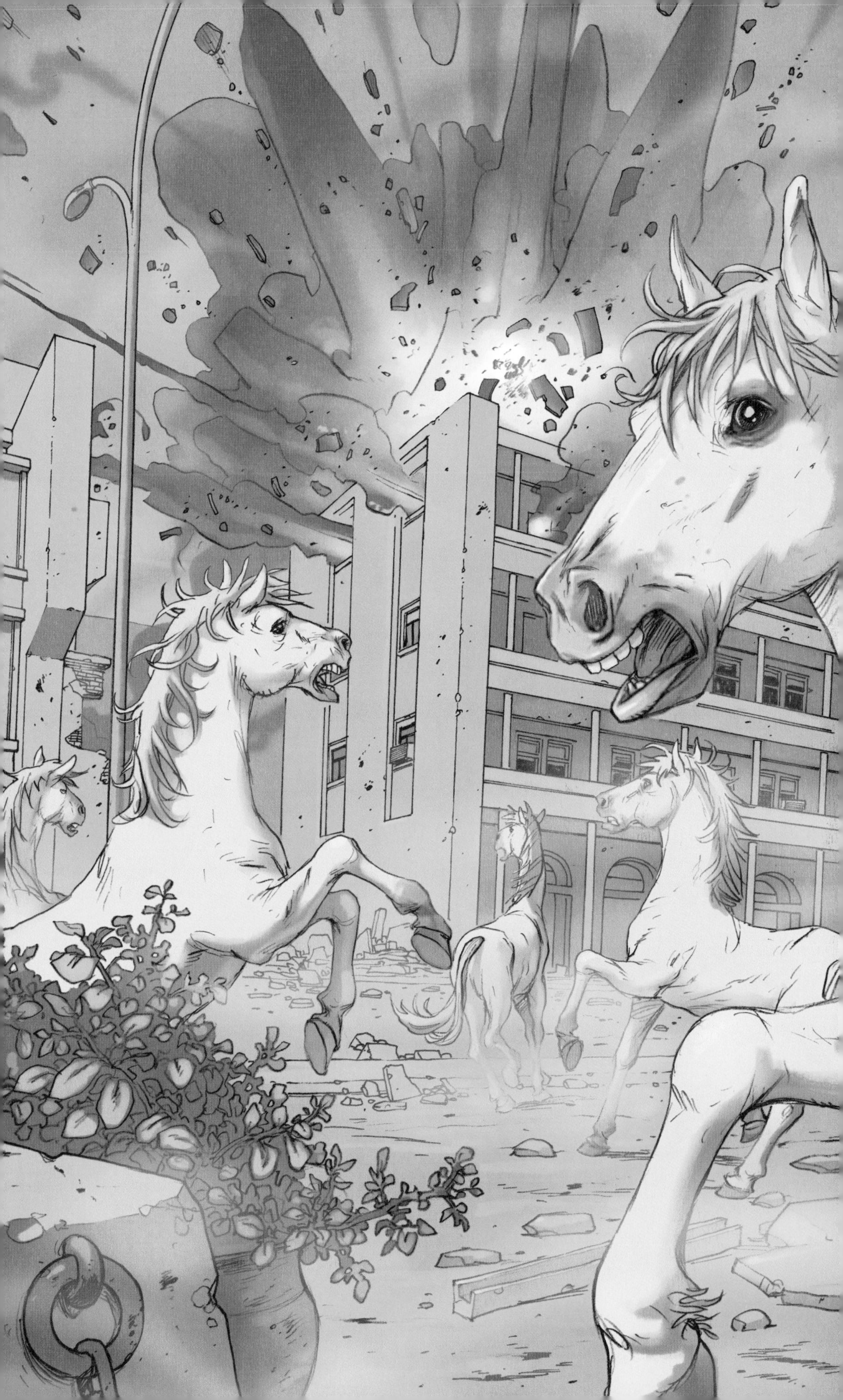

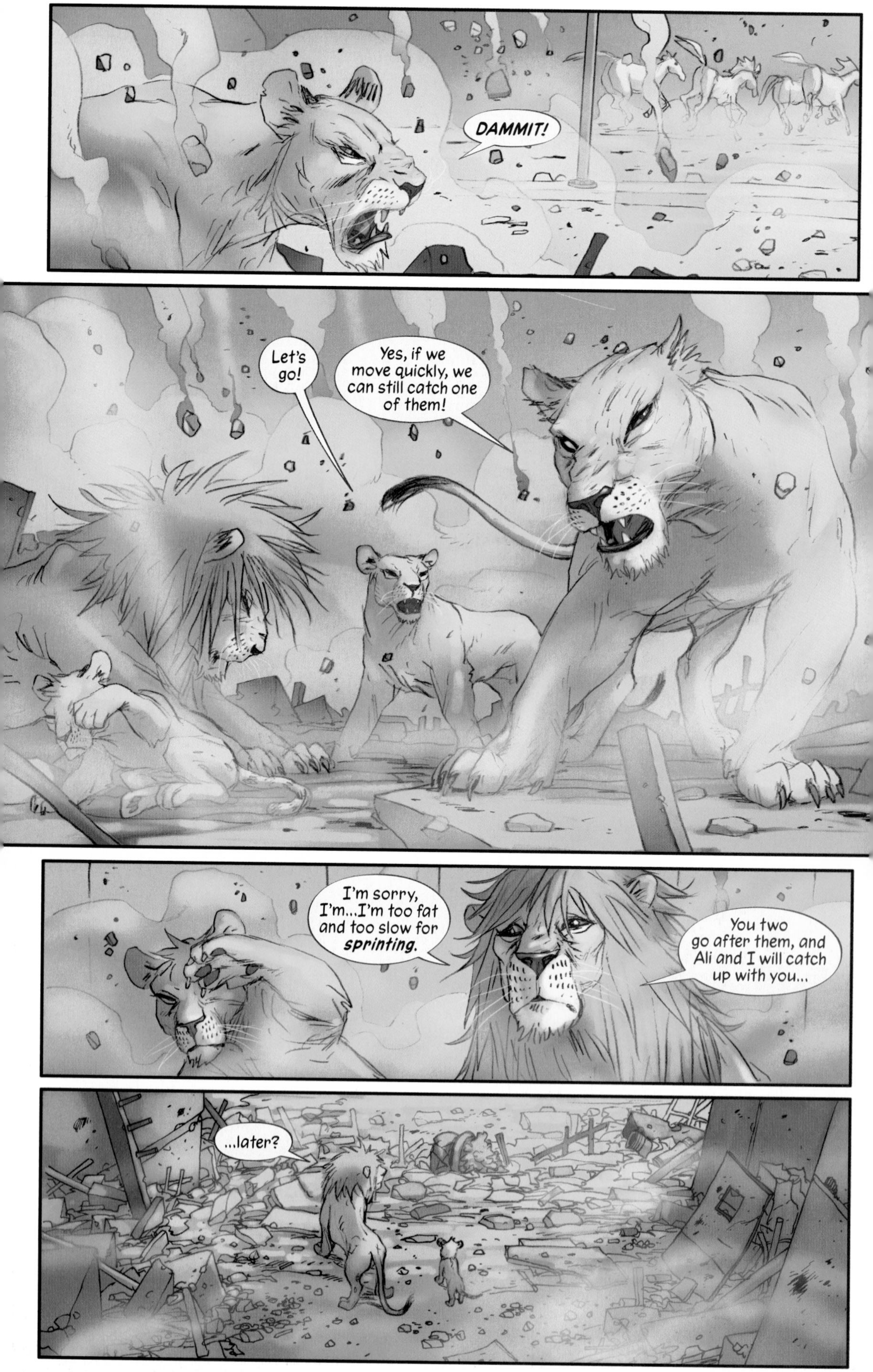
DAMMIT!
Let's go!
Yes, if we move quickly, we can still catch one of them!
I'm sorry, I'm...I'm too fat and too slow for **sprinting**.
You two go after them, and Ali and I will catch up with you...
...later?

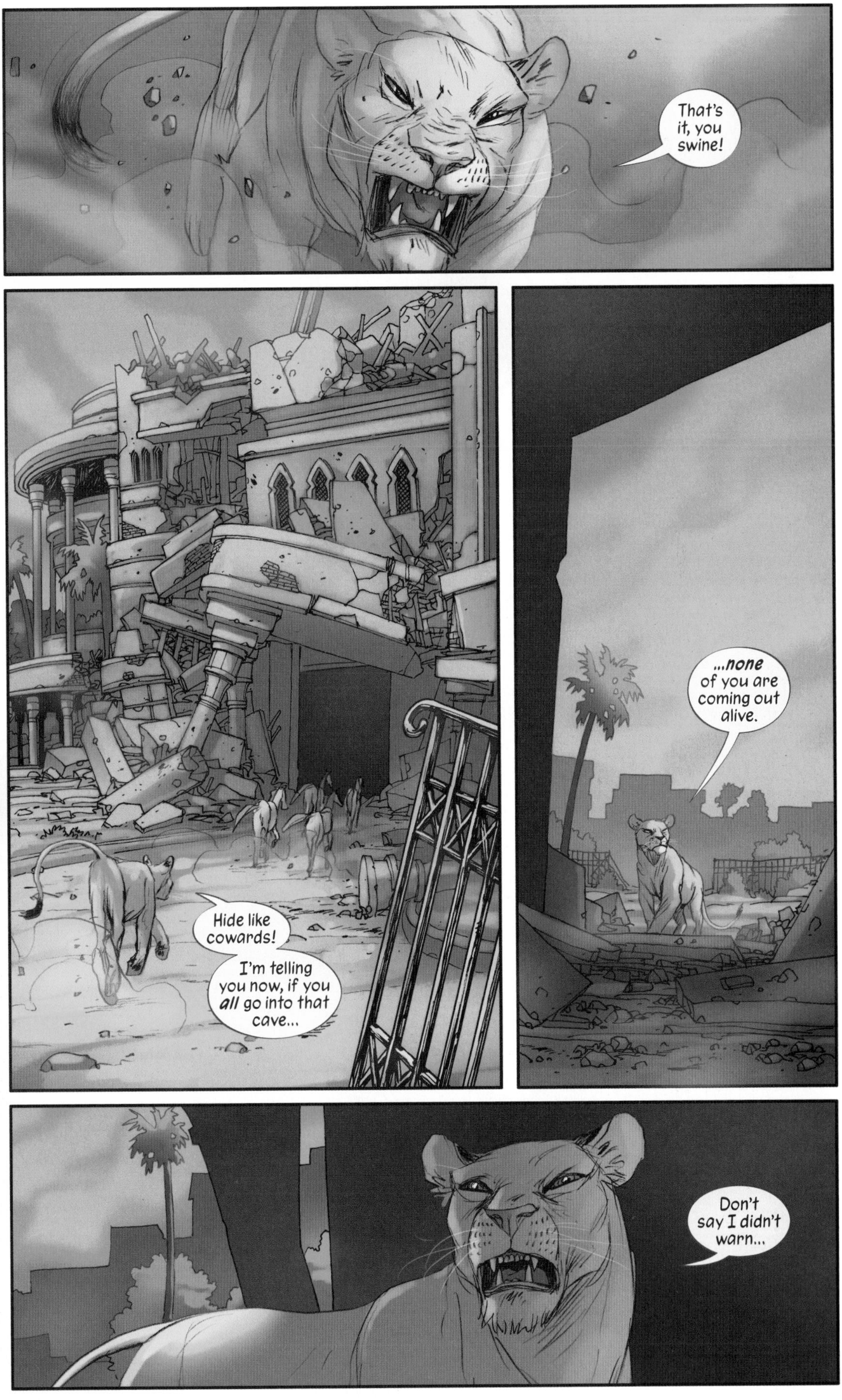
That's it, you swine!
Hide like cowards!
I'm telling you now, if you *all* go into that cave...
...*none* of you are coming out alive.
Don't say I didn't warn...

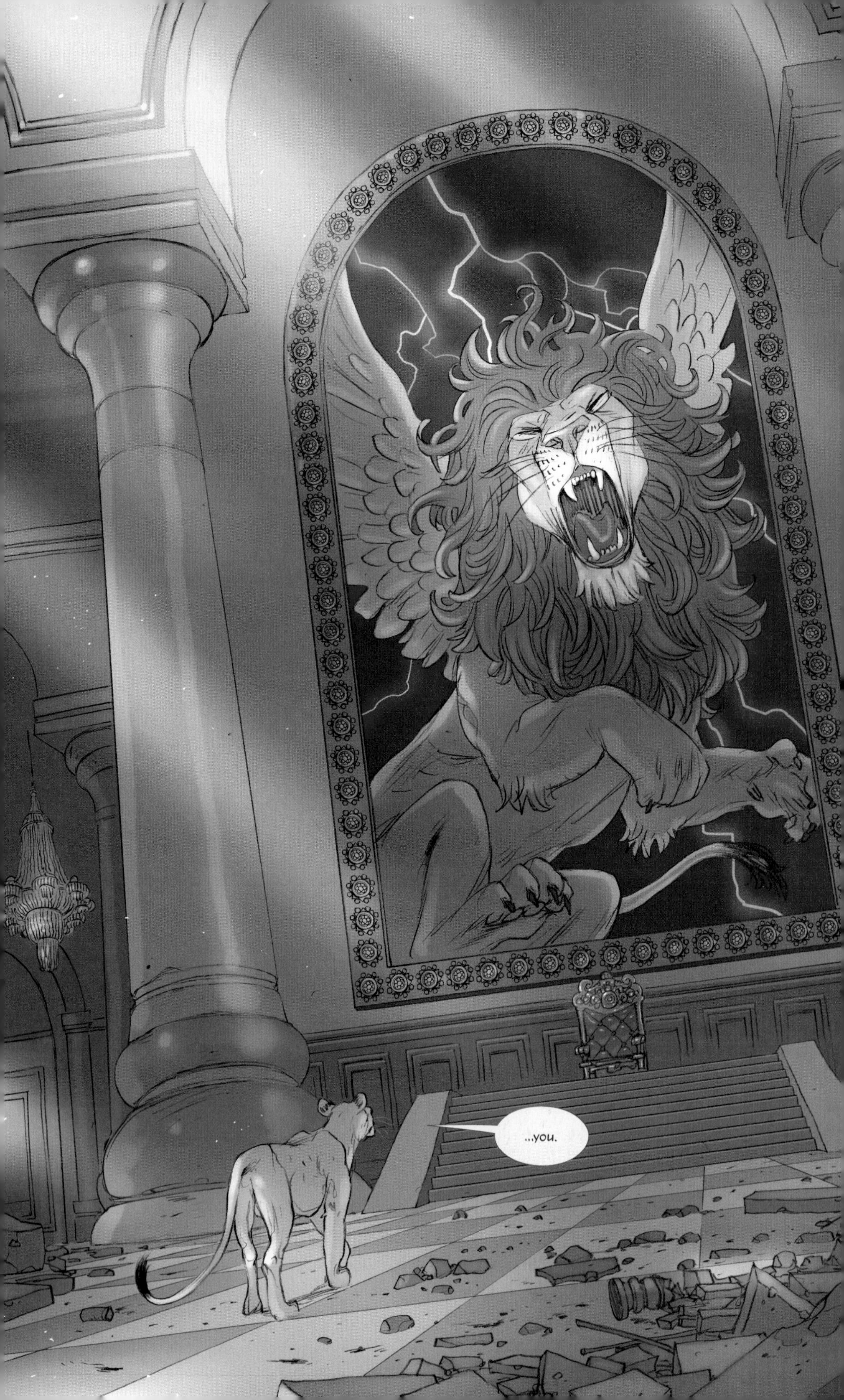
...you.

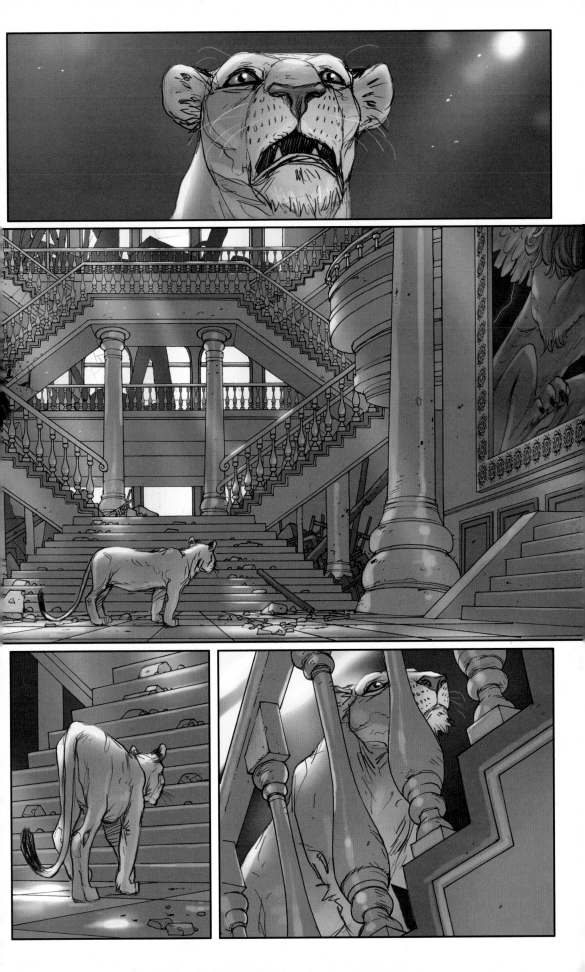

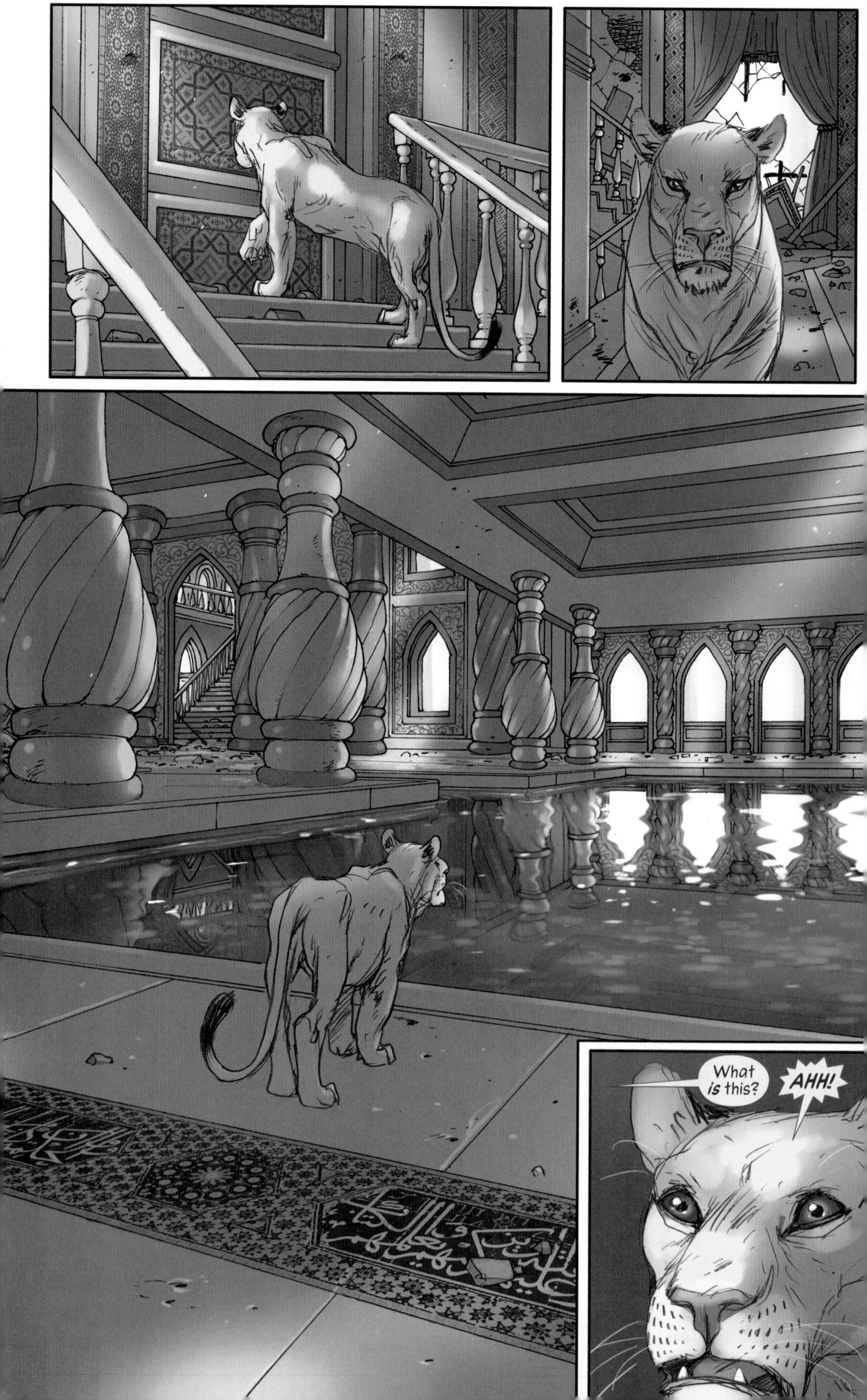
What *is* this?
AHH!

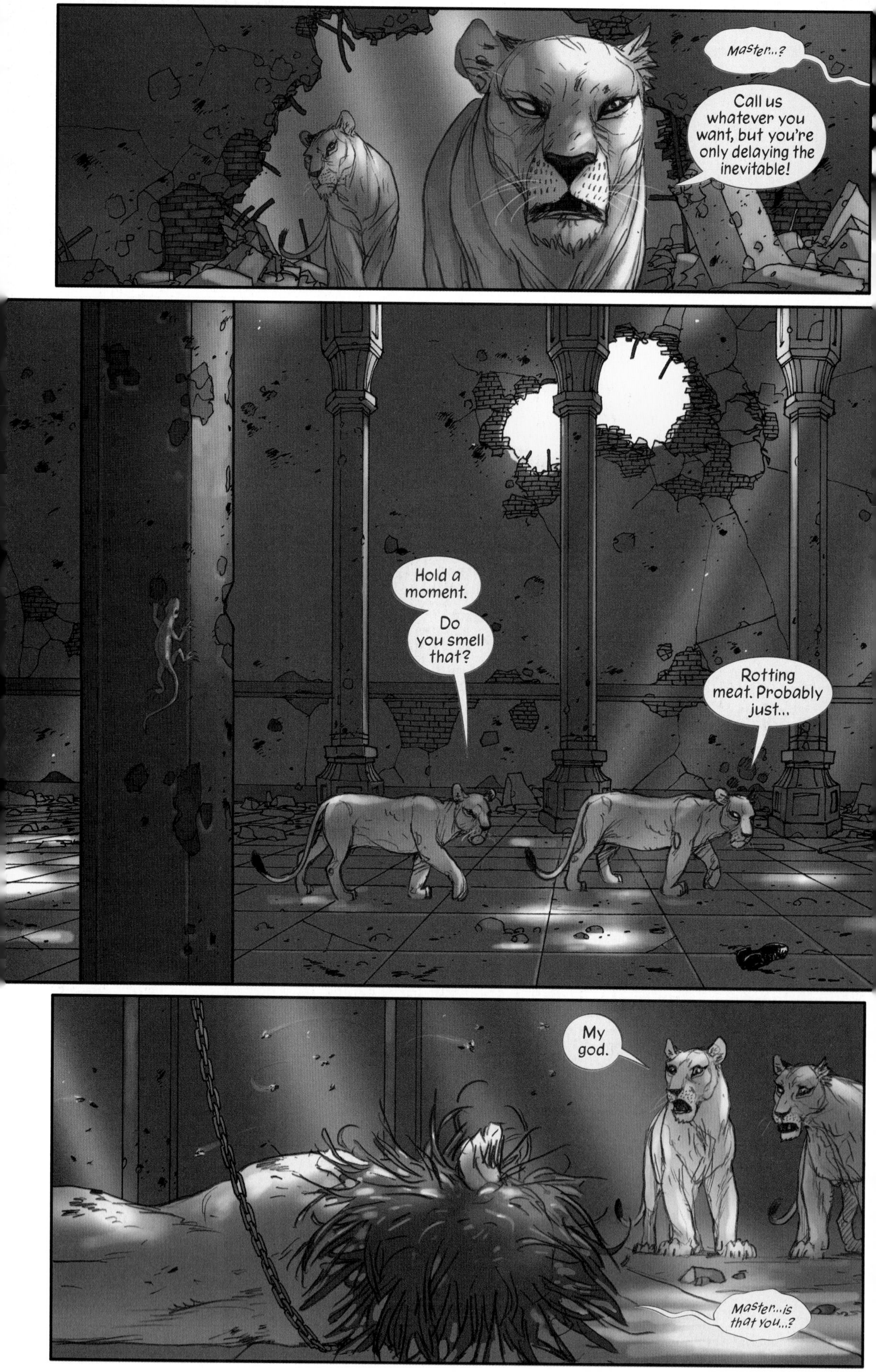
Master...?
Call us whatever you want, but you're only delaying the inevitable!
Hold a moment.
Do you smell that?
Rotting meat. Probably just...
My god.
Master...is that you...?

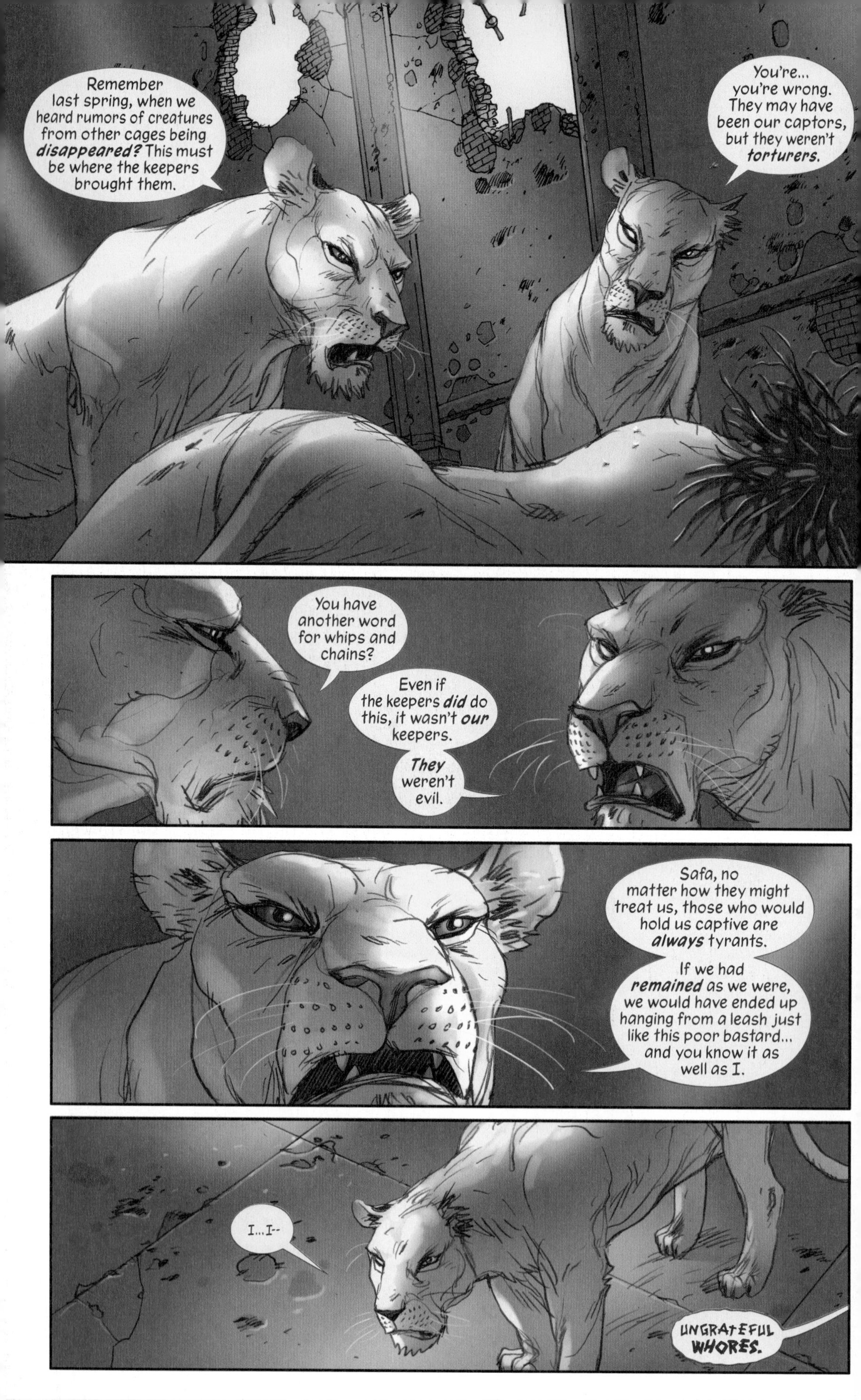
Remember last spring, when we heard rumors of creatures from other cages being *disappeared?* This must be where the keepers brought them.
You're... you're wrong. They may have been our captors, but they weren't *torturers.*
You have another word for whips and chains?
Even if the keepers *did* do this, it wasn't *our* keepers.
They weren't evil.
Safa, no matter how they might treat us, those who would hold us captive are *always* tyrants.
If we had *remained* as we were, we would have ended up hanging from a leash just like this poor bastard... and you know it as well as I.
I... I--
UNGRATEFUL WHORES.

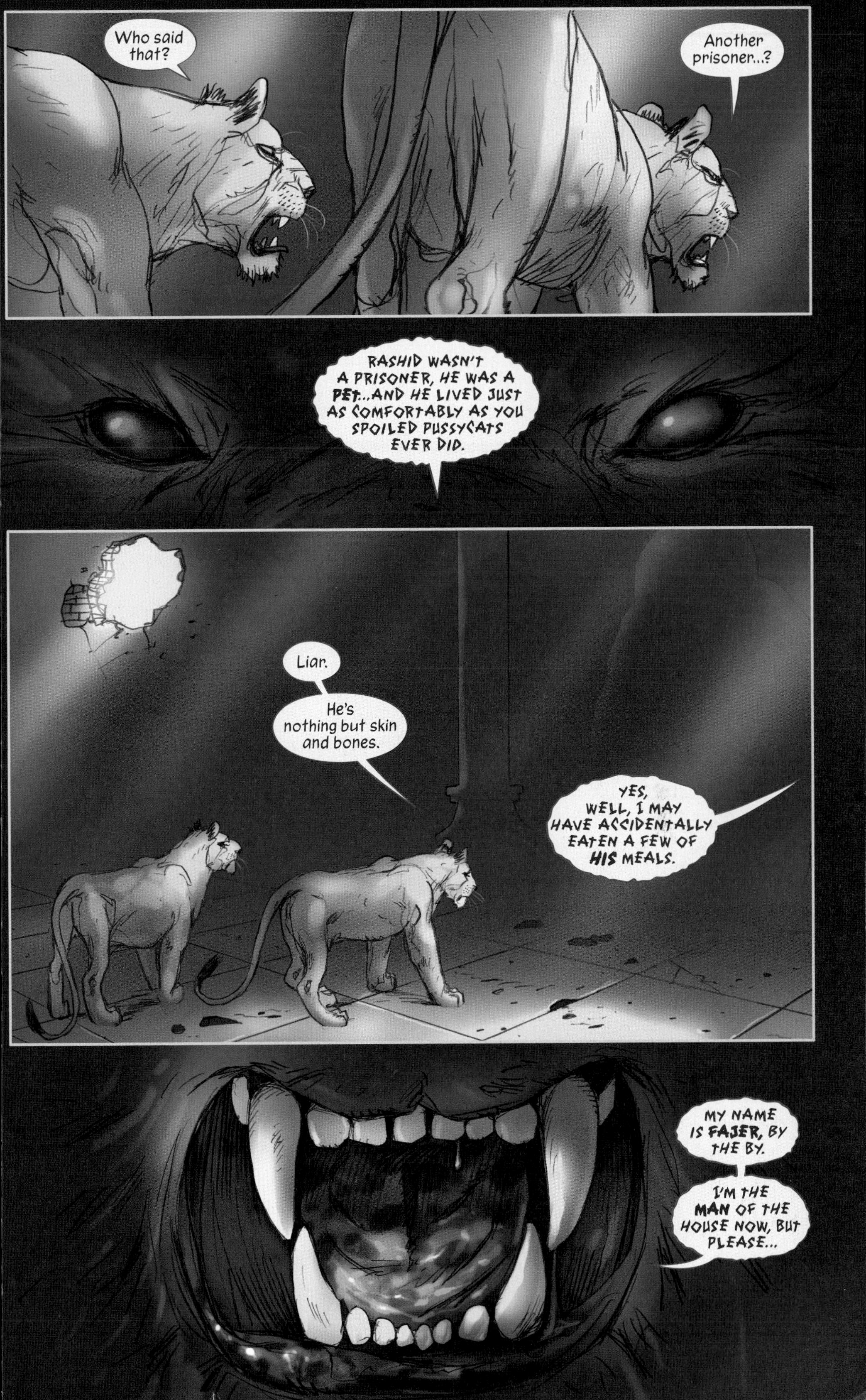

Who said that?
Another prisoner...?
RASHID WASN'T A PRISONER, HE WAS A PET...AND HE LIVED JUST AS COMFORTABLY AS YOU SPOILED PUSSYCATS EVER DID.
Liar.
He's nothing but skin and bones.
YES, WELL, I MAY HAVE ACCIDENTALLY EATEN A FEW OF HIS MEALS.
MY NAME IS FAJER, BY THE BY.
I'M THE MAN OF THE HOUSE NOW, BUT PLEASE...

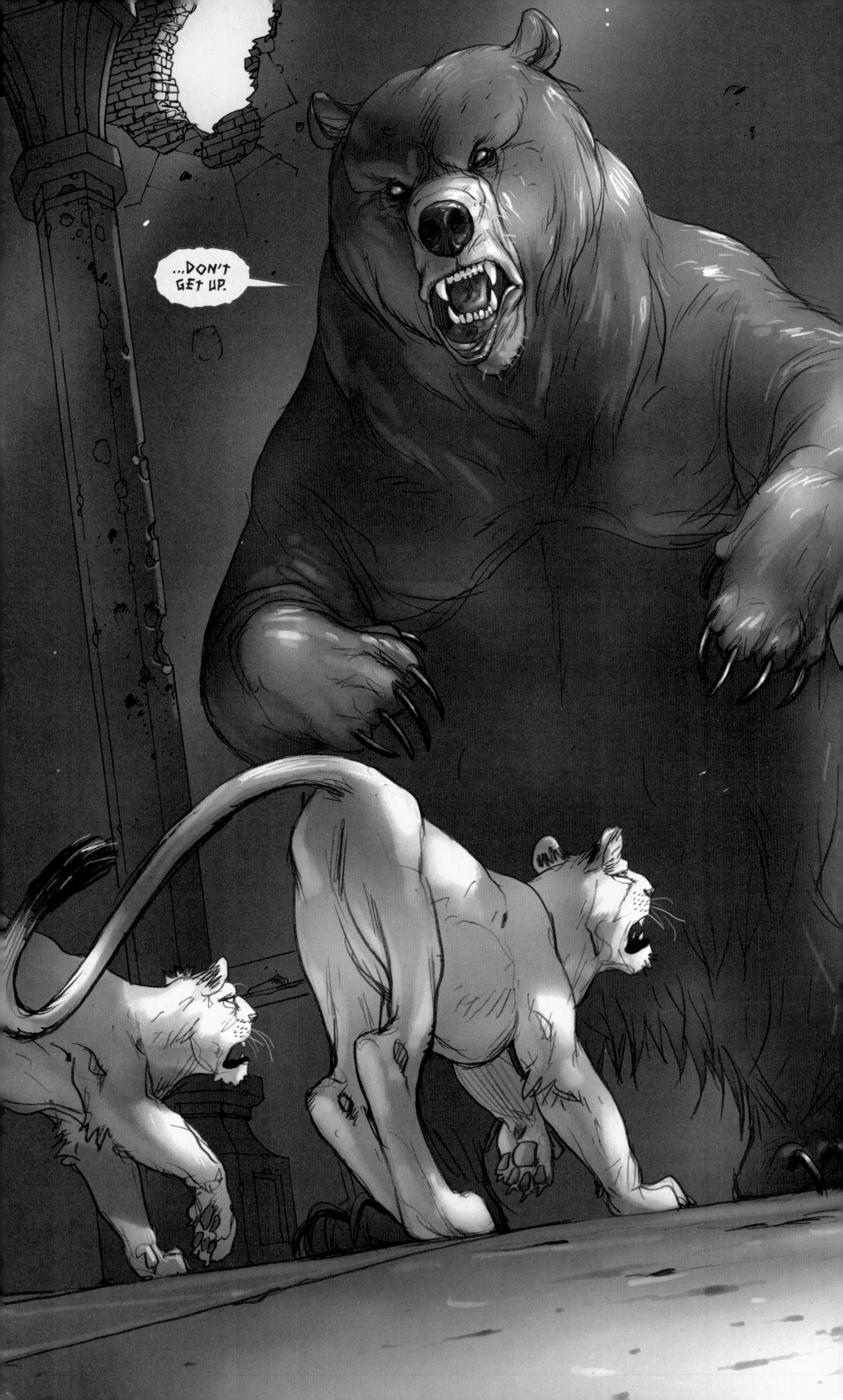
...DON'T GET UP.

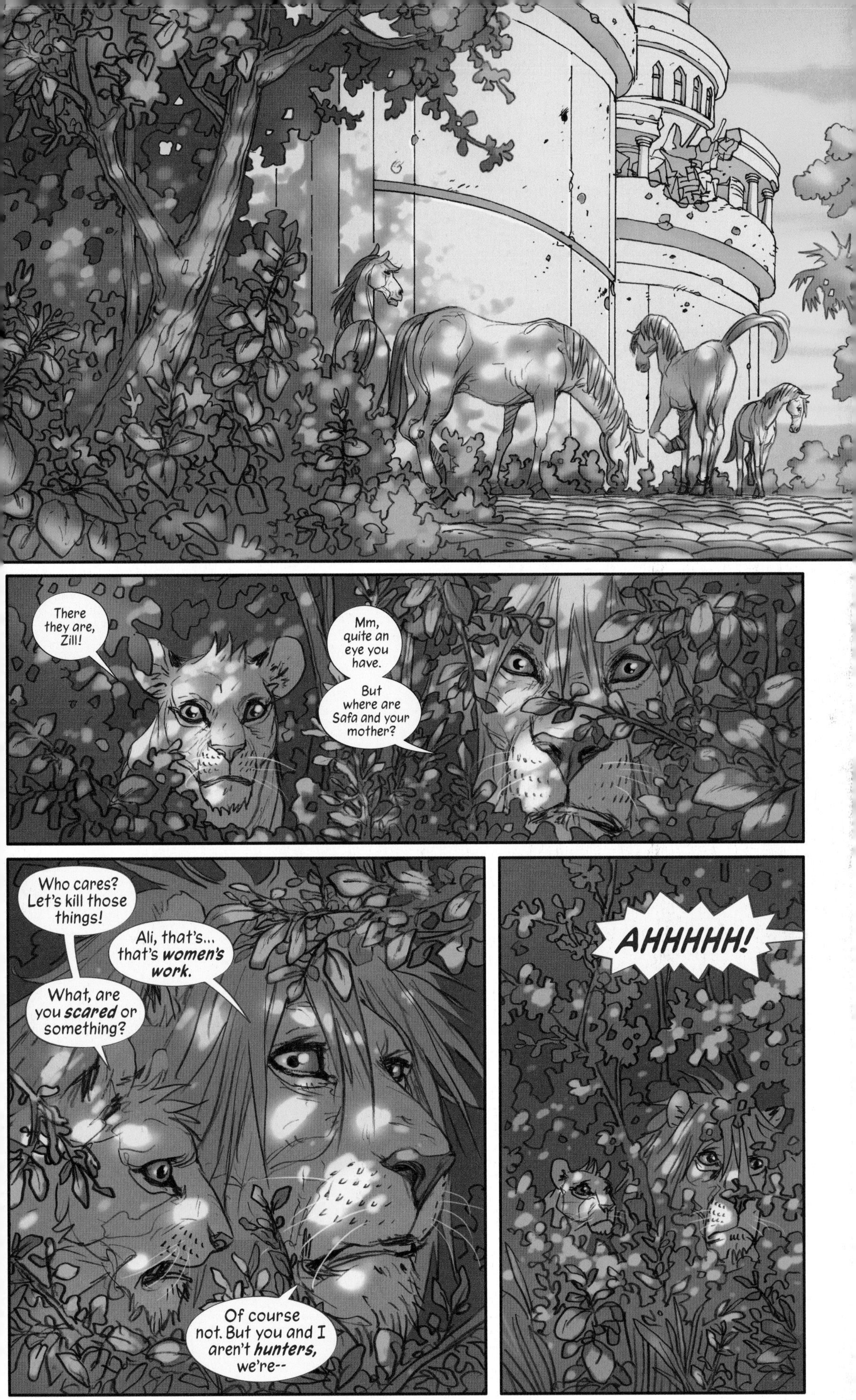
There they are, Zill!
Mm, quite an eye you have.
But where are Safa and your mother?
Who cares? Let's kill those things!
Ali, that's... that's **women's work.**
What, are you **scared** or something?
Of course not. But you and I aren't **hunters,** we're--
AHHHHH!

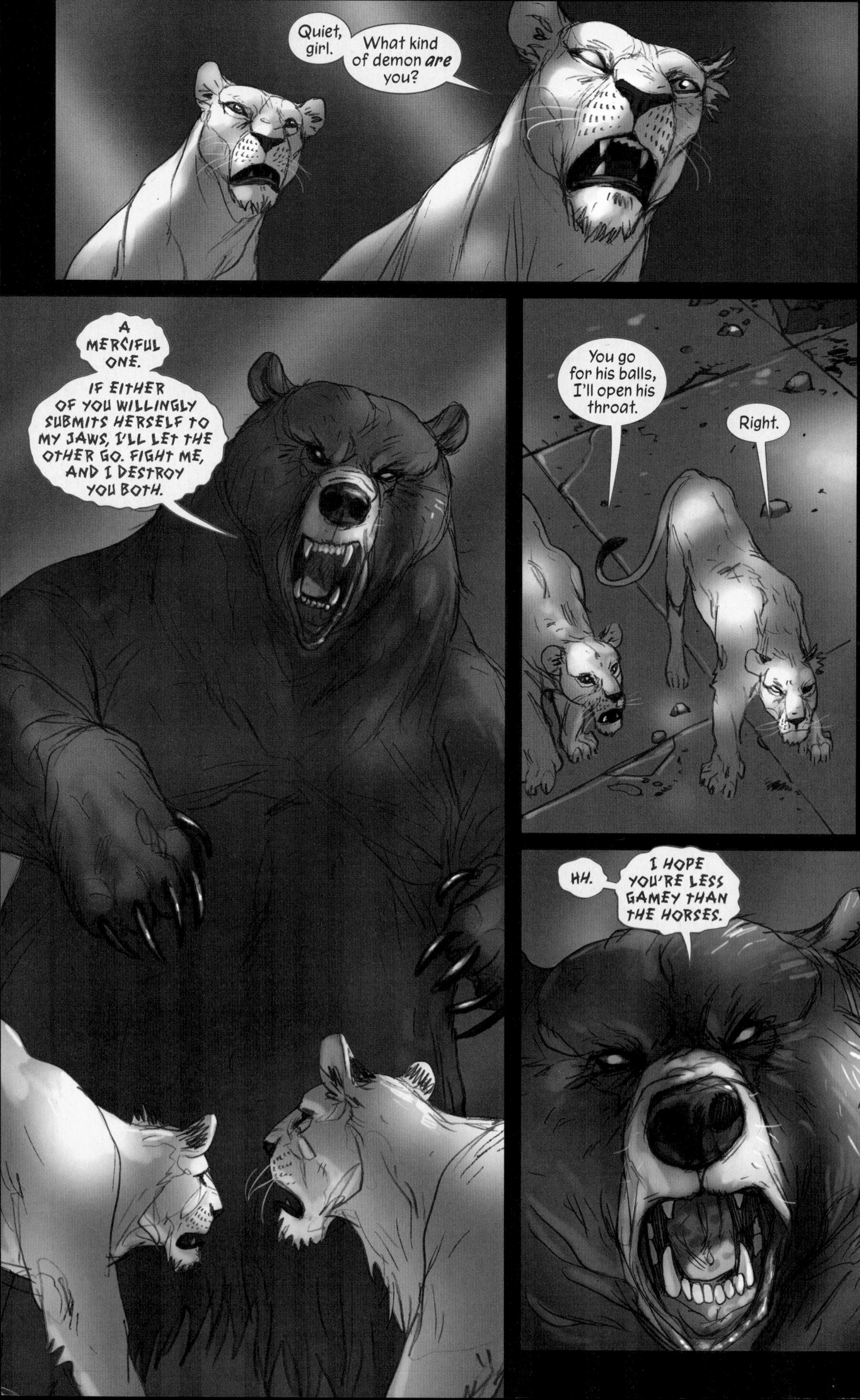
Quiet, girl.
What kind of demon *are* you?
A MERCIFUL ONE.
IF EITHER OF YOU WILLINGLY SUBMITS HERSELF TO MY JAWS, I'LL LET THE OTHER GO. FIGHT ME, AND I DESTROY YOU BOTH.
You go for his balls, I'll open his throat.
Right.
HH.
I HOPE YOU'RE LESS GAMEY THAN THE HORSES.

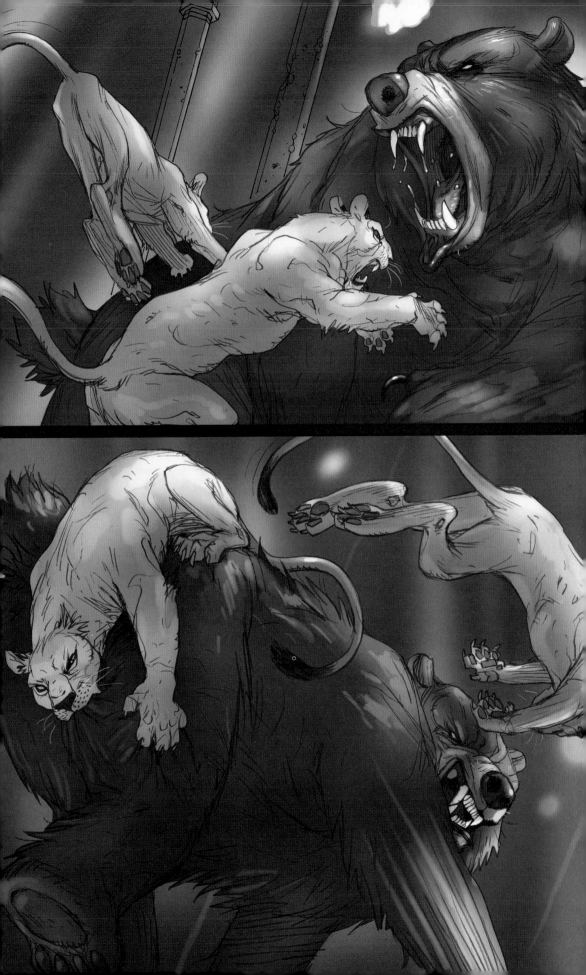

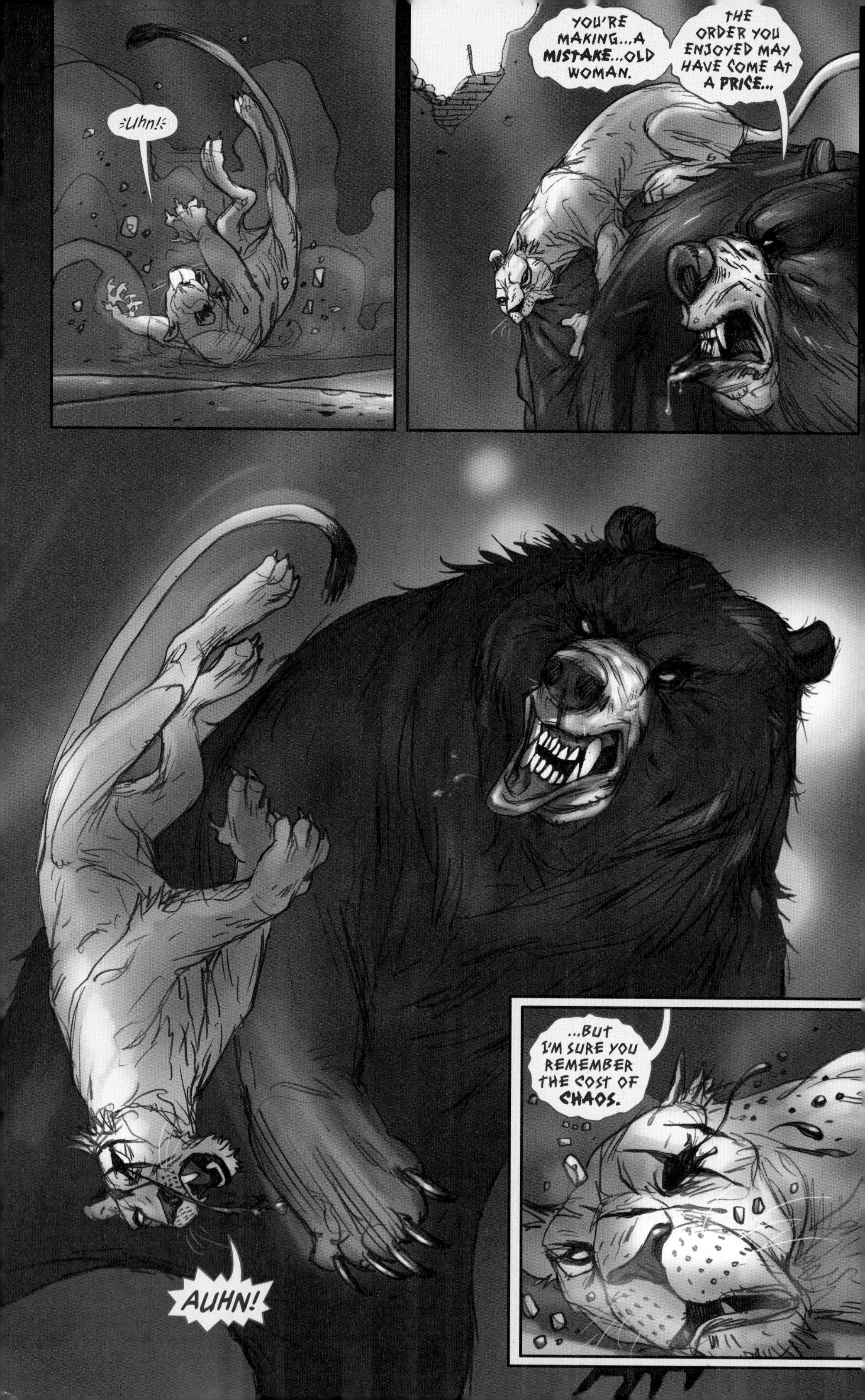
Uhn!
YOU'RE MAKING...A MISTAKE...OLD WOMAN.
THE ORDER YOU ENJOYED MAY HAVE COME AT A PRICE...
AUHN!
...BUT I'M SURE YOU REMEMBER THE COST OF CHAOS.

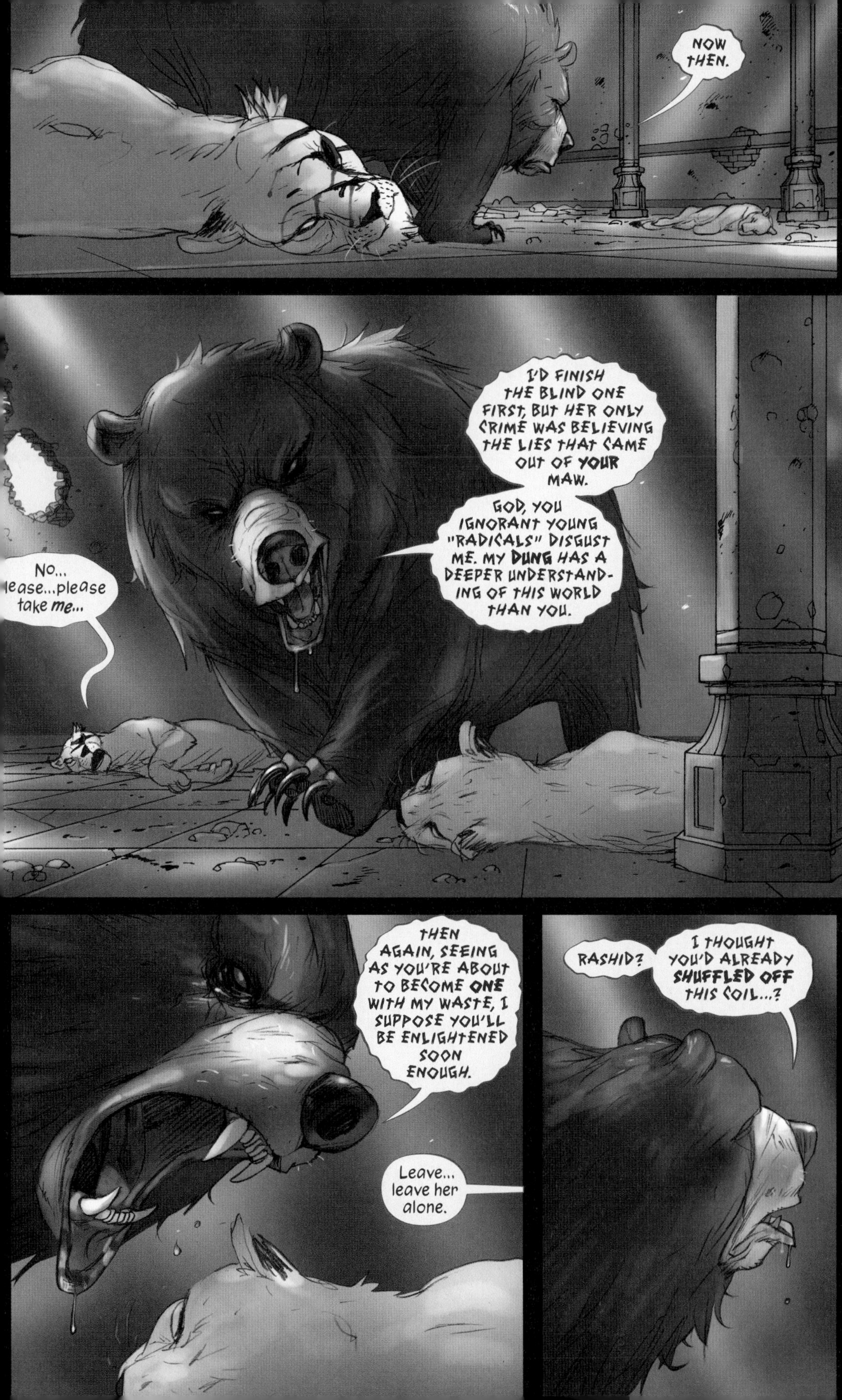
NOW THEN.
I'D FINISH THE BLIND ONE FIRST, BUT HER ONLY CRIME WAS BELIEVING THE LIES THAT CAME OUT OF **YOUR** MAW.
GOD, YOU IGNORANT YOUNG "RADICALS" DISGUST ME. MY **DUNG** HAS A DEEPER UNDERSTAND-ING OF THIS WORLD THAN YOU.
No... lease...please take *me*...
THEN AGAIN, SEEING AS YOU'RE ABOUT TO BECOME **ONE** WITH MY WASTE, I SUPPOSE YOU'LL BE ENLIGHTENED SOON ENOUGH.
Leave... leave her alone.
RASHID?
I THOUGHT YOU'D ALREADY **SHUFFLED OFF** THIS COIL...?

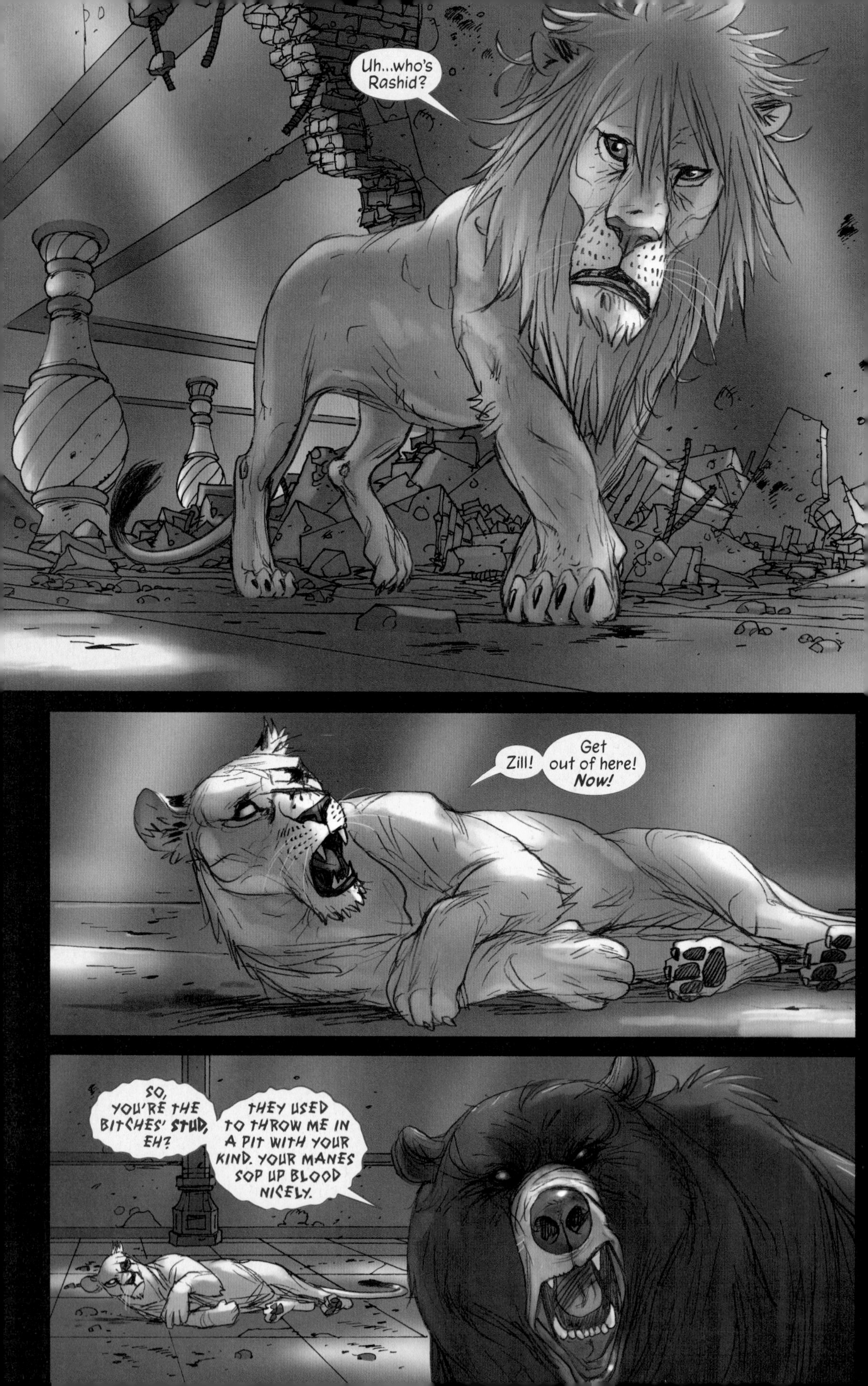
Uh...who's Rashid?
Zill!
Get out of here! Now!
SO, YOU'RE THE BITCHES' STUD, EH?
THEY USED TO THROW ME IN A PIT WITH YOUR KIND. YOUR MANES SOP UP BLOOD NICELY.

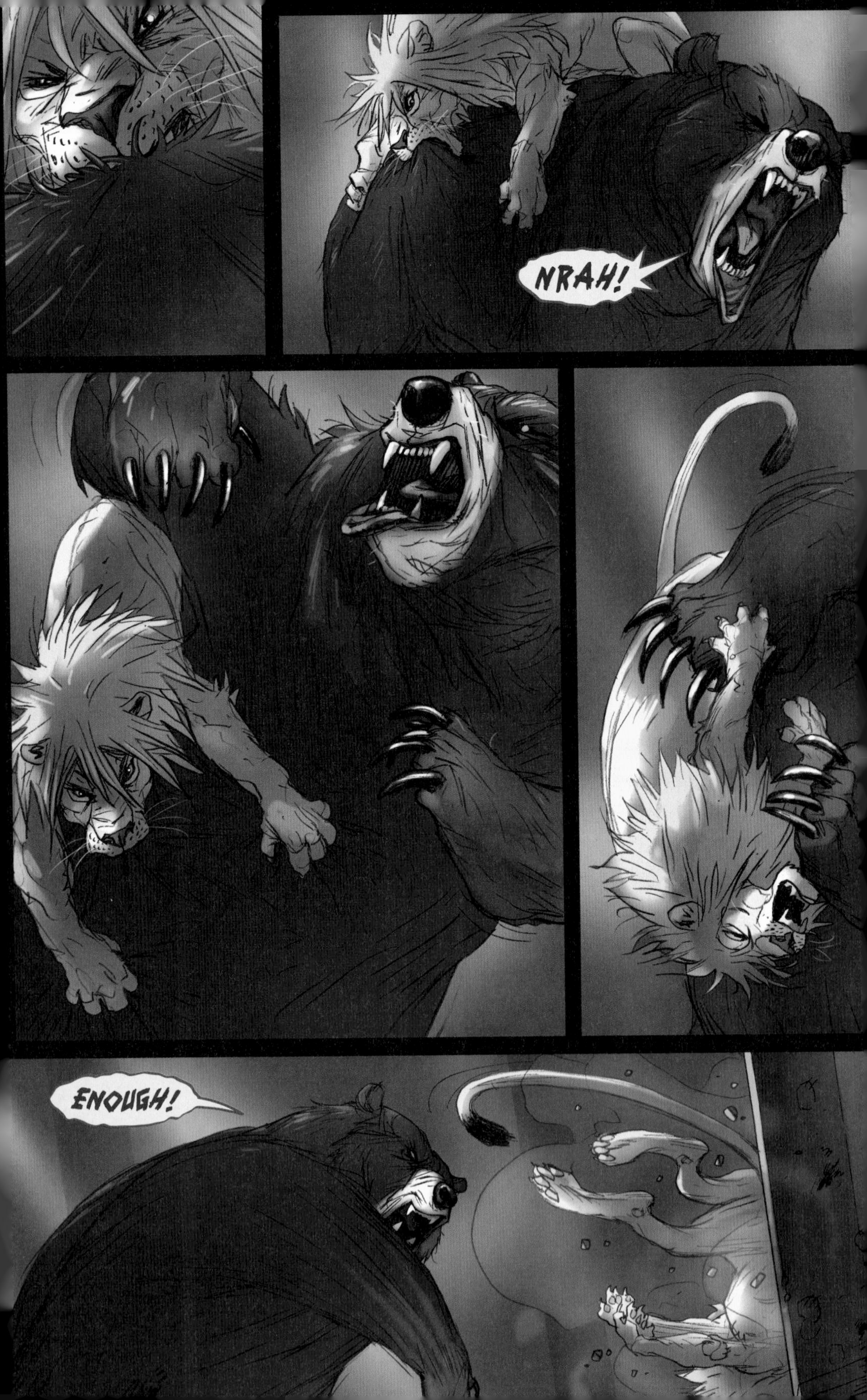
NRAH!
ENOUGH!

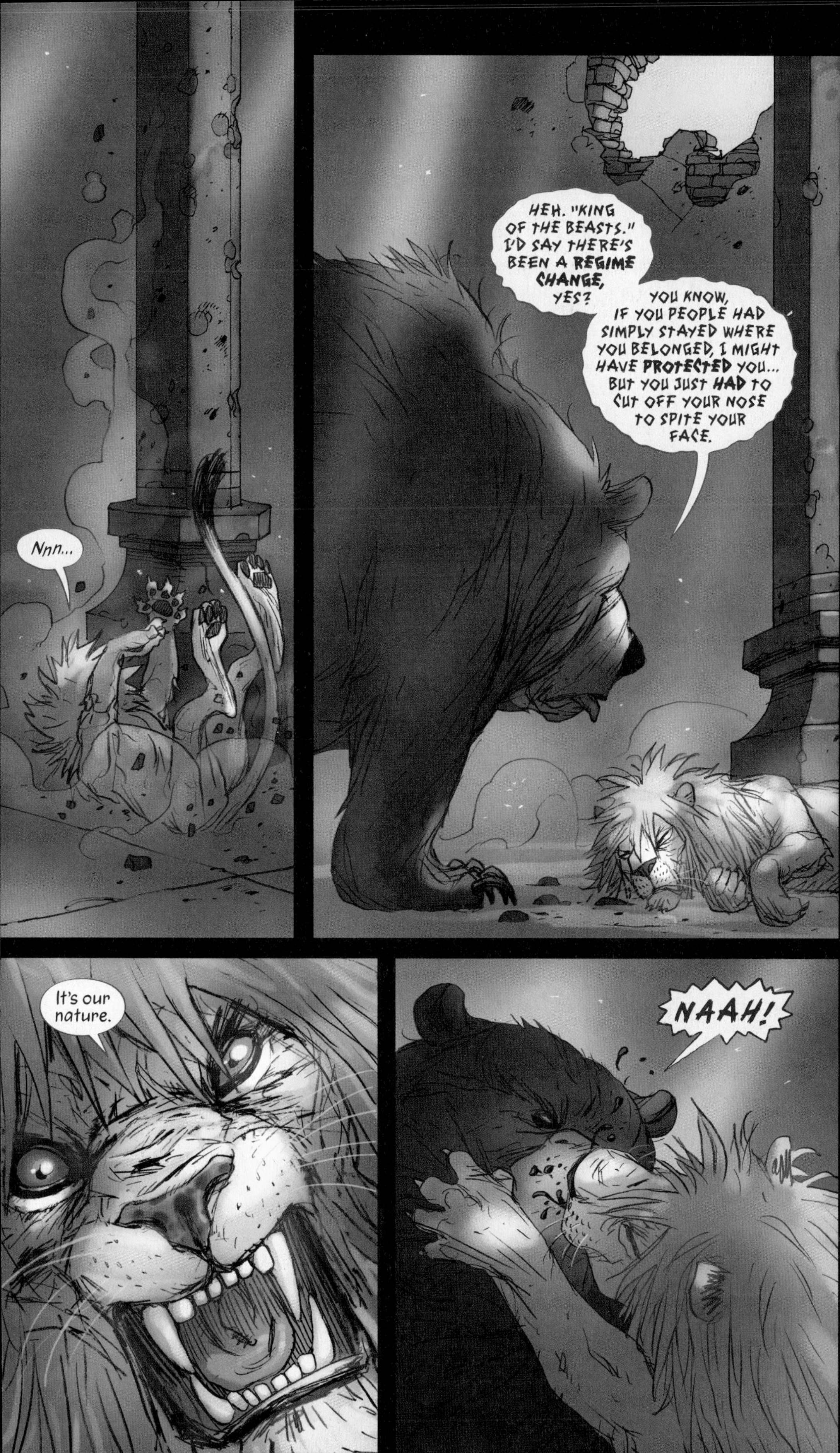
Nnn...
HEH. "KING OF THE BEASTS." I'D SAY THERE'S BEEN A **REGIME CHANGE**, YES?
YOU KNOW, IF YOU PEOPLE HAD SIMPLY STAYED WHERE YOU BELONGED, I MIGHT HAVE **PROTECTED** YOU... BUT YOU JUST **HAD** TO CUT OFF YOUR NOSE TO SPITE YOUR FACE.
It's our nature.
NAAH!

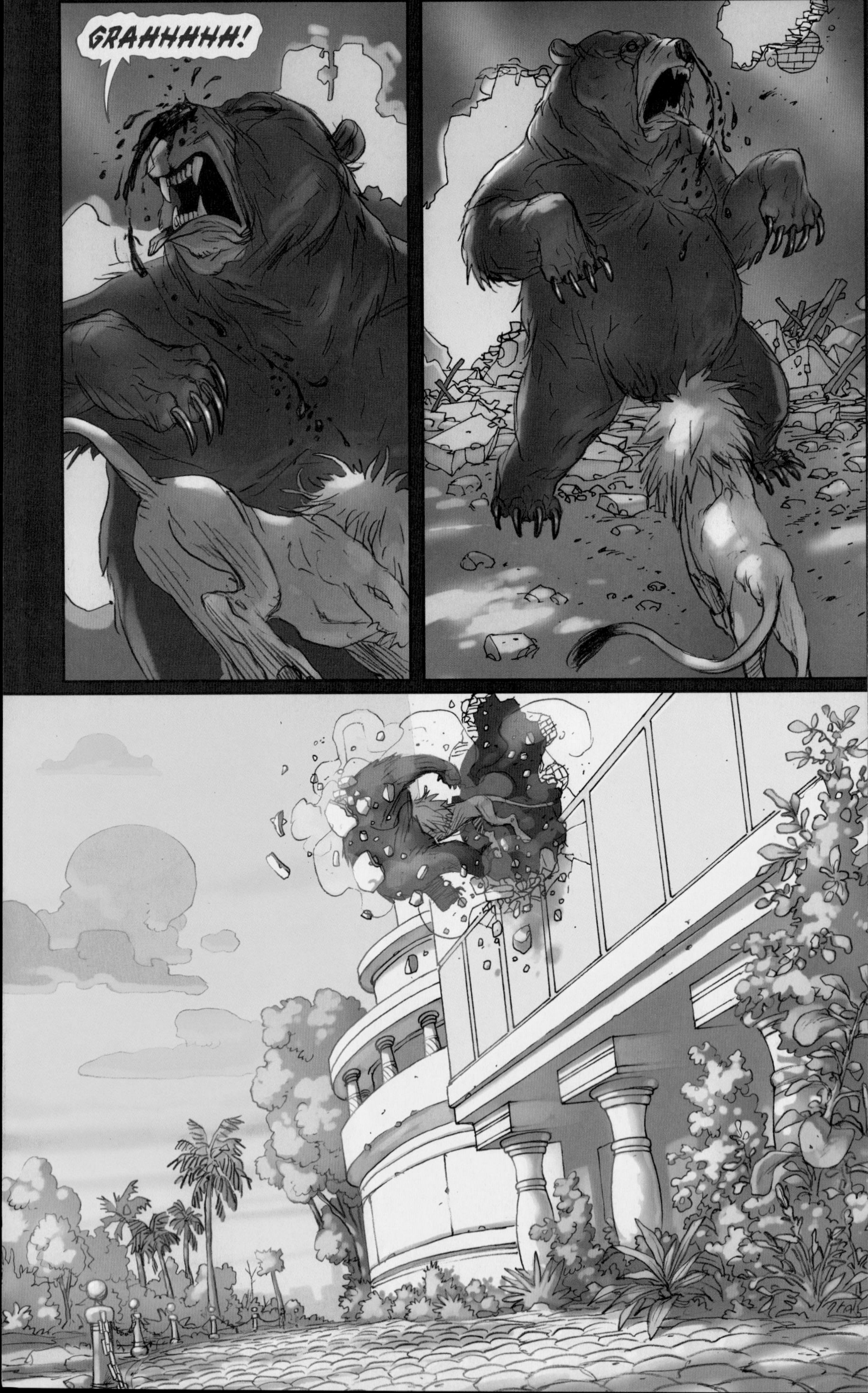
GRAHHHHH!

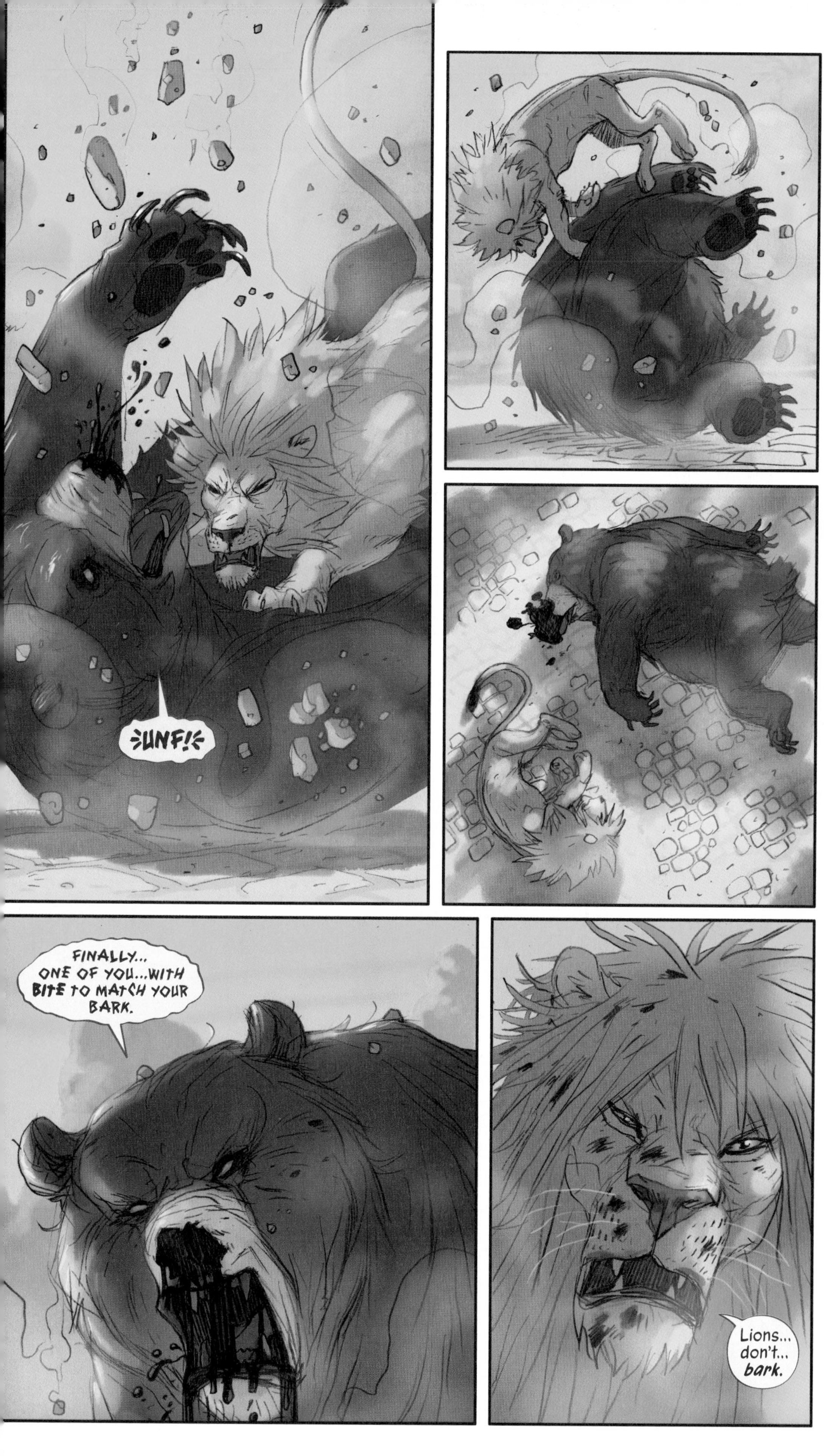
UNF!
FINALLY... ONE OF YOU...WITH BITE TO MATCH YOUR BARK.
Lions... don't... *bark.*

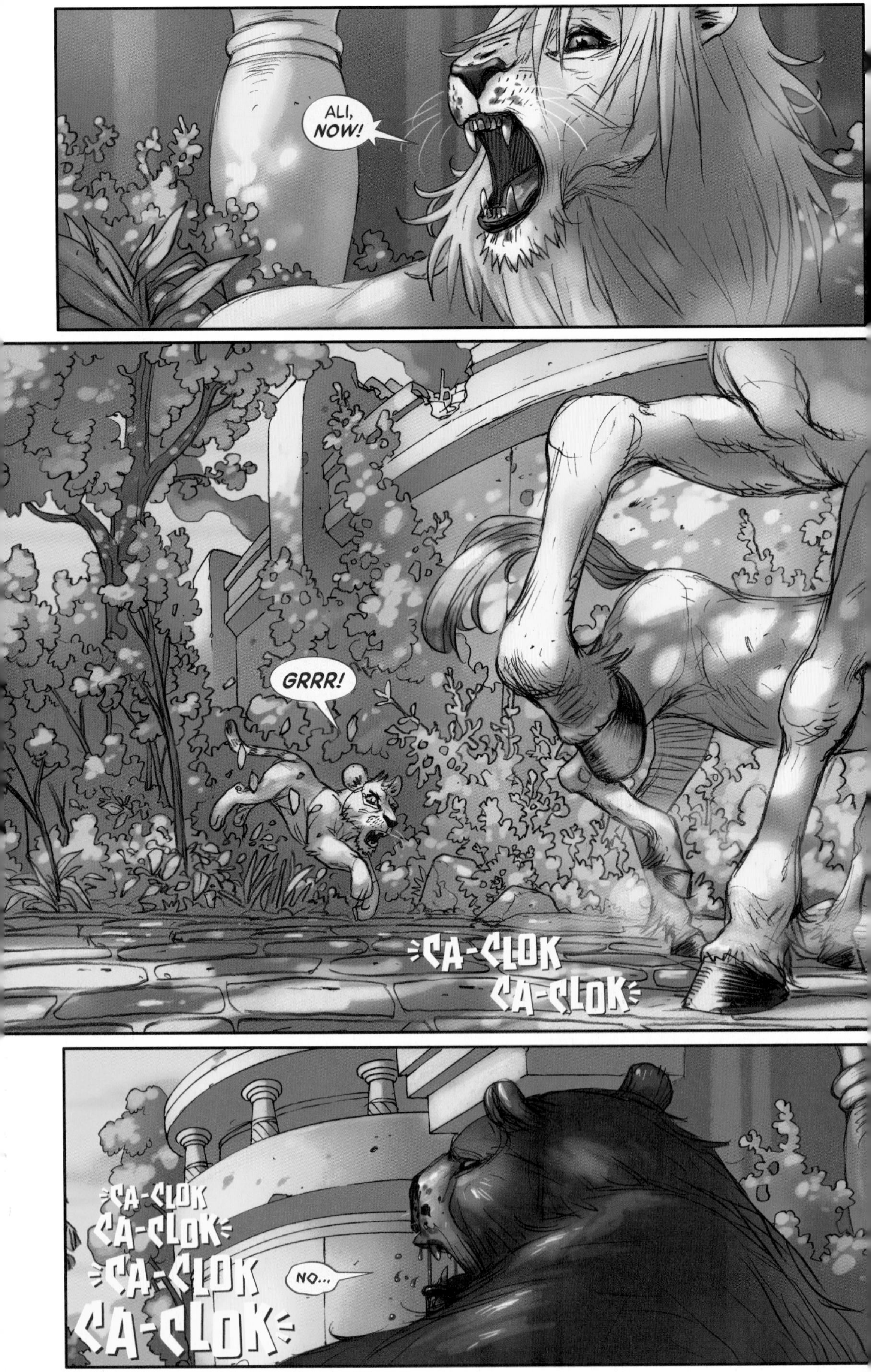
ALI, NOW!
GRRR!
CA-CLOK
CA-CLOK
CA-CLOK
CA-CLOK
CA-CLOK
CA-CLOK
NO...

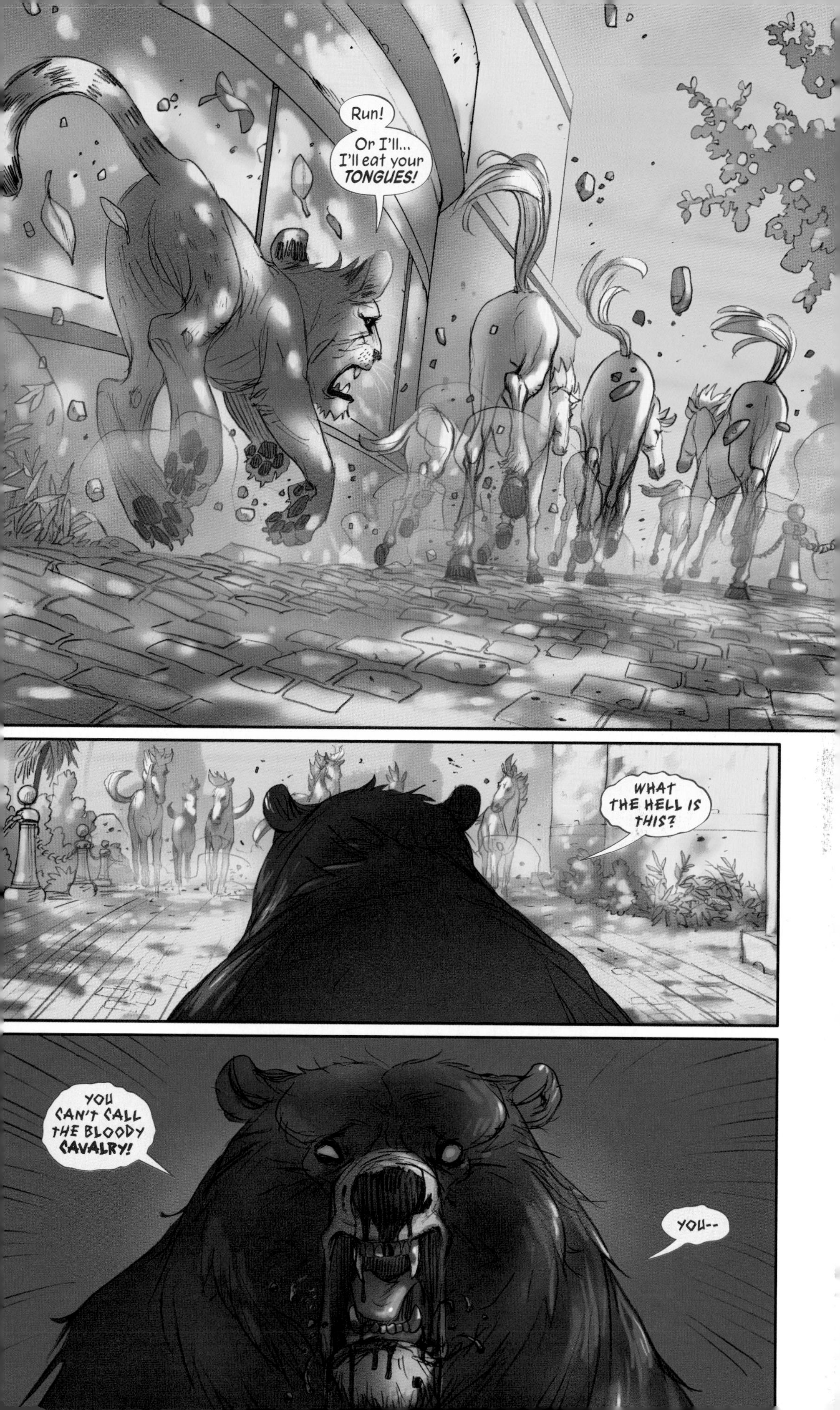
Run!
Or I'll... I'll eat your TONGUES!
WHAT THE HELL IS THIS?
YOU CAN'T CALL THE BLOODY CAVALRY!
YOU--

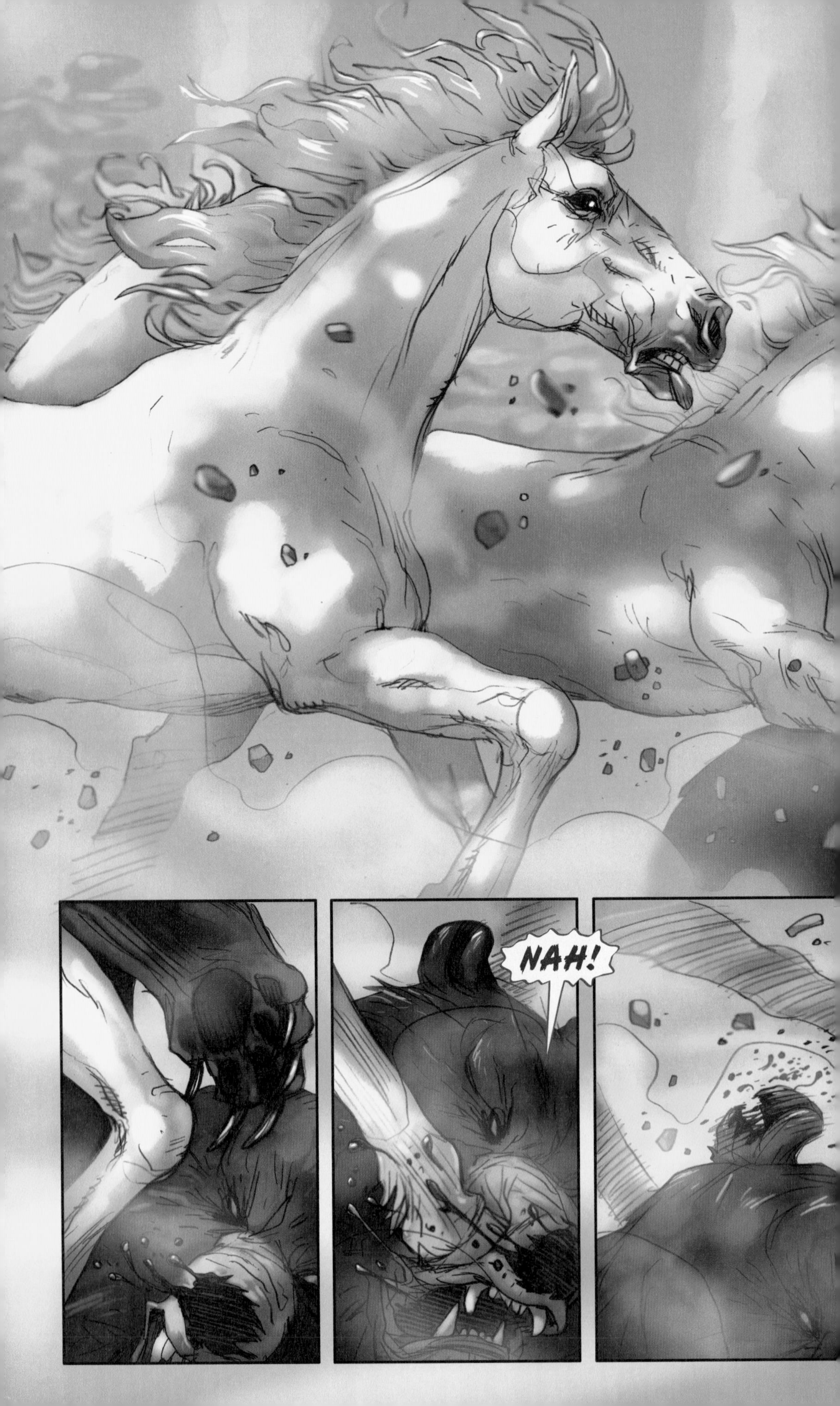
NAH!

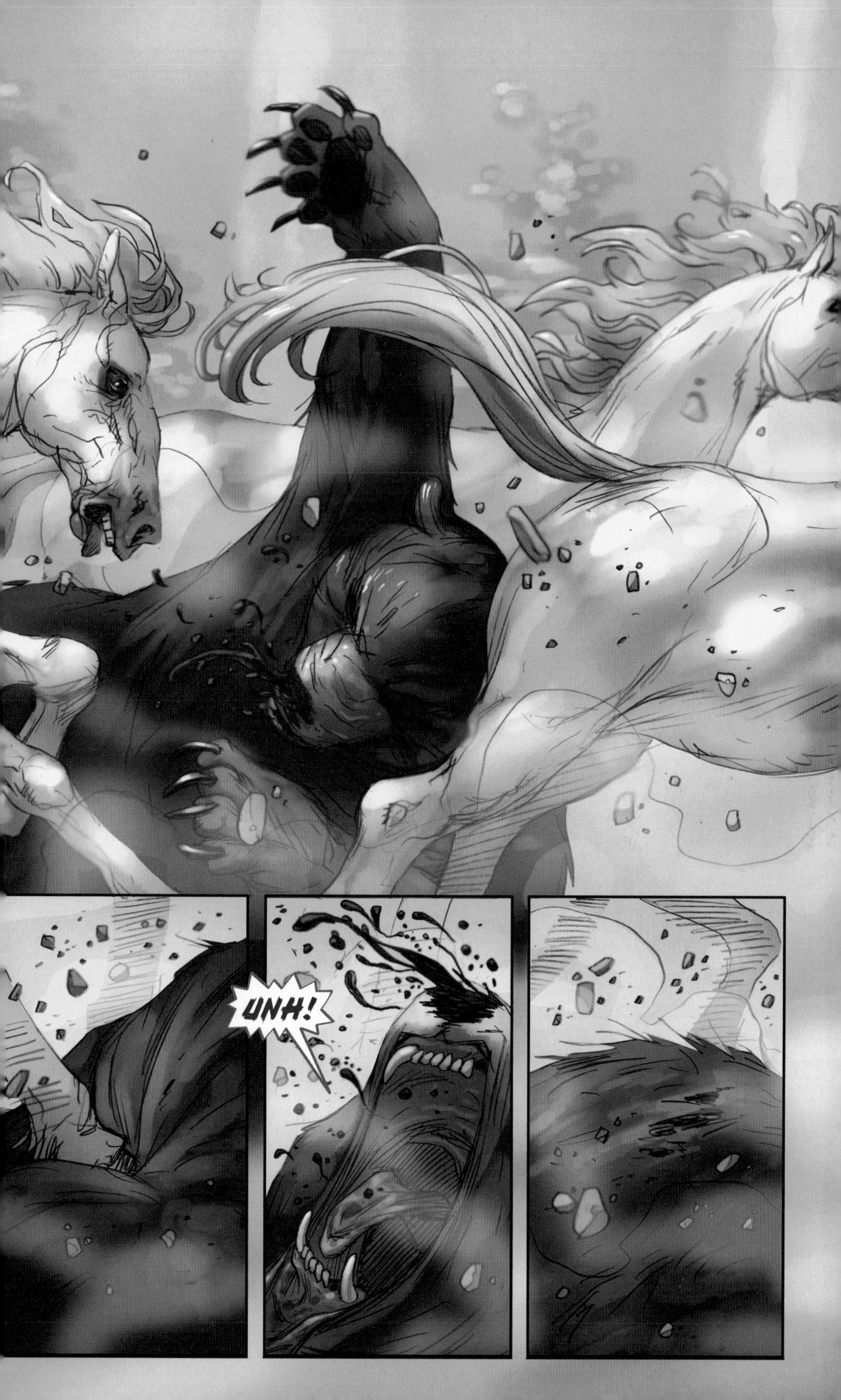
UNH!

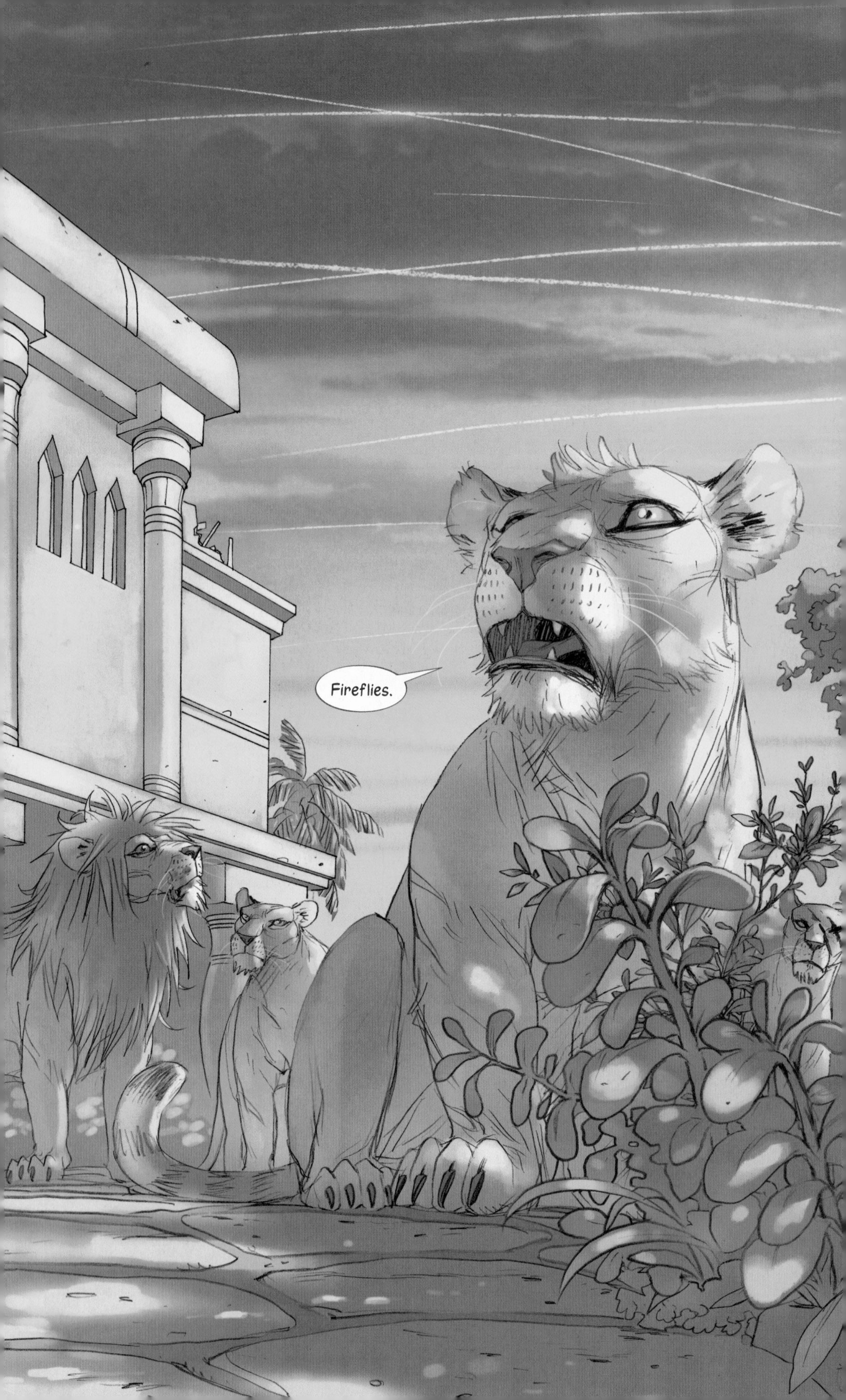
Fireflies.

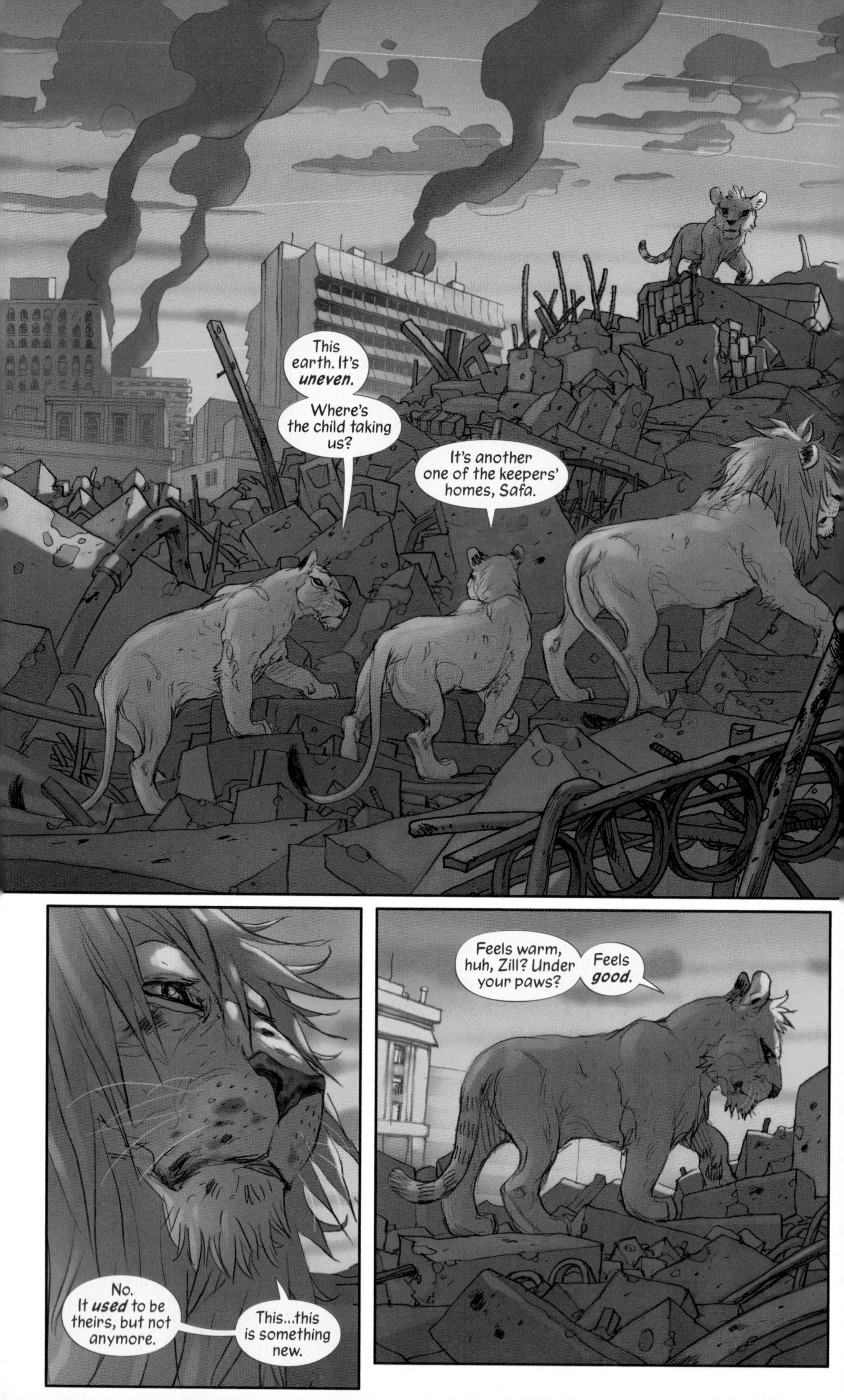
This earth. It's *uneven.*
Where's the child taking us?
It's another one of the keepers' homes, Safa.
No. It *used* to be theirs, but not anymore.
This...this is something new.
Feels warm, huh, Zill? Under your paws?
Feels *good.*

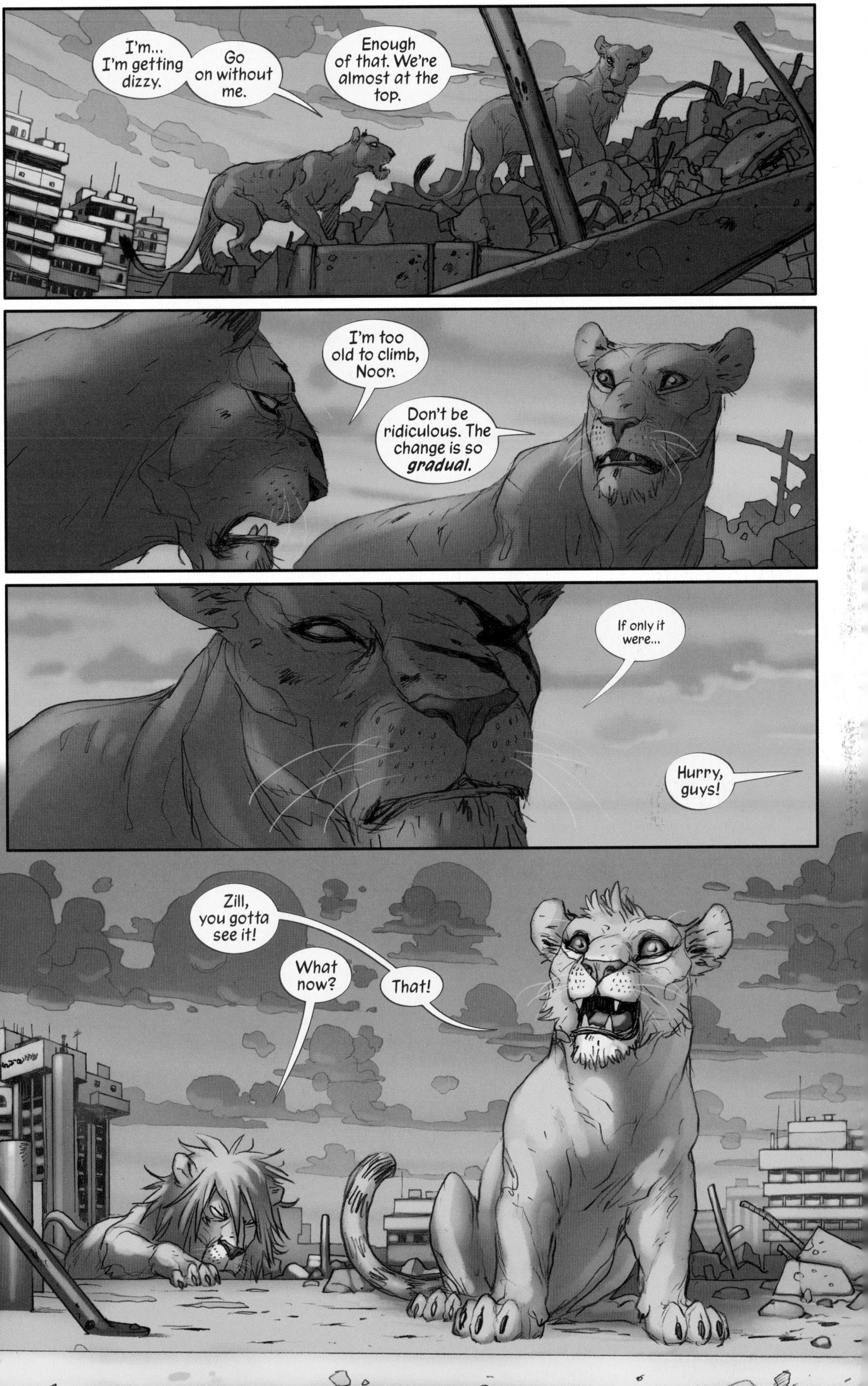

I'm... I'm getting dizzy.
Go on without me.
Enough of that. We're almost at the top.
I'm too old to climb, Noor.
Don't be ridiculous. The change is so *gradual*.
If only it were...
Hurry, guys!
Zill, you gotta see it!
What now?
That!

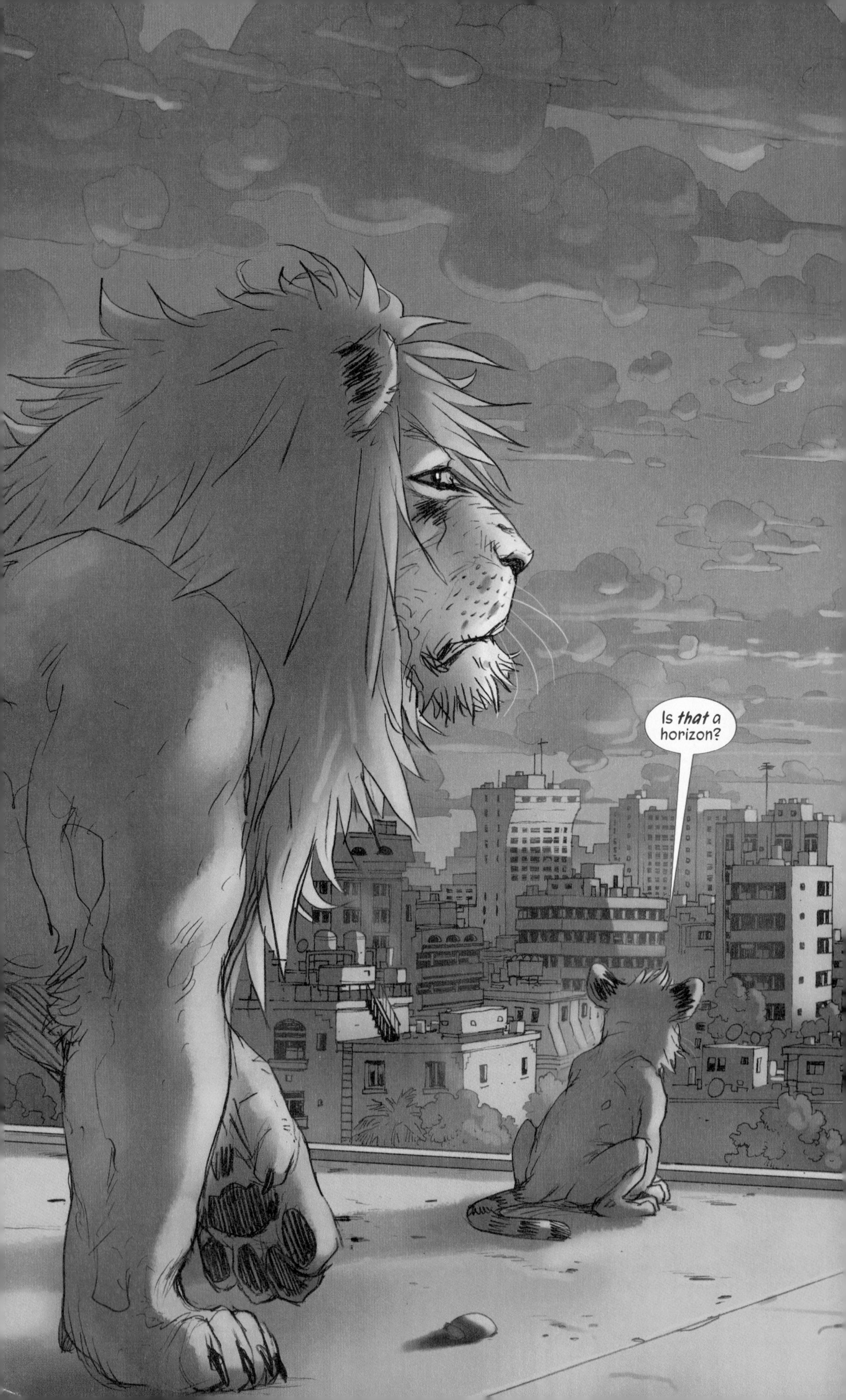
Is *that* a horizon?

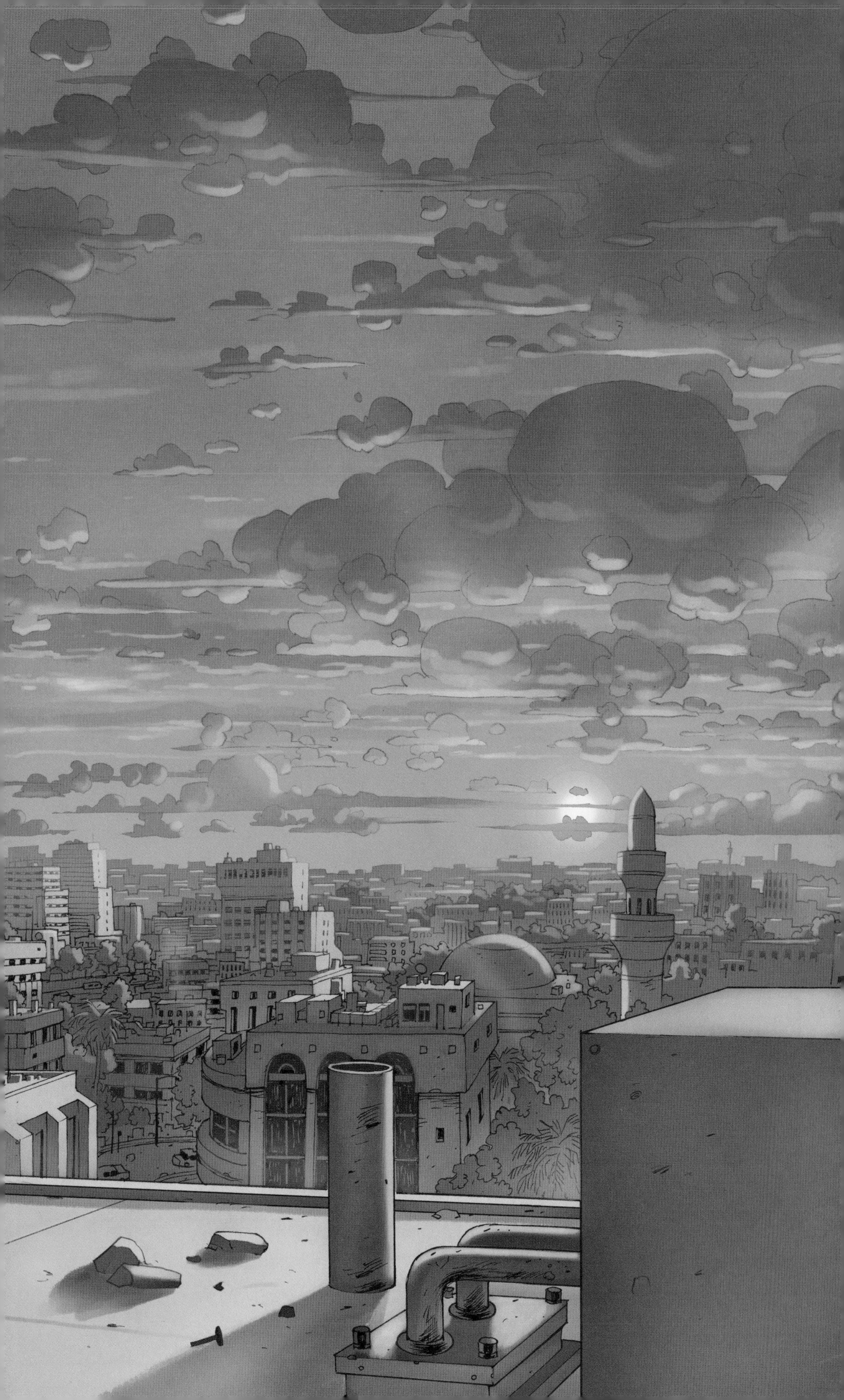

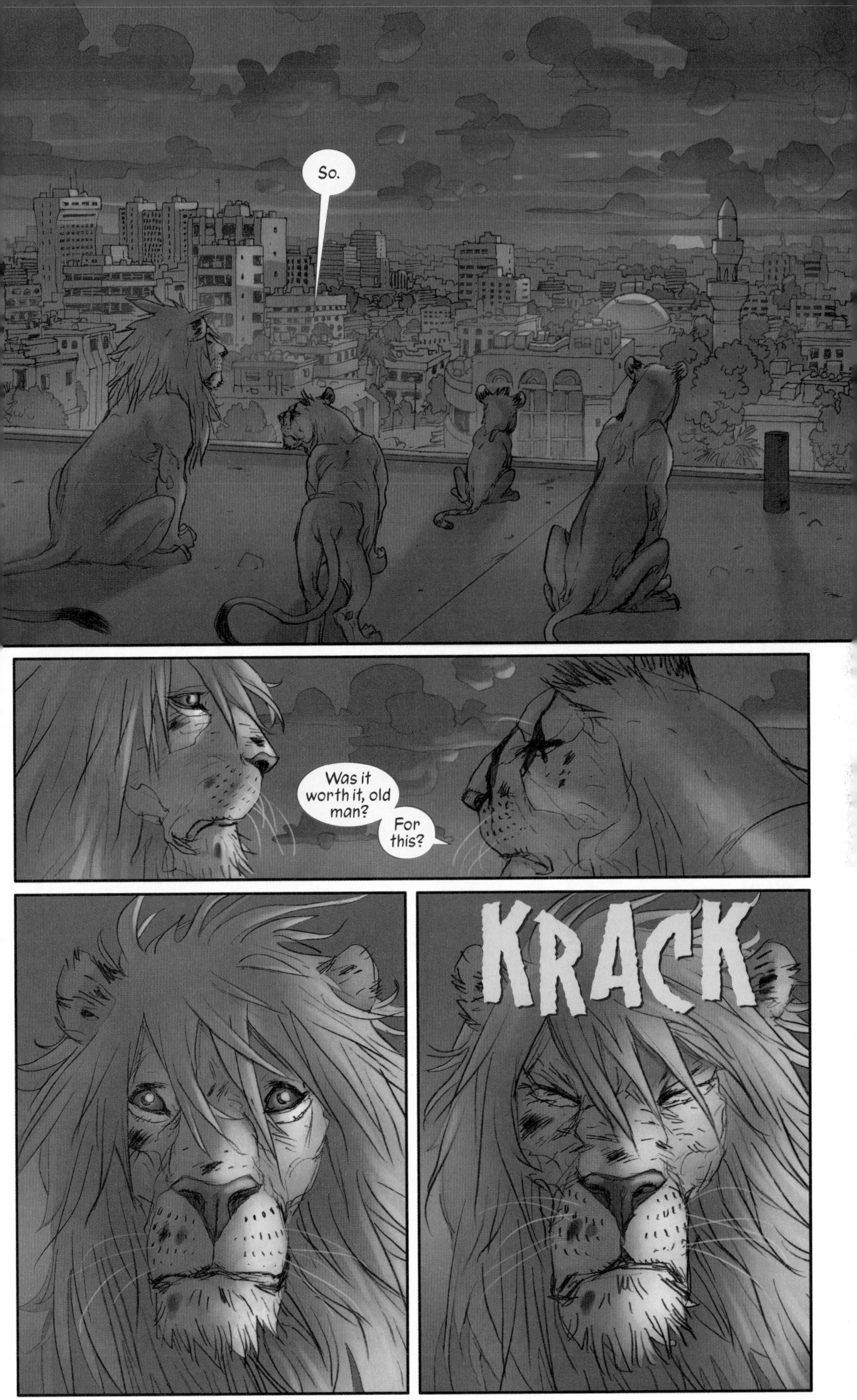
So.
Was it worth it, old man?
For this?
KRACK

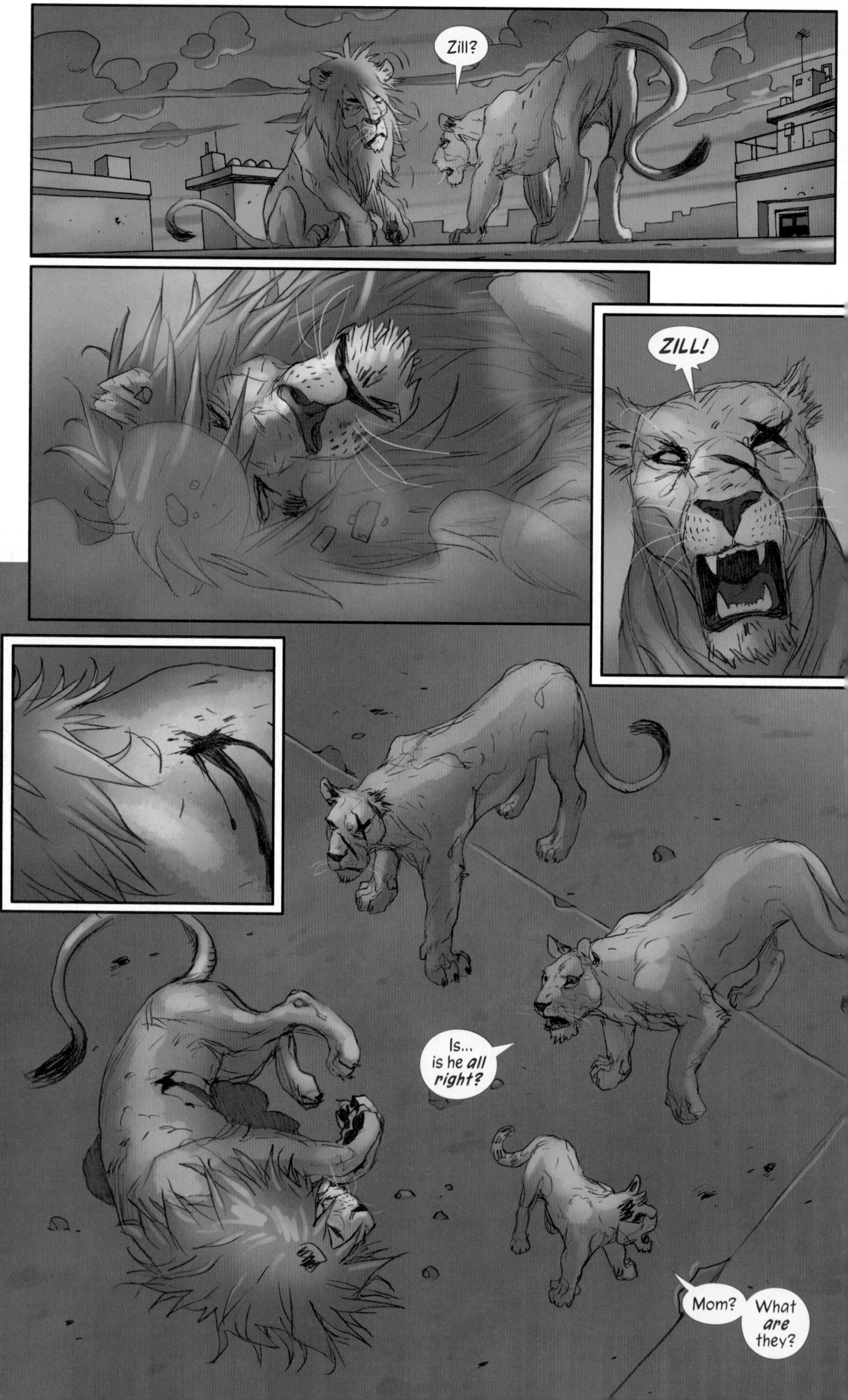
Zill?
ZILL!
Is... is he *all right?*
Mom?
What *are* they?

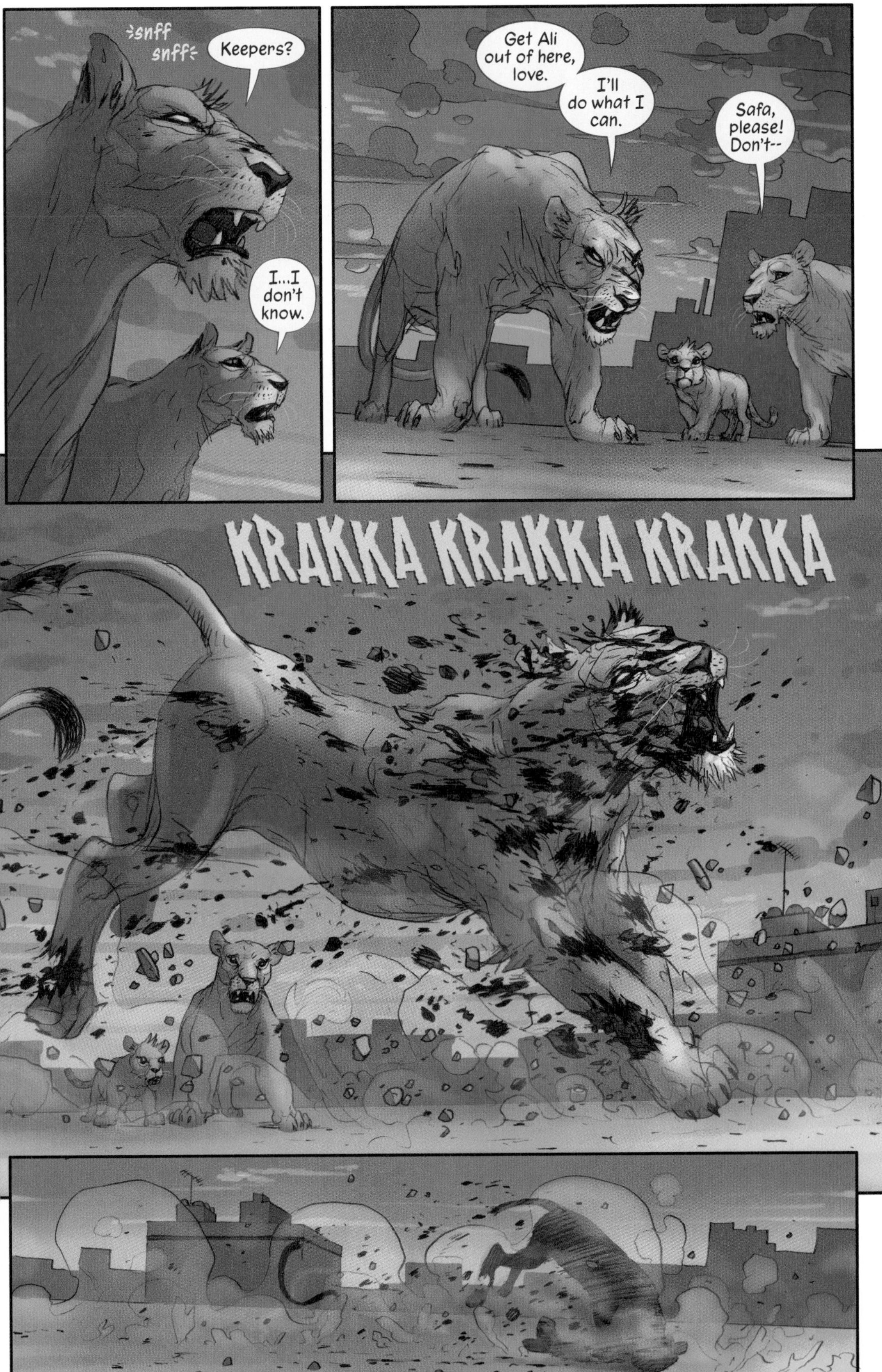
snff snff
Keepers?
I...I don't know.
Get Ali out of here, love.
I'll do what I can.
Safa, please! Don't--
KRAKKA KRAKKA KRAKKA

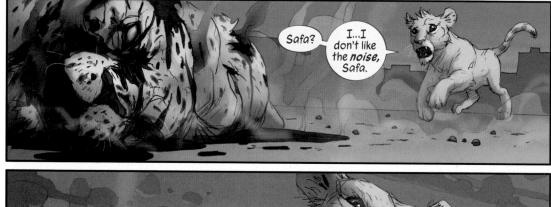

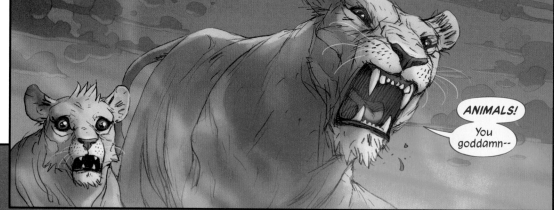

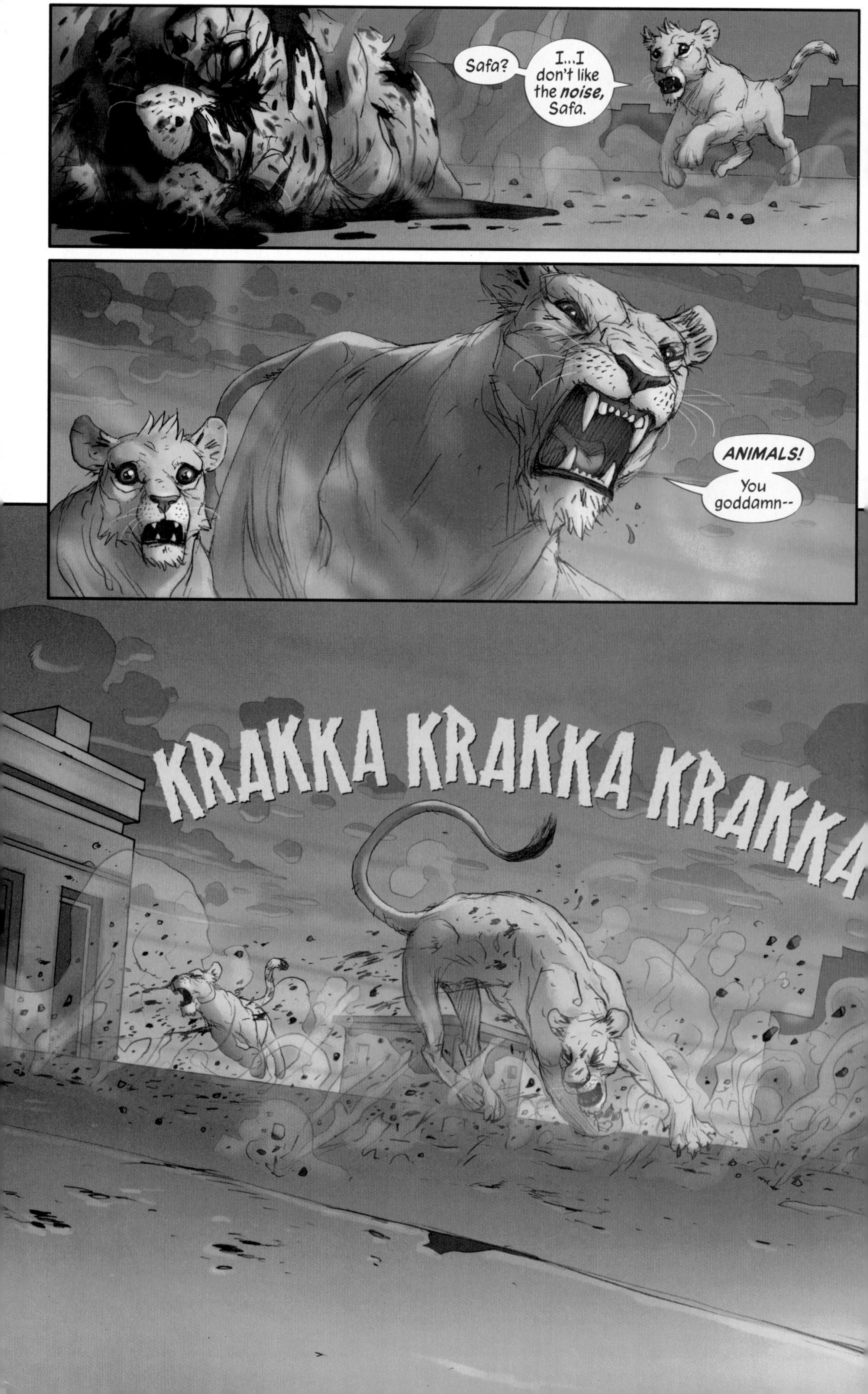

Safa?
I...I don't like the *noise,* Safa.
ANIMALS!
You goddamn--
KRAKKA KRAKKA KRAKKA

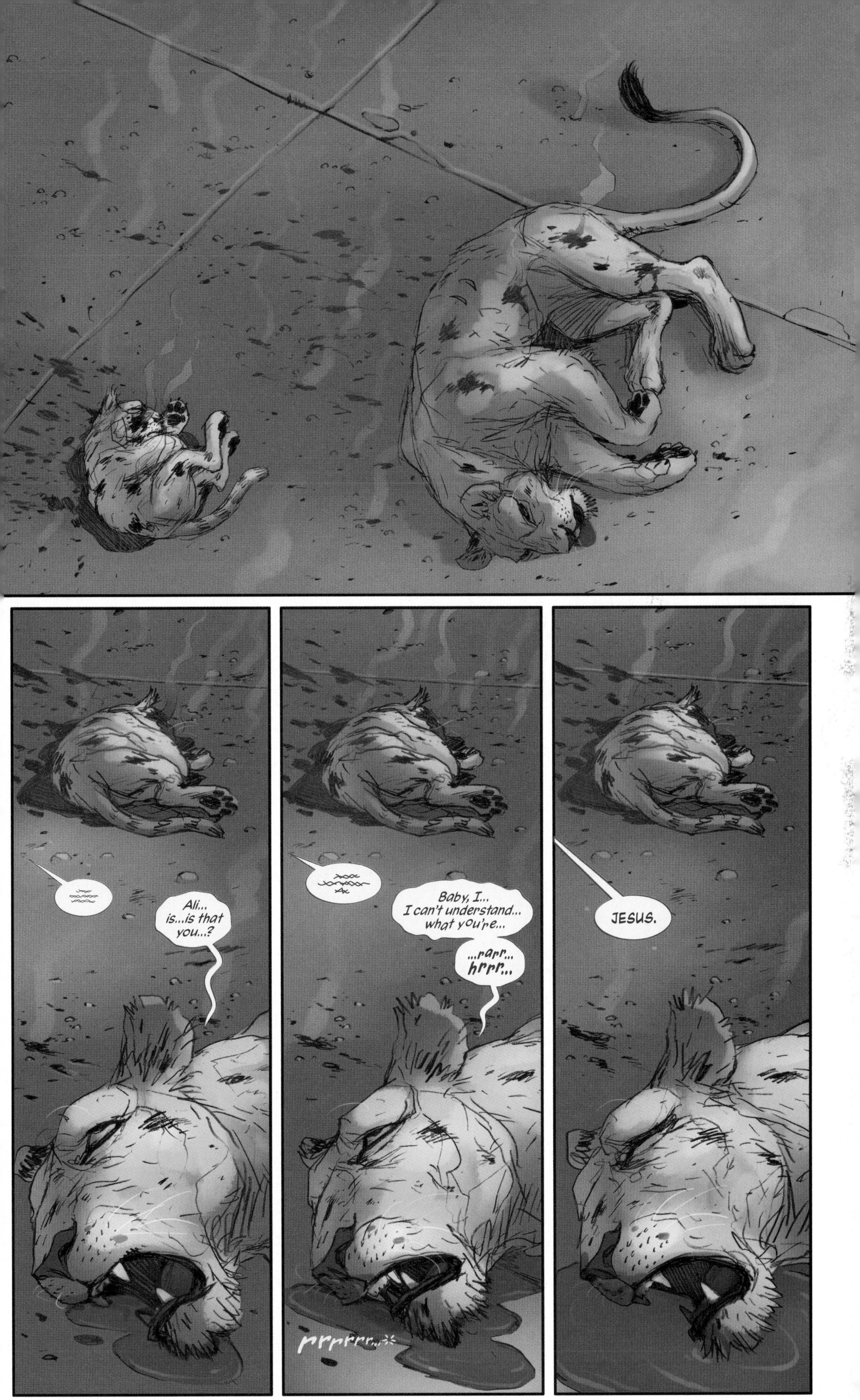

Ali... is...is that you...?
Baby, I... I can't understand... what you're...
...rarr... hrrr...
prrrrr...
JESUS.

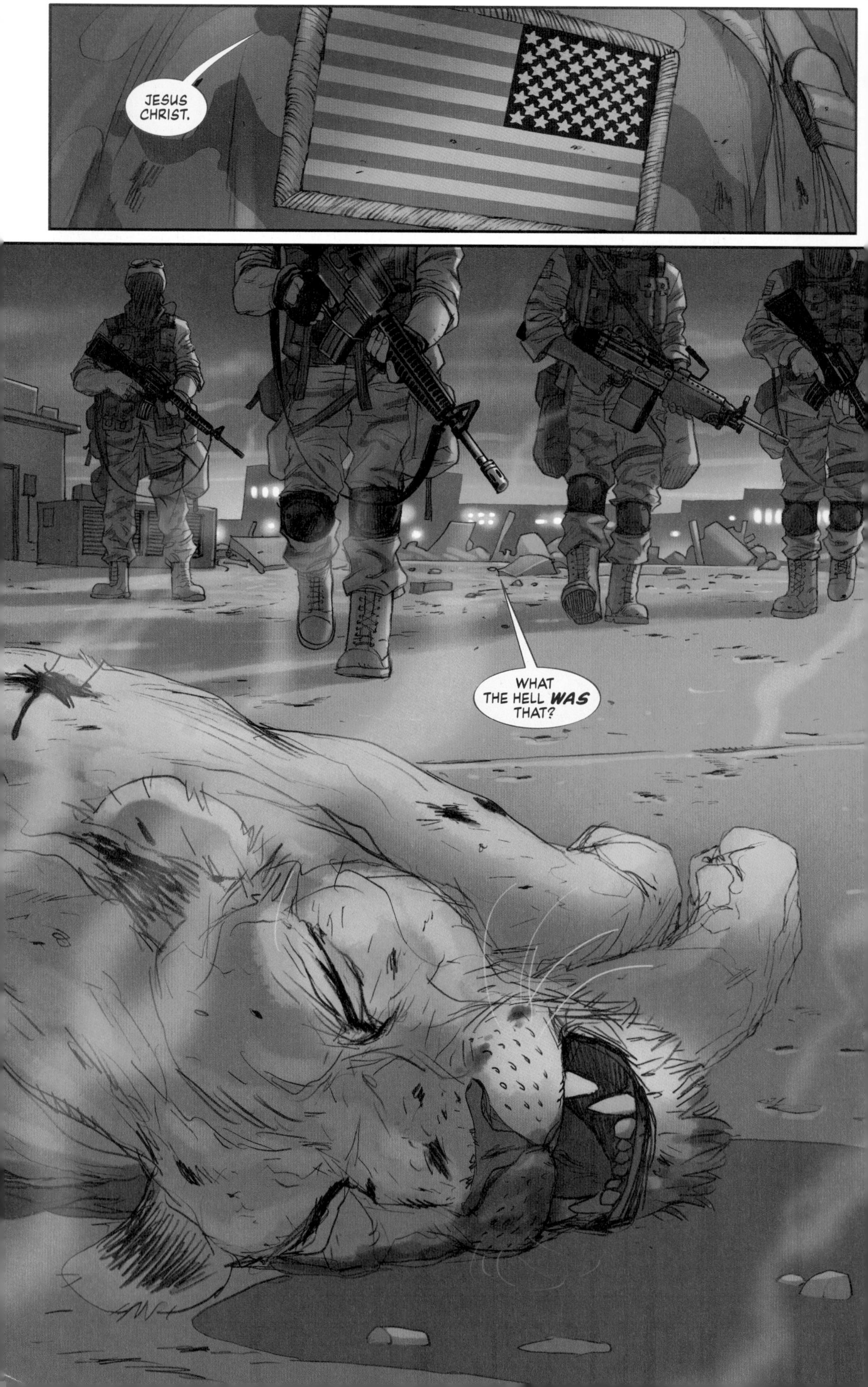
JESUS CHRIST.
WHAT THE HELL WAS THAT?

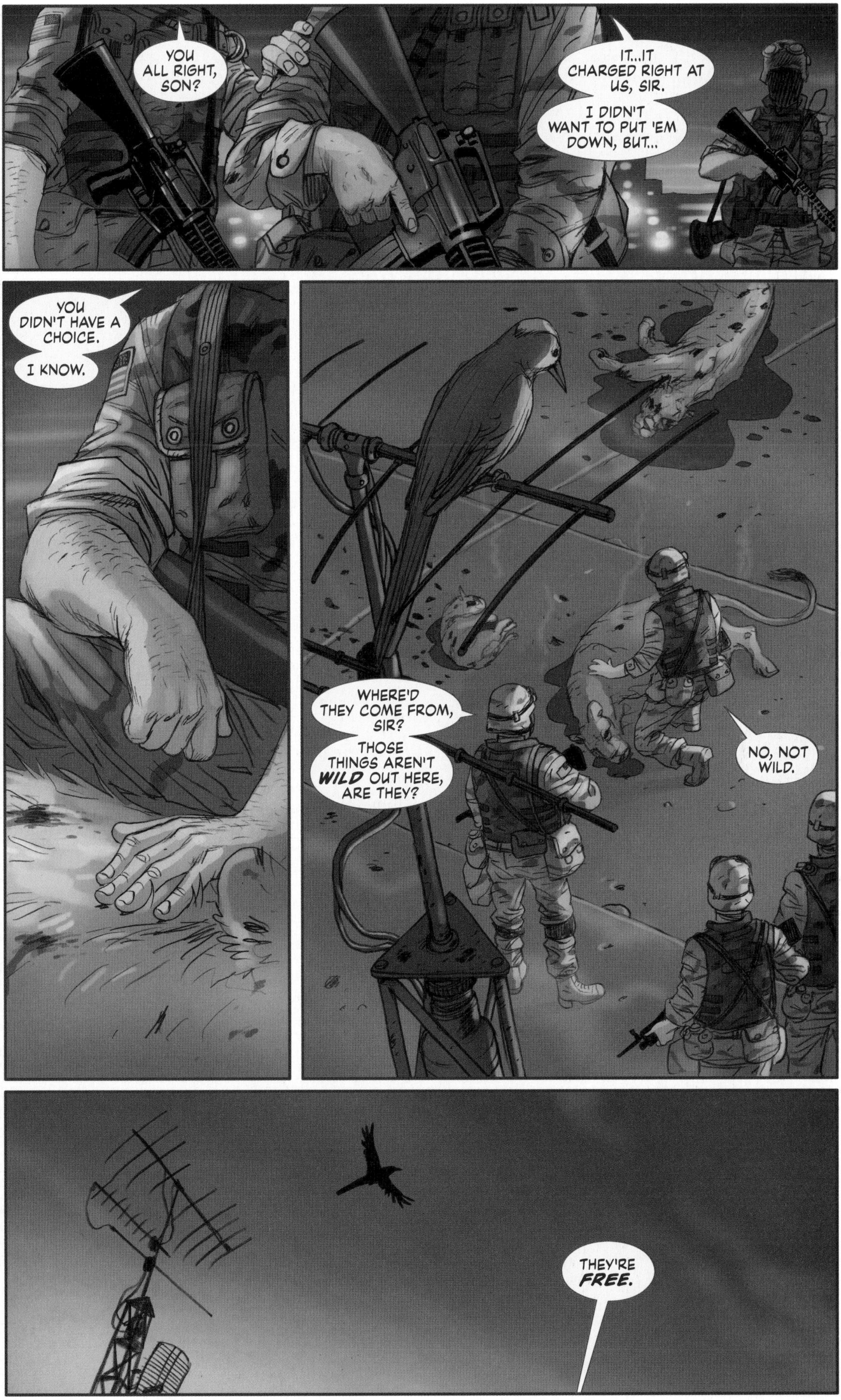
YOU ALL RIGHT, SON?
IT...IT CHARGED RIGHT AT US, SIR.
I DIDN'T WANT TO PUT 'EM DOWN, BUT...
YOU DIDN'T HAVE A CHOICE.
I KNOW.
WHERE'D THEY COME FROM, SIR?
THOSE THINGS AREN'T *WILD* OUT HERE, ARE THEY?
NO, NOT WILD.
THEY'RE *FREE.*

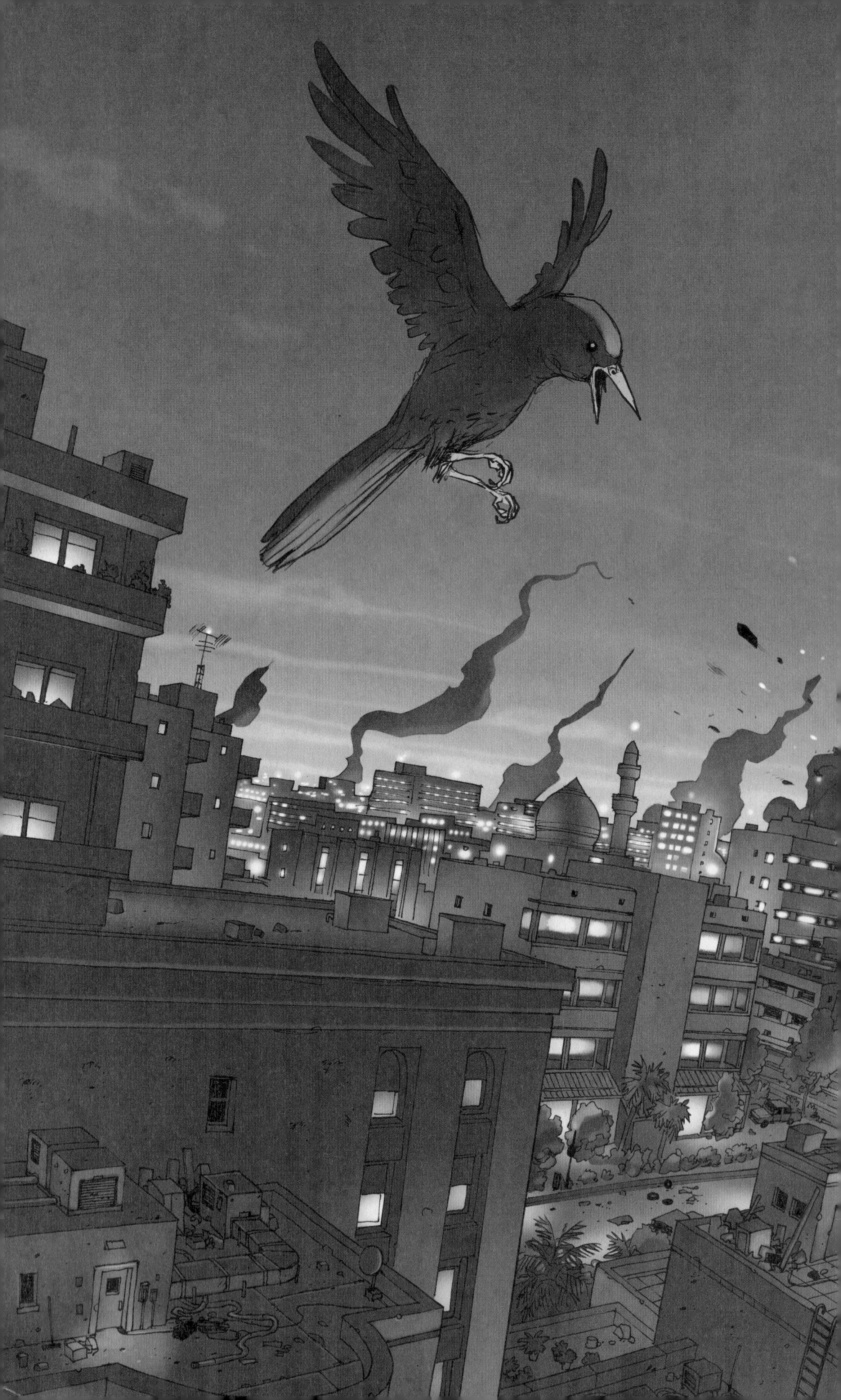

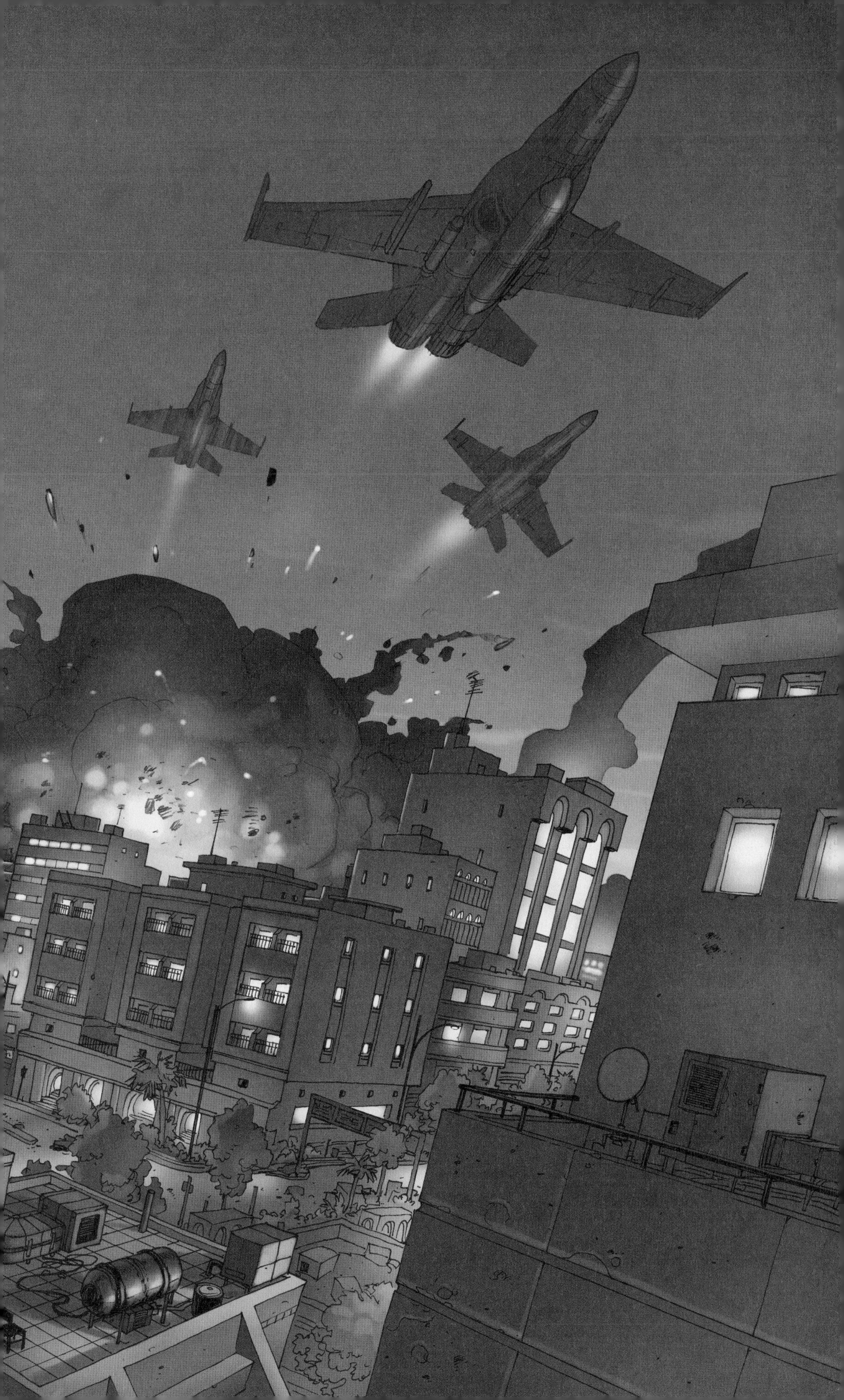

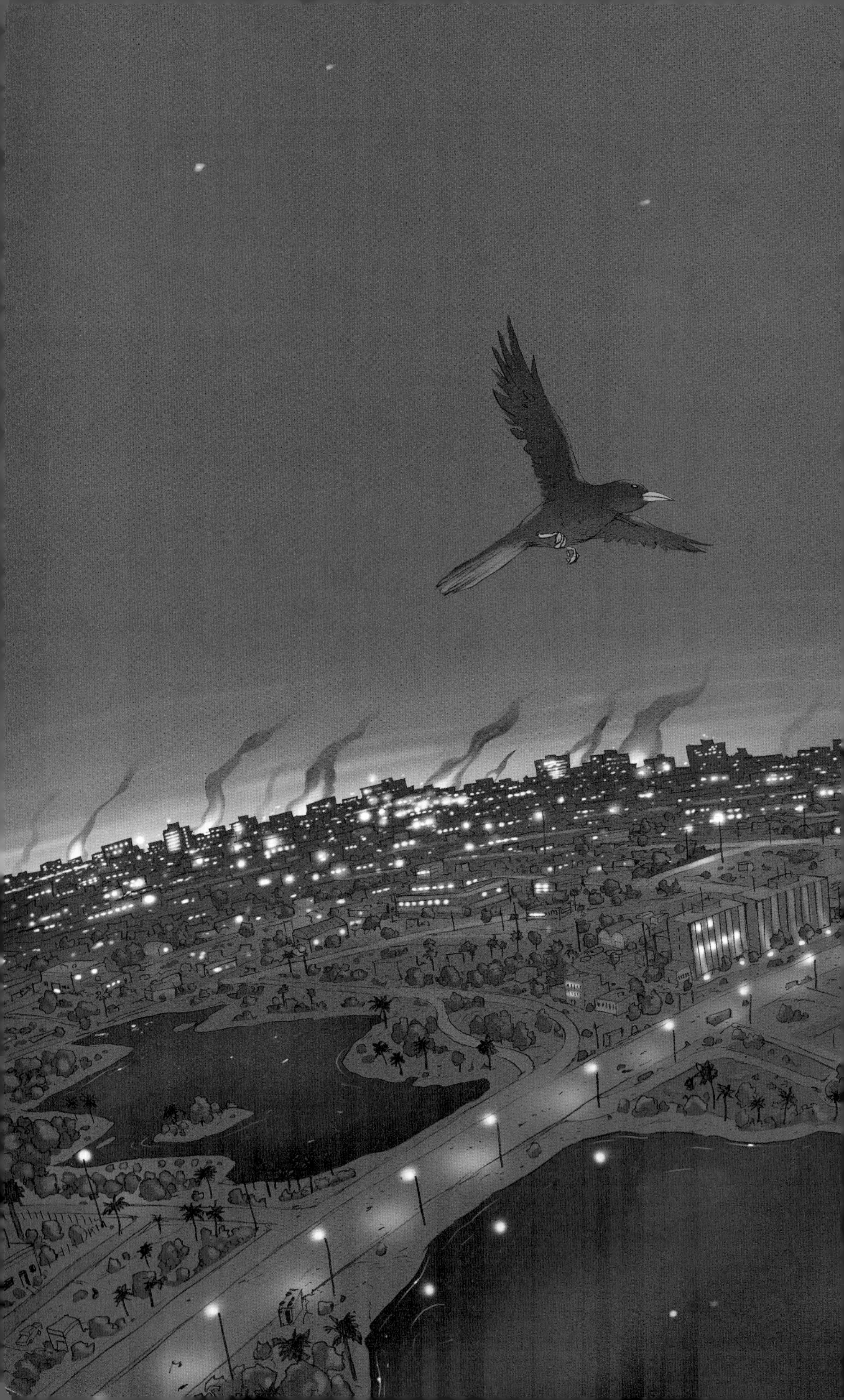

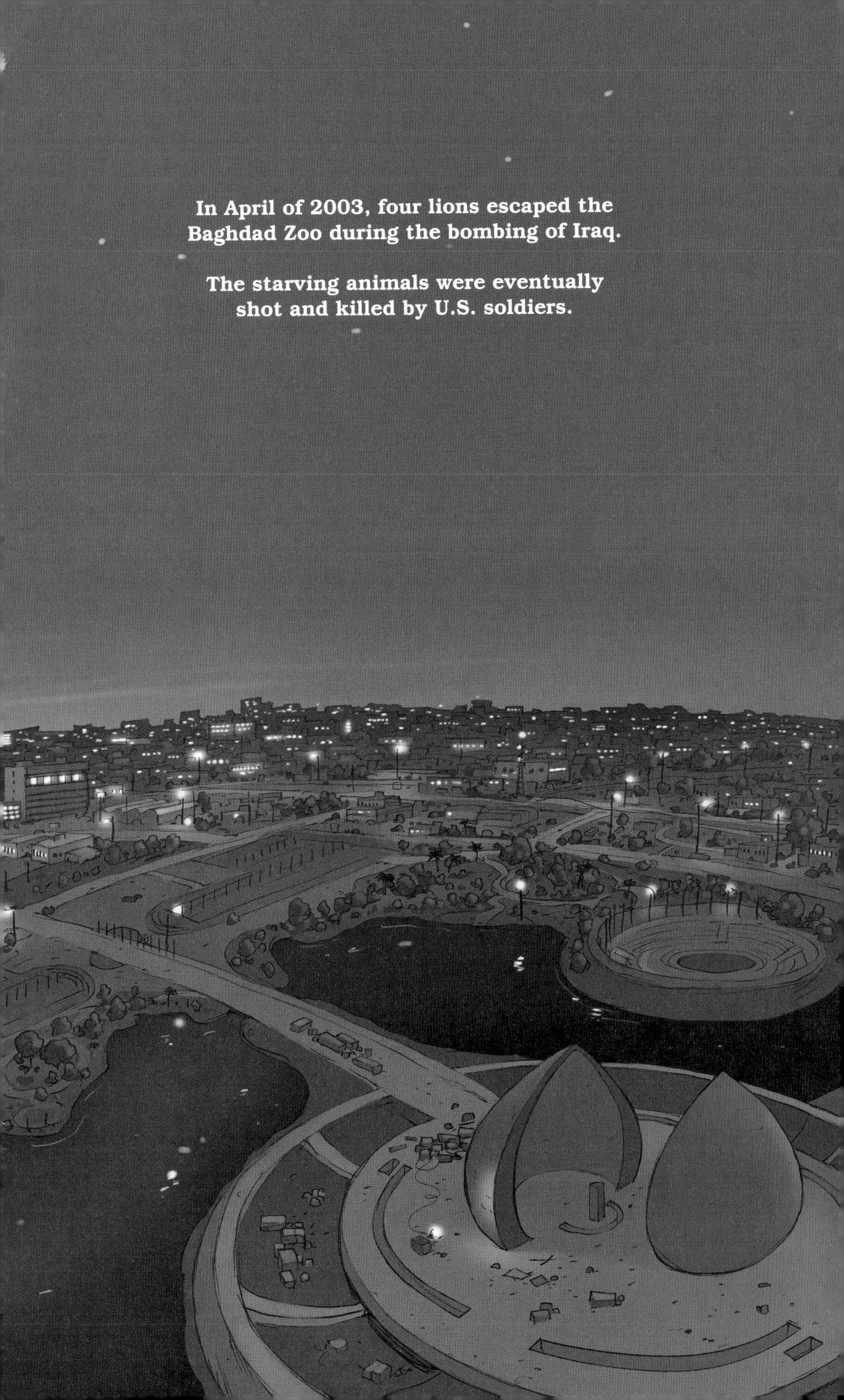
In April of 2003, four lions escaped the Baghdad Zoo during the bombing of Iraq.
The starving animals were eventually shot and killed by U.S. soldiers.

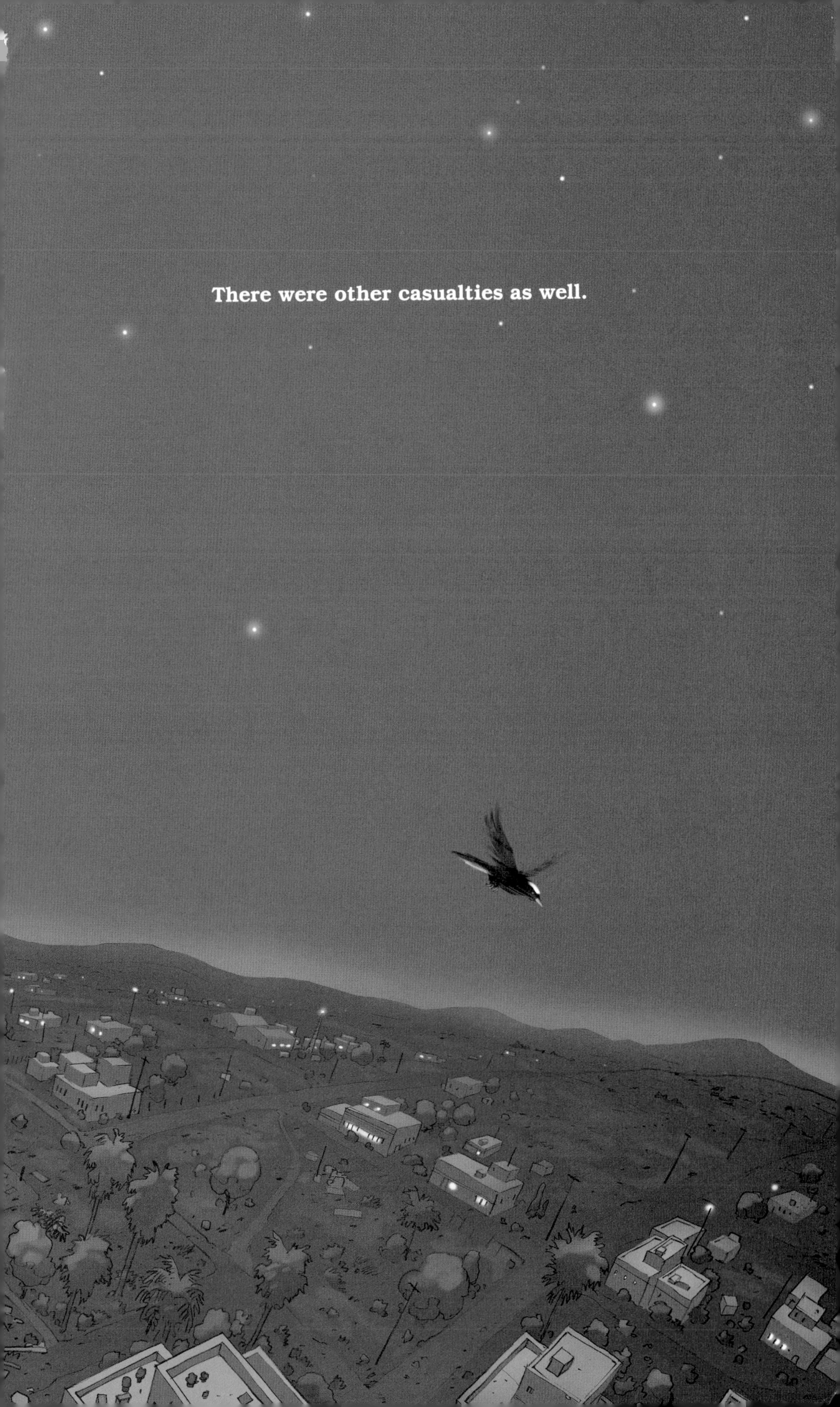
There were other casualties as well.

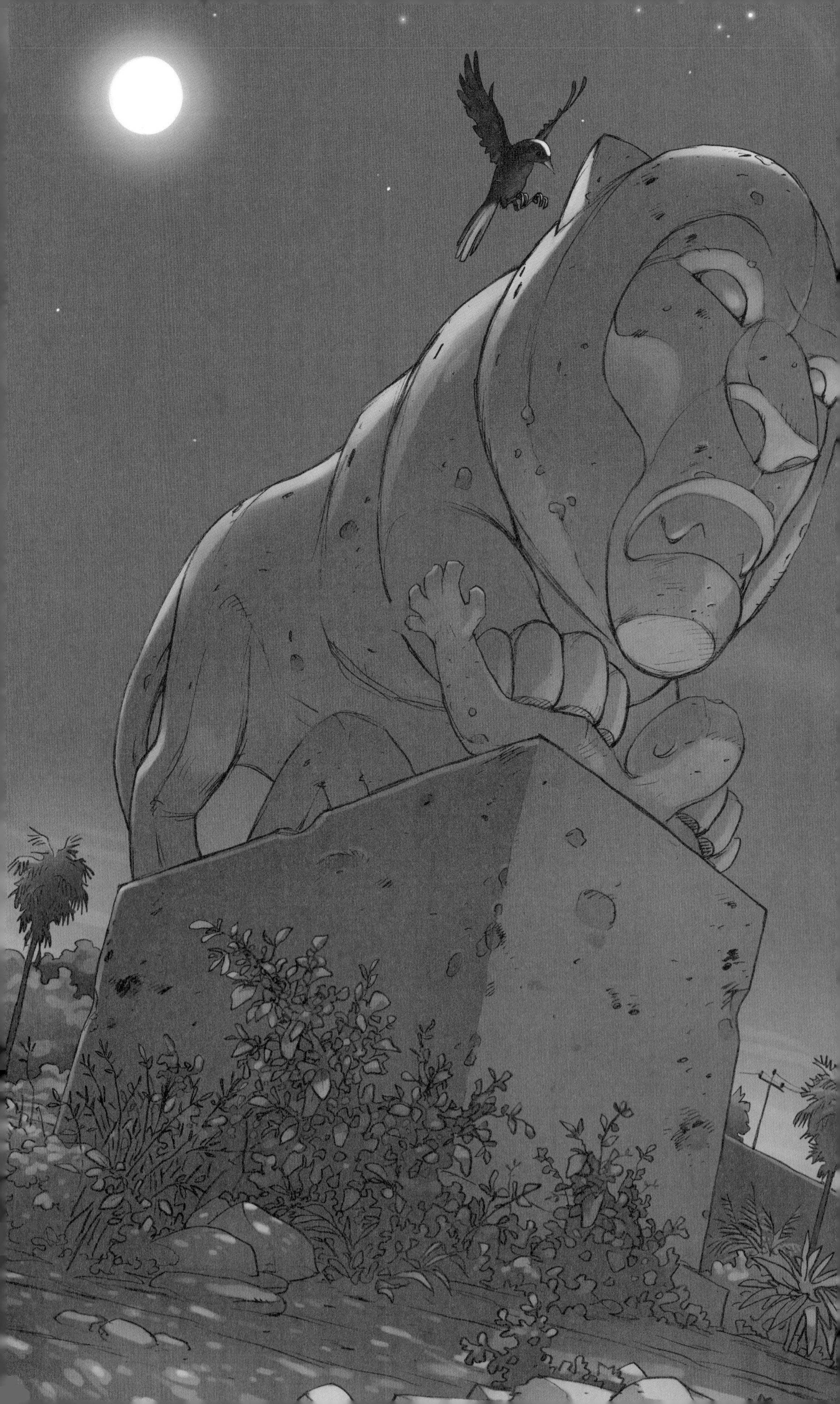

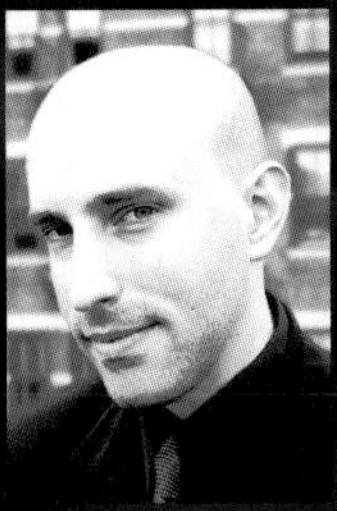

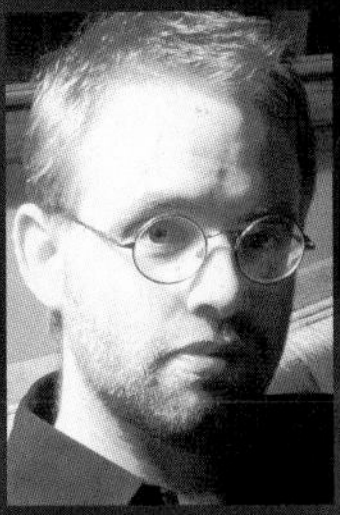

BRIAN K. VAUGHAN

I'd like to thank the following people for their assistance and/or inspiration:

I owe a tremendous debt of gratitude to Chris Cutter and Sarah Scarth at the International Fund for Animal Welfare (www.ifaw.org) for putting me in touch with the incomparable Mariette Hopley, who spoke with me at length about her work leading an emergency relief team to the Baghdad Zoo back in 2003.

I'd also like to recognize the civilian population of Iraq, especially those bloggers who generously shared their experiences with the world. And very special thanks to the dedicated men and women of the United States Armed Forces, particularly everyone from the Army's 3rd Infantry Division.

This story is inspired by true events, but the interpretation and viewpoint(s) are obviously mine and Niko's and don't necessarily reflect the feelings and opinions of the many people who kindly offered us their help. Any artistic liberties are my responsibility and mine alone, as are any and all errors of fact.

Oh, and thanks to my favorite wife, Ruth McKee, for letting me borrow her membership card to the San Diego Zoo.

Brian is the Eisner Award-winning writer of Y: THE LAST MAN and EX MACHINA. He lives in California with his wife.

NIKO HENRICHON

I would like to thank my friends and my family who have provided me support during the whole year it took to produce this book. It is also important to thank the people—citizens, reporters and soldiers—who were and still are in Iraq, for sharing their experience in written form or through pictures, despite the drama they are witnessing daily. I couldn't have made this book believable without them.

Niko lives in Québec City with his wife and cat as well. PRIDE OF BAGHDAD is his second graphic novel.

Karen Berger VP-Executive Editor Will Dennis Editor Casey Seijas Assistant Editor Louis Prandi Art Director Paul Levitz President & Publisher Georg Brewer VP-Design & DC Direct Creative
Richard Bruning Senior VP-Creative Director Patrick Caldon Executive VP-Finance & Operations Chris Caramalis VP-Finance John Cunningham VP-Marketing
Terri Cunningham VP-Managing Editor Stephanie Fierman Senior VP-Sales & Marketing Alison Gill VP-Manufacturing Rich Johnson VP-Book Trade Sales
Hank Kanalz VP-General Manager, WildStorm Lillian Laserson Senior VP & General Counsel Jim Lee Editorial Director-WildStorm Paul Lowitt Senior VP-Business & Legal Affairs
David McKillips VP-Advertising & Custom Publishing John Nee VP-Business Development Gregory Noveck Senior VP-Creative Affairs Cheryl Rubin Senior VP-Brand Management
Jeff Trojan VP-Business Development, DC Direct Bob Wayne VP-Sales